The Power of

Synne

LP O'Bryan

Copyright © 2024 LP O'Bryan

All rights reserved. No part of this publication may be reproduced, distributed, or transmitted in any form or by any means, including photocopying, recording, or other electronic or mechanical methods, without the prior written permission of the publisher. For permission requests, write to the publisher at the address below.

Ardua Publishing

Argus House, Malpas Street

Dublin 8,

Ireland

http://arduapublishing.com

Ordering Information: Contact the publisher.

This novel is a work of fiction.

The role played by real historical figures in this narrative is entirely fictional.

The imagined characters, however, abide by the generally known facts about the period in which the novel is set.

"We fall bound to our fate like raindrops in a storm."

> The Prophecies of Gytha.

Historical Background

This novel takes place between 1068 and 1069 in Ireland and England. William the Conqueror is consolidating his hold on his new kingdom. The recent Norman conquest of England is having an impact far beyond its shores.

1

"I'm off to see the king," Magnus shouted. He was at the door already.

"I'll join you," I replied from the other side of the hall, where I'd been checking some herbs hanging from the roof.

"I won't be long, stay here. You need to get on with your preparations," he shouted back.

I should have gone with him, but he blew me a kiss and gave me a big smile and I fell for it.

I was also in no mood for dealing with the King of Dublin. He enjoyed keeping visitors waiting and always answered questions with another question.

I thought little more about him until that afternoon, when I found myself listening to the sounds from the street, wondering what was taking Magnus so long. Was the king showing even more disrespect than usual?

That was when I heard a street urchin shout something about me I couldn't quite make out as he passed by. Some of them called me the-seer-that-blessed-the-Normans, but his words, except my name, were lost in the shouts of the hawkers along our street, so I went back to the list of preparations I'd been obsessing over.

I loved one gift I'd been given, a blue silk ribbon I'd wear in my hair on the big day. The way it slipped through my fingers reminded me of water and how everything was changing, flowing fast. We didn't have ribbons like this when I was growing up, but I'd heard about them, and I'd always hoped that on my wedding day I'd have one. And now, my dream was coming true.

Or was it? I had a lot of doubts, because we were going ahead without either of our families present.

But perhaps I was worrying too much? Perhaps I should just be happy. What I'd known was impossible, was happening to me. That should be enough. Right?

It had been a long year since we'd escaped from London. The good part was that the hall we were living in was one of the best in Dublin. We had servants, and guards, and a well for water just outside our front door. Some other parts we'd get to.

Our wedding would be the best thing ever, though I half expected it would be delayed, again, because of Magnus and his dithering or something the king would say. Why was he late?

The never-ending rain that April day meant, I hoped, that there'd be few visitors to the king to delay Magnus and few interruptions when we ate, which should be soon.

I walked around the darkening hall lighting candles as I went, my thoughts mostly on the celebrations we'd been planning for in two days' time, after a small ceremony at the tiny church nearby.

These thoughts circling inside me all that day were my best excuse for not being aware of what should have been blindingly obvious.

But I'd never felt like this before. Being in love was about lying to yourself, wasn't it?

A hammering on the door broke my blissful chain of thoughts. The hall guard, Bjorn, went quickly to see who it was.

"Mistress," he called to me from the door. "Someone needs your help."

I went to see who was there. Women in this city had been coming to me since soon after we'd arrived, ahead of a big mid-winter storm. They said our safe arrival, when others had perished at sea the same day, meant I was favoured by the Queen of Heaven. People here also liked that I'd escaped a battle-torn England and was with the man I loved, the son of a king. Everyone soon knew what had happened in London, the fighting we'd been involved in. I was fortunate that lots of people here needed healing.

Getting paid for healing turned out to be lucrative.

At the half-open door stood a child of about ten summers, shivering. A long well-patched cloak reached down to his bare muddy feet. The cloak was splattered all the way to his elbows.

"Healer, please, please come, please," he said, holding his hands out, speaking the tongue of the city, that mix of words from near and far, which I'd come to understand, barely.

I looked along the muddy, stinking street. There appeared to be no one with him. Only a few distant figures could be seen, all hurrying away from us.

"What happened?" I asked, leaning down, putting a hand on his shoulder to steady him. I was wary. It wasn't unheard of for people to try a trick to lure you out of your house, but the gates of the city would be closing soon, and the sun was about to go down, so escape would not be easy for an outlaw.

"It's me ma," said the boy, in a frightened voice. "You helped her a few months ago. She needs you. The baby is gonna come."

I hesitated for only another moment. There was something familiar about him. I grabbed my cloak, wrapped it around myself, gave the boy one of our old cloaks to keep him warm and went with him. Magnus would likely get angry at me for giving another cloak away, but I didn't care. Bjorn followed us. Magnus had insisted I always bring a guard with me. I didn't bother arguing with that. There were plenty of other things for us to argue about.

We ended up at a long hovel near the river wall, where many families lived in what had once been a fish market.

The boy's mother was inside, lying flat out on a mound of skins near the hearth at the centre of the low-roofed hall. Thankfully, a fire was going. A pot of water and another of stew were bubbling over it. Around the woman a crowd had gathered, all of them other women. They parted as I approached.

I went down on my one knee beside the woman and spoke a prayer as I went down, a hymn I'd learnt from Ulf: *Humbly we honour heaven's guardian, humbly we honour the great maker, humbly Queen of Heaven we pray to you.* The words were for those watching as much as for the woman, but also to still my racing mind, for the task ahead.

The woman was on her back with her legs wide, breathing fast, puffing. I turned to the women around us, tried to speak as calmly as I could. "Bring hot water," I said, my words coming fast. I breathed deep, said the prayer again. I must not hurry for this task.

I reassured the woman about to give birth with a hand on her knee, a nod, and a wide smile, then tested the water one of the other women held towards me.

"Good, it's hot," I said.

I felt the belly, slid a hand lower. She was open, wet, ready to give birth. I felt the baby kick, hard, then again. He wanted to come out and soon.

"A boy," I said. "He has a kick like a young bull."

A cheer rose up around us. The woman about to give birth smiled, but only for a moment, then reached towards me.

"You're not safe here," she whispered. She clutched at her belly and groaned after she spoke. Her eyes were wide with fear.

The racing in my mind was back. What did she mean? I'd been afraid when we first came here that the Danes looking for me would find us, but the fear had subsided as all the days slipped into each other with no one ever appearing looking for me. I narrowed my eyes, tried to look fearless. "I am," I said. "I have a guard."

She shook her head as if to tell me that wouldn't make any difference.

"It's not these people you're in danger from," she said nodding to the crowd. "'Tis someone else."

"Who?" I leaned closer, my skin prickling. Had I missed some danger? We'd done our best to fit in with the people here and the local king. He'd been welcoming. Perhaps Magnus had annoyed someone with his constantly cajoling talk of returning to England to retake his father's throne.

That was the moment she screamed. It sounded as if a wolf had taken a bite from her. "Quiet, keep breathing," I said as calmly as possible as echoes of her scream died slowly.

"More water," I shouted.

It was past dawn before the baby came. I'd already sent Bjorn back to our hall to tell Magnus what had happened. I was bleary-eyed when I finally stepped outside the hovel, but I did notice the river gate was open and beyond it the long dock was busy already. Ships came and went every day in Dublin.

Watching these comings and goings was a game many loved in the city. I walked towards the black pool, a shortcut to get back to our hall. As I got closer, I saw a Viking ship was pulling out of it, its sail still only a quarter way up and oarsmen rowing to get their ship out into the fast-flowing river channel beyond.

I stared.

That looked like the Godwin banner, a red boar on a black background flying on top of the mast. Who was on board? Someone was standing by the mast, his hands on his hips. My heart squeezed, as if a hand had come up from inside to grab it. I laughed; could I believe my eyes?

Magnus was at the mast, as clear as day now. You couldn't miss his new iron helmet, and that stupid silvered mail shirt he'd insisted on having made for him here. He was looking out to sea. He wasn't even looking back at the city.

With a sick, sinking feeling, I knew what this meant.

He was off to join his brothers and his mother. He'd planned to go to them a week after our wedding, but he was going before. And he hadn't told me. There could be no doubt what this meant.

He'd changed his mind about our marriage.

I went up on my toes, staring at the ship as disbelief followed by anger rose up inside me.

He wasn't even looking back.

The ship had a full complement of rowers too, and a mound of cargo covered in skins near the mast. And there was a woman near the cargo, her hood up, black hair streaming from the edge with the wind. Who was that?

"Bastard," I shouted, my face twisting, my voice lost amidst the endless cries of seagulls that filled those streets.

The woman was standing beside Magnus now. A sharp stab of jealousy made my chest tighten and my teeth clench. What was going on? I'd have cut his balls off at that moment, if I could have.

An old woman across the street shouted at me, "They're all the same, love. Don't fret. There's many more good men 'ill keep you company this day or any day."

I hurried on. I was shaking inside, still taking in what I'd seen, going over the implications in my mind.

The next few days would be a nightmare, not a dream come true. Everything I'd planned, everything we'd planned, was dust, no, stinking shit. I'd have to explain to a lot of people why our wedding was off.

And try to understand it myself.

They'd all look at me with pity too and with blame in their eyes. I should have known he was getting cold feet. What had happened to my so-called powers of prophecy? People would laugh.

And who was that woman? I groaned at the thought of them rutting. Perhaps I could kill her too?

What had happened?

Tears threatened. I raised my hand and wiped one away. No more. Stop.

I should have guessed this was coming.

Sure, I'd been happy with him, at times, but too often wanting to gut him too. He could be arrogant and rude, if occasionally caring, usually when he wanted what men always want.

I sent him into rages sometimes, especially when I talked about scouring the country for my sisters. He didn't like the idea of me disappearing, looking for them, even if I had a guard with me. He also didn't understand why I cared so much about finding them, even though I told him how our mother had rammed into us almost every day that as three sisters we had to help each other, and that family was the weave that made life bearable and how I'd come to believe it.

The summer after we'd arrived here, I'd travelled all over the south of this island looking for my sisters. I didn't care about his petulant shouting. After I returned to Dublin, I'd come to the conclusion that my sisters were most likely in the far north of the island, and he refused to provide an escort for me to go there, because of some stupid dispute with a local king and the risk of me being kidnapped.

I was grateful for one thing now. I was not pregnant. That was such a relief. I think he'd been hoping I would be, but I wasn't, because of careful planning and a few clever tricks I'd played.

When I got back to our hall, I found a small and battered leather purse with a few gold coins in it on our bed and a simple message he'd left for me with Bjorn. I dropped the purse as if it was hot as I shook with rage after seeing the coins. I wanted to kick it far away, but I didn't. I hid it instead along with the few silver coins that had been pressed on me for healing and a few other small things I needed to keep safe.

"Stay pure until I get back. That is all Magnus said to tell you." Bjorn repeated the message twice. He had a look on his face that made it clear he'd been asked to keep an eye on me too. No apology. No explanation. Just instructions. Magnus all over.

Despite my rage, I smiled at Bjorn. "I'm always pure, Bjorn. You know that."

He gulped. The poor boy was smitten. Magnus was either stupid to have him watch over me. Or very clever.

I hid the beautiful silk marriage-binding ribbon and paced the hall for the rest of the day, as I raged, imagining the retribution I'd inflict on Magnus. I wasn't going to take his manhood off with my dagger anymore, but a vision of threatening it in his ardent moments pleased me.

That night I washed and put on a hard face and a clean tunic and went to the King of Leinster's hall. He was not there, but his mother was. Aoife was white-haired, elderly, and unable to walk far, and confused at times, but I'd helped her recover from the coughing sickness. She spotted me and called me to her as soon as I came in their door.

I told her what had happened. The words came out slowly, as if they didn't want to be said, but I had to say them. She reached towards me, bent her head, and gripped my hand. Something about the gesture made all the feelings I'd had that day come bursting up again as strong as ever. I wiped at my eyes, pushing the tears away. I could not let anyone see my weakness.

She hugged me.

"Have no fear for your position here, Synne. You are welcome in this hall anytime, whatever you decide to do." She held my shoulders, looked at me with narrow eyes, a half-smile on her face.

"He could have told me," I blurted out.

"I'm sure he'll be back." She smiled.

She did not mention what might happen if he did not come back to marry me or that her son, the King of Dublin, would most likely presume a say in my future if Magnus didn't return. That family liked to have their say in too many things.

"Who else went with him?" I asked with a shrug, as if I wasn't that concerned about who'd been on the boat.

She looked me up and down. That was the moment I knew there was more to Magnus's departure than I was being told. Her pensive expression made it abundantly clear she knew more than me.

"Did you try this bread?" she asked, avoiding the question. "It's from a new baker from Francia." She broke a small piece from a pale loaf on the table and handed it to me with a fake smile. I was about to ask her again what she knew about Magnus's departure when she shook her head at me and looked around. I did too. A few other people sitting near us at the long table were quiet and listening.

I took the bread. It was good, light, but I could not eat much. I moved closer to her and told her about the woman I'd helped the night before. After that, she agreed that I could use two of her messengers to send word to the various families who were due to attend our wedding.

I was grateful for that.

When I got back to our hall, I felt utterly alone. I wondered how many other people knew what Magnus had planned before me. I shook my fists when I realised I was probably the last person to know our wedding would not happen. I wanted to break something, but it passed. Slowly.

What irritated me most was that he must have known about this for some time, including while he was agreeing with all the plans I'd been making.

At cock crow, as a grey mist from the marsh downriver lay its fingers over our roof, a gentle knock came on our door.

I knew Bjorn, who slept on rushes near the door every night wrapped in a wolf skin, would rise to see who it was this early. He came running and called for me through the wool curtain we used for privacy.

I raised myself from our low bed and slipped on my soft leather boots. Something was wrong. People only come to your door at dawn with bad news.

"It's Frida, the king's daughter. She wants you," Bjorn called out.

"Let her in."

"He did," came a soft voice.

I stood, smoothed my thin night tunic, and pushed the curtain aside. He looked awestruck as he backed away. And not just by me. Frida was one of the few real beauties in this land. Her rope-thick strands of red hair framed a pale face.

After greeting her, I said, "Let me put on another tunic, Frida." I went to the chest where I stored my clothes.

"Dress for the road," said Frida.

I stopped, my hand on the lid.

"Why?"

"The woman you helped give birth a few nights ago died. Someone in her hall claims you put a spell on her."

I groaned low and long and pulled out my thickest tunic. Such an accusation could change everything for me.

Frida was staring at me.

"You must leave the city at once," she said softly.

The Power of Synne

"What? Who said this?" It wasn't like Frida to give orders.

"Grandmother." The woman I'd been with the night before.

"Where will I go?" I hated the thought of running away. I'd been out of Dublin many times, but I had no real friends outside the city and few enough in it.

"I've a horse for you outside and a guide who will show you where to go until this blows over," she said. "Hurry, come on." She looked and sounded panicked.

"I'm coming," I said. "I'll be with you in a moment. Wait for me outside." I waved at her to go, and again she stared at me, a strange look on her face. When she was gone, I went to get the silver coins from where my purse was hidden. I would leave the gold ones until I needed them. They were too valuable to wander around with. I hid the purse again quickly.

The idea of leaving and not knowing when I'd be back made me uneasy. But I strapped my best boots on, filled a shoulder bag quickly with an extra tunic and a comb, wrapped my cloak around myself, and headed for the door.

Bjorn was nowhere to be seen.

I should have taken notice of that and headed out the back door, but I heard Frida calling.

"We're waiting. Hurry, Synne."

I thought Bjorn was with her. But when I pushed open the main door, I saw what "we" meant. Standing beside her was the head of her father's guard, a thug of a man with a wide face like a bear's and a scar where one of his eyes should be.

"Take her," he shouted.

Men came out of the shadows at each side of the door, and I was grabbed, roughly, silently. I knew at once what had happened. There would be no reports of Magnus's hall being invaded, a crime some claimed was equal to a rape. I'd been taken in the street.

I pushed away the first man to my right trying to grab me, but soon there were four men holding me. I stopped fighting then. I would wait for my chance.

"What's this all about?" I shouted, holding my arms wide. "I cannot be taken without knowing why." Two women had come out of the house opposite. They were watching and would no doubt spread the word about what had happened through the whole city by noon.

"You've been accused of causing a death," said the leader of the guards, equally loudly.

"I helped a woman give birth," I replied. "When I left her, she was alive." I took a deep breath, tried to calm myself. "The monk Ulf can vouch for me. He told your king that I'm a healer and not to be blamed if people die after my care."

"The monk Ulf is not here anymore," said the man. He waved at the men to bring me and was helped by another of his guards to get onto his horse.

I was taken straight to the king's hall, while being poked constantly to walk faster, by the two men beside me and the two behind, some of them muttering about what they'd do to me if I ran. A big enough crowd, maybe twenty people, was waiting for me inside the hall. I didn't recognise many of the faces, but as soon as I entered, they all began shouting and pointing at me as if they knew me. I was stunned into silence.

The two men at the top table were staring down at me with hard expressions. I knew them. One was the son of the King of Dublin. The other, the king's half-brother. I'd only had a little to do with either of them up to that moment, as they spent many days away raiding, but I'd heard bad things about Bran, the king's half-brother. He liked to force himself on women. I had to be careful.

"She's an evil English witch, sent to destroy us," shouted a woman.

"I am no witch," I shouted, struggling against the men marching me forward.

I was released in front of the top table while the crowd bayed around me. They could not decide my fate, I knew that, but the men at the top table could. They could judge me now if my crimes were proven or put me in a hole while they gathered witnesses to a crime someone claimed I was guilty of.

"Quiet," roared Bran. He smashed his fist down on the table. The room hushed.

I waited for an opportunity to speak.

Bran was eyeing me with a sneer, as if he knew something bad about me. I stared back, my face hard, my breath coming fast. One thing most men like him do not like is a woman who will not bend for them.

Was the fact that Magnus was not here anything to do with this?

"What is the charge against this woman?" said Bran.

I turned, looked for an accuser, ready to question them.

And I saw him.

The boy who'd come to get me to help the woman was sauntering towards me. An old woman was beside him, whispering in his ear. He blinked when he saw me and paused. She pushed him forward.

"This one came to help my mother," shouted the boy. "Now my mother is dead. I demand she pay the blood price for this as I am an orphan because of her." He pointed at me, began crying, but in a weird unnatural way.

"I tried to help this boy's mother. That is all," I said. "I do not kill people! If God decides to take someone a healer tries to help, the healer cannot be blamed."

The boy's eyes were on me. They were red, as if he'd been up all night, and there was a hollowness to them, as if he suffered with grief. I felt sorry for him.

"I feel for this boy. I will help him," I said. "But the mother was perfectly healthy when I left her. I want to see her, see what killed her." Anything could have happened after I left her.

"We will set someone to examine the body," said Bran. He banged his fist down again. "This trial will resume tomorrow. You will be kept in the hole until then."

I shuddered, closed my eyes. The hole was a dreadful place, a pit with iron bars over it, where prisoners were kept for a day or more until it was decided what to do with them. It was a good place for breaking people, a place where nightmares became real.

I was grabbed and taken, my feet barely touching the ground.

I swore to myself as they lifted the iron bars that I would not start crying down there and would never admit my guilt to get out of the place as some I'd heard did, but as that day dragged on and on and on, I weakened a little.

The portion of stale bread and the skin of water that were dropped to me did not comfort me. And thinking about the change in my fate in a few short days did not help. I hoped at one point that I might wake up. But I didn't. And the cold and the mud down in the hold did not help.

The pit was in the yard at the back of the king's hall. From it, I could hear servants and slaves moving about until it grew dark and started to rain. That added to my misery. I held my cloak over my head and prayed for the rain to stop. I prayed for my sisters too, that I could find them or maybe they could find me. There was much we needed to talk about.

Slowly my cloak became too heavy to hold up with the rain pouring into the hole. I sat down in a layer of mud and wondered how many prisoners had died down here, like this, their death a judgement on their guilt. I half slept leaning on my arms.

"Synne," a voice hissed.

I was dreaming, surely.

The voice came again.

"Synne, take the rope."

I looked up. Frida's pale face was looking down at me anxiously, lit by moonlight. A grey rope was hanging, just a little out of my reach. I stood.

"I can't get to it," I hissed. Was this a trap? Escaping from custody was a crime. I knew that. Should I refuse this offer?

No. I couldn't. I had to get out of this place.

The Power of Synne

A little more rope came down. I grabbed it with both hands. Then, with a jerk that almost pulled my arms from their sockets, the rope was pulled up. I was at the top of the pit moments later. Two big men had pulled me out of it. Frida had a dry cloak under her arm. She handed it to me.

"Come on," she said. A faint light had appeared in the east. Dawn was not far off.

I laughed quietly, like an idiot, looking around for guards.

"Why should I trust you?" I asked. Always be wary was the best way to live, Magnus had told me often enough. He loved such phrases, teaching me things I already knew.

"I'm trying to help you, Synne." Frida looked one way then the other. "I did not know they would put you down there." She shook her head. "I did not know what they'd planned, I swear." Her words came out in a believable tumble.

I put the cloak she'd handed me on, hugged it. It was so good to have something dry around me.

"Where will we go?"

"We'll go to the hall of the high seers at Tara," she said. "They will help you. I know them."

I'd heard of the place. Everyone in all these islands had. Tara was a school for seers I'd wanted to go to before, at the harvest festival, but you had to be invited.

"You have an invitation?"

"I can go there any time."

"The king's guard will pursue me."

She leaned closer. "You cannot stay here, Synne. I heard talk about making you a slave. The charges against you have been proven."

"They can't do that." This was sick, an old nightmare returning. Could the Danes have found me?

"They can, Synne. You must come with me. The seers will help you."

Could I trust her?

She seemed to read my mind, and held a dagger out, its sharp end pointed back at her. "Take it. Stab me if I'm lying," she said forcefully. "The king's son knows I'm taking you away. Trust me." She hissed that last part.

"He didn't speak up when I was ordered into the hole," I replied, pointing back at the pit, my hand shaking.

"He did not speak against you."

I took her dagger. I could still fight. "Which way?" I asked. If the king's son was on my side, if agreeing to this was his way of helping me, I had to take the chance.

Frida waved at the two men. They went to the high wicker fence around the yard and pulled at a corner. That part of the fence moved. A gap opened up for us to get through. Beyond it was a muddy path leading to the cornmarket. We hurried along it. The market was empty, the usual bustle of the stalls replaced by the insistent hissing of the rain that had started up again.

We ran through it to where four horses were tied up under the extended thatch at the side of a tavern.

We rode at an unhurried pace towards the main gate to the west of the city. We reached it as it was being opened. A line of damp-looking leather-covered carts was waiting outside. The gate guards just nodded as we went out. They'd probably report Frida's departure if they were asked, and that there was someone with her.

We rode at a canter along the muddy road leading inland, the occasional thatched hovel on either side, passing a few carts along the way, heading for the city markets. Soon the road narrowed and passed into a deep wood, the start of the endless forest that covers most of this land.

We slowed then and soon after took a side track heading north, winding through the forest. The rain stopped after we crossed a swollen river at a ford. Frida spoke to me a few times, but I barely answered. Everything that had happened in the past few days made me tired and worried. Yes, I'd escaped the city with her help, but was I now an outlaw? How could I have gone from preparing for my marriage to running for my life as an outlaw?

Outlaws had to look over their shoulders constantly as there was often a price on their head and someone wanting to claim it.

Why had Magnus left so suddenly? Was my arrest connected to his departure? Had he a hand in all this? Did he want rid of me?

I'd grown truly fond of him since we'd left London, but he also annoyed me at times, and I'd told him. Was that my mistake?

Being held in that horrible pit had reminded me of how much you can lose at any moment, and what waited the unfortunate.

I fought an urge to question Frida. She was hiding things from me, I knew that, but I should wait for a good moment to question her and push her for information.

We passed a few tiny villages with low, thatched-roof houses. We also passed two small forts surrounded by mounds of earth and high wicker fences.

Some fields cut from the forest had the first small growths of wheat and barley sprouting in them as we headed north towards Tara. Frida rode beside me as the road finally straightened late that day, heading directly towards a distant hill, which I assumed was our destination.

Smoke rose in a black pillar high into the air above the hill.

"When the time comes, answer all things truthfully when they ask," she said, turning to me.

"I will do nothing else," I said, bristling at the implication that I might lie.

She put her hand out towards me. "I don't mean disrespect. The seers at Tara are…" She paused, took a deep breath. "Able to see inside hearts and minds." She raised her hands. "They can show the future and turn men into animals just like that." She clicked her fingers.

"Does Yann know where we're going?" I asked, changing the subject. I'd heard a lot of wild stories about the seers at Tara. Yann was her brother, the King of Leinster's youngest son, the man who'd supposedly agreed to me slipping away from their city. Though his authority only existed if his brothers weren't in the city.

Frida smiled. "He does. He's coming. He'll be at the feast."

"Which feast?" We were a week away from the fire festival at the start of summer, when cattle were driven between bonfires and women and men who wished for fertility jumped over them.

"You'll see. Everything starts early at Tara," she said.

There were many things about this island I was still learning. One, which was unsettling, was the treatment of slaves here. We'd just passed a string of them being led away from the distant hill. There'd been twenty of them, at least, all roped together, stumbling as they went.

Being turned into a slave was a deep fear. Without family to protect you or a husband, such things were always possible.

I'd spent too many days, to Magnus's annoyance, visiting the slave markets in Dublin, trying to track down my sisters by getting close to the traders to find out if they knew anything about them. Every trader I spoke to claimed to know nothing about my sisters, all had crooked smiles, and one told me they wouldn't tell me anyway, even if they knew exactly where my sisters were. It wasn't worth the trouble, he said.

But I didn't give up. I kept looking and asking. Our mother had fed us on the importance of family. She'd made us promise out loud every year that we'd never desert each other. I'd heard some families were not like this and I wondered what nourished their hope.

A family of Northmen ran the Dublin slave markets. One market was for women and children, the other for men.

I'd spoken a few times to Magnus about organising men to go north with me, to search that part of the island, but he'd told me to wait until more of his supporters arrived. I'd pressed him on it, and eventually he'd promised it would happen after we were married.

Another lie.

We went through two barriers on the road as we approached the Hill of Tara. One had a group of young men with polished axes on their belts and intricately woven cloaks, who eyed both Frida and me as if we might become available to them. At the next barrier, a large stone in the road, two old women with white hair waited. We were allowed past them but the two guards who'd been with us since Dublin weren't.

Frida told them to wait in one of the low huts nearby. There were people milling about there with pigs and a few cattle being herded into wicker pens while a biting wind blew and sullen grey clouds marched overhead. A few women there were staring at us, pointing in our direction as we went up the hill. I assumed these were women who hadn't been allowed to go up as easily as we'd been.

The road was wider here and lined with ancient yew trees that looked as old as the island itself, each one with multiple trunks and branches reaching high into the air.

Frida smiled as we passed under their high boughs.

"If these trees are ever cut down, our island will lose all its magic, so they say."

"I thought you and your family were all followers of Christ," I said.

"We are, but we believe in the old ways too. We can do both."

At the end of the line of yew trees, an embankment blocked us going any further. We slid from our horses and walked with them along a narrow grassy path around the edge of the embankment. A steep earth wall loomed high on our left and a forest of thin trees on the other side stretched into the distance. It was getting near sundown. I was wondering what would happen here. I trusted Frida and I'd not heard any bad stories about Tara, so I was willing to go along with everything. To a point.

The evening sounds of the forest, bird song, rustling from the many creatures of the trees and the wind, enveloped us as we went. I was sure, as darkness grew and we kept walking, that we must have gone around the hill more than once. Then I saw that the embankment had an opening just ahead. I hadn't seen that before.

All noise died away.

I looked around. I'd thought, with a head-turning start, that Frida had disappeared, but she hadn't; she was right behind me.

A red glow at the top of the hill had distracted me. We had to be close to our destination. My horse knew it too. It picked up its pace as we went through the opening and emerged into an open area in front of an earth mound with a series of low wattle and daub thatch-roofed halls around it. Smoke rose into the sky, twisting and mingling in the air above the halls, joining into that one column far up, which I'd seen as we approached the hill, like threads winding together.

A tingle of expectation ran through me. I knew that Christian priests and monks had tried to stop all the ancient activities on the hill, but they'd not succeeded, as most of the seers had become followers of Christ and were not even here all year round. What could the Christians do when seers mixed Christian prayers with spells and chants?

Light from each hall's doorways lit the area in front of the halls. Two young, smiling male slaves with shiny neck rings that could have been gold appeared and took our horses. We were directed to a smaller hall with a closed door and went inside, where four basins of water were laid out around a smouldering hearth. Each had different coloured water in it. A female slave wearing multiple bone necklaces sat beside each basin. The wicker door closed behind us. Frida bowed to me.

"Everything off, Synne the healer. You'll be given a new tunic after the cleansing," she said.

I didn't have much choice. The few silver coins I'd had in a purse had been taken from me before I was put in the pit back in the city, so there wasn't much I was going to lose, but still I felt uncomfortable at not knowing what was coming as I stripped off.

The cleansing process took a long time.

After we'd washed in each of the four basins, the first for our heads, the next for our feet, one for our bodies and the last for our hands, we were given new short, pale blue tunics and taken by a door at the back across a twig-strewn path into a second and larger hut where we were told to sit and pray to whatever gods we worshipped.

This hut was dark, lit only by a few candles in the centre. In the shadows near the far wall, someone was kneeling with their hood on, facing us. I felt wary until a voice called out.

"You made it, Synne the healer." The person at the back of the hut rose and pushed his hood back off his face. It was Ulf, the monk. Mightily relieved, I went to him. We hugged each other tight for a long time.

"What are you doing here?" I asked, eventually holding him at arm's length.

"Magnus told me to come here."

"Magnus?" I said his name with anger. "You know he left me just before we were to be married!" I had to stop talking for a moment to stop my tears. "Did he tell you he was planning to leave me?" I struggled to finish my thought.

"He had his reasons, I am sure of that. You must forgive him, Synne." He smiled, as if what Magnus had done was not so bad.

"Forgive him?" I laughed.

He was looking over my shoulder.

"Is he here?" I asked, turning, my heart quickening.

"No," said Ulf.

I was about to say more when a voice called out.

"Are you ready to cleanse inside?" It was Frida.

"Yes," I said, after a hesitation as I struggled to control my feelings. I thought I'd got over his painful departure, but the threads from it still gripped me like a horrible knot. I sniffed in as Frida motioned me to kneel and then to listen and breathe slowly, with her and Ulf, one on each side, Ulf whispering Christian prayers while Frida whispered chants in a language I could not understand but with words that keened to my soul.

I let myself sink into the chanting and the prayers. It felt as if a blanket had enveloped me, easing my pain, until eventually they stopped, I do not know how much later, and the door of the hut opened in front of me and beyond, the lights of another hall beckoned.

We all stood and went out. Ulf and Frida held my hands, one each side, and urged me to hush, though I hadn't said a word.

Ulf sat on a bench at the back of this new hall and pulled me to him. "Why did you come here?" he asked.

I sat, smiled. "Guess." I was not going to tell him I wanted help from the seers.

Ulf did not reply.

"Why did Magnus leave?" I asked, my smile showing my anger and pain had diminished.

"Did he not tell you about his mother needing help? She summoned him to England, Synne. That's where he's gone. His mother and his sister are marooned on some island with King William's men threatening."

"Why didn't he tell me he was going?"

"You would have asked to go with him."

He was right. I breathed in, shifted on the wolf skin covering the bench, looked around at the few other people in the hall. A strange feeling came over me then, as I watched everyone, all looking around, as if they were expecting something to happen.

"King William is freeing slaves in England," said Ulf. He leaned closer. "If the slavers here cannot sell bodies to England, a big market is gone for them. That means less silver to pay the men who man the walls of Dublin."

I knew how important slave trading was to Dublin. The slave market there brought traders from as far away as Constantinople.

"What has that got to do with Magnus?" I asked.

"Magnus should find it easier to get support here for retaking his father's kingdom because of this. That is good news for Magnus. Every cloud has a silver edge." He laughed.

I closed my mouth. I'd spoken out against slavery to Magnus. Now it might benefit us. Or was there an "us" anymore?

A horn blared nearby. The hall went quiet. Everyone stood. From the other end of the hall, a line of women emerged, all dressed in white tunics with garlands of pale flowers in their hair. They all had smiles on their faces, as if they were drunk, and each of them carried a blazing torch.

"The seers of the four provinces," whispered Ulf reverently. "We are fortunate to see this."

"Tell me again, Ulf, why are you here?" It seemed strange he was part of all this.

"To preach the word of Christ, Synne." He waved around him. "And to witness what they're up to here."

Frida had appeared in front of me with her hand out, motioning me to stand. She had a wide smile on her face. I smiled back, gripped Ulf's shoulder as I stood. My legs were still a little weak after all the riding getting here, my thighs burning in places.

She led me through the crowd to the top of the hall. The seers were standing behind a high, long table. The air here was thick with smoke and the light dim. I sniffed as the earthy smell of burning oak filled my nostrils. The women drank from yellow, almost see-through, horn goblets. Frida found one for me, filled it from a large red jug on the table and handed it to me. Then she filled one for herself and downed the contents in one go.

"Drink," she said, yellow liquid dribbling freely down her chin. "It's an insult to refuse the seer's mead. It will bring us all good luck and spread fertility across the land."

That was when I noticed the young men lined up along the walls. They looked as if they were waiting for something, looking at us eagerly.

I'd never been to a ceremony like this, and I'd no idea what was to come next. The customs here were different to what I'd been through before.

I drank from the horn. Whatever it was tasted like fire, burning down my throat. With an excited laugh, Frida urged me to keep drinking, pressing her palm to my horn, pushing it up as I raised it, then downing her second horn, then filling mine again and hers from the jug.

I felt a deep warmth growing inside me and I laughed. There was nothing to be afraid of. It was just fire water, which we had in England, though this seemed stronger than what I'd sipped at feasts a few times.

I drank more of the fire water and Frida pushed the end of the horn up in the air further this time, forcing the liquid into my mouth and down my chin. I didn't care. I swallowed some of it and more ended up on the front of my tunic and on the ground. Then I swiped her hand away.

Frida laughed, grabbed my arm, and pulled me tight to her. She kissed me on the lips. Hers were soft and warm.

I was tempted to respond, to kiss her back. I could have, but a warning voice inside me said, no, be careful, be very careful.

Frida stuck her tongue out at me as we pulled apart. "Are they all cold like you in Saxon lands?" she asked, a taunting tone to her voice and a mocking gleam in her eye.

"What do you want from me, Frida?" I asked. She'd rescued me from the pit, but there was more going on here than her wanting to kiss me.

Frida leaned close. I could smell mead all over her. "Tonight, Synne, we'll choose a new great seer." She spoke in a hushed tone, as if sharing a secret. "Tomorrow, a procession will head for the big feast in a week that'll mark the start of summer. You celebrate something similar, yes?"

I nodded.

"Do you want to go with them?" She was slurring her words.

"No." I must not be sidetracked.

"What will you do?"

I didn't reply. She'd respect my need to find my sisters, but it was hard to explain how much that need shaped me. And now I needed to find Magnus too.

Frida laughed, crooked her finger at me, her head to one side. "Have you forgiven him already, like a good follower of Christ, turning the other cheek?"

I sniffed and thought about my reply. She was goading me. That was clear. But it was true that Magnus leaving me had disturbed me deeply, as if I'd lost something I had to find quickly.

"No, I have not forgiven him."

"Good, I have something for you."

She raised her hand high. One of the young men by the walls came running. In his hands was a bough of hawthorn, as long as his arm, with green buds all over it, ready to bloom.

"This is for you, Synne. It symbolises the affection someone has for you, not fully bloomed yet, but full of promise. You have a new admirer if you are open to it." She winked at me, stuck her tongue out.

I shook my head, slowly, tempted by her words. "I cannot take it." I knew what it would mean to accept the bough. A commitment would begin.

"You do not care who sends this before you decide?" Frida looked shocked.

I wanted not to care, but I could not resist asking.

"Who is it?"

Frida's eyes sparkled, reflecting the glowing embers from the fire. "The bough is from Yann, a son of the King of Leinster." She raised her eyebrows and grinned, as if I must surely jump at an offer from him.

"He wants you. He expects to be king too, unlike your Magnus." She flicked her hand, dismissing Magnus's chances of succeeding his dead father.

"Magnus says he will be a king too," I replied.

Frida laughed, took my hand, rubbed the skin on the back slowly with her thumb. Her touch was reassuring. "Magnus has run off to rescue his mother, Synne. He may not even live to summer's end."

"I need to speak to Magnus or learn of his death before I turn to someone else." I sounded more confident than I felt. I knew he might never come back, but I would not be rushed.

Frida laughed. "Yann told me you'd say something like that. This is his offer, to take you by ship to where Magnus is, so you can learn the truth about him."

My mouth twisted. This was a welcome surprise, but also a dangerous offer. Yann might expect something from me. But saying no to a member of a king's family was something that had to be done carefully.

"He expects something from me?" I said it without emotion.

She shook her head, fast. "No. This is not a trick to rut with you."

It was hard to believe, but not impossible. I'd heard stories of love-struck men following the object of their desire with no expectations. Agreeing to this would help me find out what had happened to Magnus. And if it was a trick, I would deal with that when it happened.

"On these terms I agree," I said. I looked in her eyes, put my hand out for her to clasp to seal the agreement.

She reached towards me. "You have bewitched him, Synne the healer. I hear he is not the only one."

I gave her a thin smile.

"There is one small thing Yann asks." Frida looked serious now.

Here it comes.

"What small thing?" I pulled my hand back. Here comes the price.

"You have a ring that belonged to Odo, the brother of the new King of England. Yann asks that you give it up for safekeeping."

My chest tightened. This was not just about me. Someone, possibly from his family, wanted something that belonged to a member of King William's family, probably so they could cast spells on him. There'd been talk in Dublin about how to protect the city and all Ireland against William and his Norman lords. Many were afraid the

Normans would soon come to Ireland looking for more spoils.

Magnus must have told someone I had Odo's ring. I hadn't said it to anyone here. Apparently there'd been talk about finding something that belonged to the new Norman king or his family.

"I expect something in return," I said softly. She had to lean forward to hear me.

"What?"

"I need help to find my sisters." My words came out loud. "They are in the north of this island, I'm sure. But I've not been able to go there because Magnus wanted me to wait for the right moment." I said it all in a rush.

I would happily hand over Odo's ring to find Gytha and Tate.

Frida laughed. "You have a long neck," she said.

"I do." I leaned close to her, put my hand on her leg, rubbed it gently, while smiling. "Will you tell him? He can send messengers out while we go to find Magnus."

"I will ask."

"You should worry about the Normans coming here, Frida. They will gladly destroy all this." I waved my hand around. It was a stretch to think the Normans would want to take this island, seeing as the Romans had never wanted it, but the threat of it had to make these people think.

Frida nodded, stood, told me she was hungry, as if all this talk had developed her appetite. She went off and found mutton stew with soft onions in shiny red bowls. I was offered more fire water but refused. I was still feeling the effects of what I'd taken earlier. I swayed while watching everyone around me, listening to the different accents from all over this island and beyond, many of which I could not understand at all. I'd kept to the major towns when I'd travelled around and there'd always been someone who'd understood my tongue, but the people here were from every place.

Frida left me alone after she finished eating. She returned a little later to tell me that Yann would be ready to travel in the morning. That news sent a shiver through me. What he expected from me might be very different from what Frida had told me.

The threads of fate can weave a bad turn in one direction and then a good one in another.

I slept a little under a bench in the hall after some of the other women lay down in the rushes. Some of them lay close to each other. Frida lay beside me, but she did not try to kiss me.

***

Just before dawn, we were roused.

The procession would head off soon on a journey to the hill at the centre of the island, where celebrations to welcome summer and to mark the death of winter would be held. The old seer, who had been leading the seers on the island for seven years, would be escorted to a great fire at the top of the hill.

As the sun rose, with a small crowd of us observing, an old woman in a gold embroidered cloak headed inside the larger cairn nearby.

She was expected to emerge later, wearing a long grey cloak, and follow the procession as an ordinary seer. They did not sacrifice their seers any more, as happened long ago, but it still felt as if something momentous was happening. The followers of Christ had changed many things on these islands.

I had a vivid dream the night I was there, and that morning as I watched all this, it came back to me.

In the dream I'd seen Normans with their strange haircuts, here on this hill, laughing, killing.

A row of guards with spears and axes was waiting near the cairn. I was about to turn away when another guard, dressed in a knee-length green tunic, approached Frida, who was standing beside me. He stared at me as he spoke. I could not understand a single word he said, but Frida looked at me when he was finished.

"The seer has requested you talk with her," said Frida.

I was surprised and wary. "Why?"

"She will tell you." Frida smiled, but not with her eyes. She pointed at the guard. "He'll take you. Go with him, Synne. We must not keep the old seer waiting." She waved her hand to hurry me.

It all felt rushed, but I was curious about what the seer wanted from me. I went with the guard. He walked beside me, making sure I only went where he pointed, towards the entrance to the cairn. The other guards stood aside as we came to the passage that led into the cairn. The guard with me waved me to go straight in.

I did, bending as I went. The kerbstones on both sides of the passage were giant flat stones with carvings, swirls, and an array of rune patterns carved into them. The roof was a little too low to walk upright.

Ahead, a single shaft of light from a hole in the roof beckoned. A thick smell of earth and decay filled my nostrils. Sounds from outside, the neigh of distant horses, seemed far away, as if from across a lake.

I took a deep breath and went on.

I would not be afraid, especially of someone who could help me. As I came close to the cave-like central chamber, my hand brushed the cold stone wall, and then I saw the old seer just beyond a shaft of light. She was on her knees with her head bent, as if praying in the Christian manner. Her hair was wound up on her head now, in an ash-grey spiral.

Words I did not understand spewed from her in a torrent as I came near. Dismayed at my lack of understanding of her words, I wondered if any good could come of this. Then she switched to the Dublin tongue.

"Kneel with me, Synne the healer." Her accent, lilting like the sea, was a lot like the accents where I grew up near York. Shocked, I opened my mouth, then closed it.

She put her head to one side. "Yes, I am from near where they tell me you come from." She was a mind reader, too.

"But how?" I'd heard the lilting accents of northern English traders in Dublin a few times, but this was the first one so similar to mine she could have been from the next village.

"I was taken as booty by Danes after a battle near York many moons ago. And now I am here." She opened her hands, then breathed in deep through her nose. "The weft of life turns again with your arrival."

I knelt opposite her on the same smooth stone slab she was kneeling on. She didn't have to tell me what to do. A shaft of light fell between us with specks of silvery dust dancing in it. I could hear my breathing, but not hers and I could smell her too; she smelt of sweat and candle grease. My breathing sounded loud. I was sure she could hear me.

She raised her hands, palms towards me, as if to calm me.

"Give me your wakening stone," she said.

My mouth opened. The small amber bead the seer in England had given me was beneath my tunic. Only the thin leather string around my neck that it hung from was visible, and only Magnus knew about it. I'd not shown it to anyone else. But no special powers had descended on me because of it, not yet. Perhaps Magnus had told someone about it. He had a big mouth.

I pulled the bead out.

She motioned me to lift it from my neck. I pulled it over my head and passed it to her. She laid it in the shaft of light between us.

"With this, the power of a seer can be woken in you, Synne," she said softly.

A tingle of excitement rose inside me. This was what I wanted, what I'd dreamed about. To have my powers awakened.

"You… can do this?" I asked, stumbling over my words.

How I could open the powers that my mother could have helped open, if she'd lived, was a question I'd been asking myself since soon after she'd died. Could I ever have the same powers she had displayed and been famous for?

The old seer smiled at me. "This is why you are here," she whispered.

I shivered as if an icy draft had blown across me. If this seer could awaken my powers, the legacy of my mother and of hers, and hers before her, could finally come to me.

I'd suppressed all such hopes when I was with Magnus, but now they sprang up again in my mind as if a crack had opened for them to pass through.

I nodded, then nodded again.

"I feel many powers in you, Synne, deep inside, wanting to get out. You will surely become a great seer." She paused.

I waited as another shiver passed through me, this one like a snake curling all around me.

"Now, you must learn to pray to the winds," she said softly. "For only they can awaken your powers. Recite after me…

"Grant my soul's desire.
Grant my soul's desire, from earthly cares to rise.
Grant my soul's desire, deep within to rise.
Grant my soul's desire, from earthly cares I rise."

I recited the incantation after her.

"Again," she whispered. She leaned across the shaft of light and grabbed my wrists, one bony hand on each.

She pulled me forward until the shaft of light was on my hands and they were over each other and over the bead.

Her nails dug into my arms.

"Again."

I recited the chant again.

She reached up with both hands, touched my forehead with her middle fingers, and traced circles with her fingers around my eyes.

"Recite the chant when you truly need help," she said.

I looked past her at the dark shadows moving behind her. It looked as if someone else was there. I thought about my mother. She would have loved to be here, to be part of this.

With a snake-like movement, the seer slapped my cheek, hard.

I groaned loudly at her gall as the sting of the blow spread out and my skull shook inside. I raised a hand to ward her off. She grabbed my raised wrist and pulled it down again over the bead.

"Do not be distracted by the past, Synne. You can be the greatest of your line." She said it as if she knew what I'd been thinking. "Keep the bead close," she said. "It can be a weapon. Use it to survive. If you do, you will outlive them all."

I held the bead. What did she mean it could be a weapon? It felt hot.

The Power of Synne

"Do not doubt this. Seers do not need to prove themselves like men prove themselves for women. Women bring life forth. Seers save lives. You are a seer now."

Warmth spread through me from the bead. I opened my mouth, unable to stop myself asking the question that had come to mind.

"Do you know where my sisters are?"

She smiled. "One will find you near the black pool," she said.

Dublin was the city of the black pool.

"When?"

"Soon." She opened her mouth wide. Her front teeth had been filed into points. She waved me away. "Go now, Synne the seer."

She waved me away more vigorously, put her head down, and mumbled again in that tongue I could not understand. I moved backwards. As I went, the light shaft grew dim and her face disappeared. I put the string over my head and pushed the bead under my tunic.

Frida was waiting for me outside. I did not want to talk to her. She did not ask me any questions.

More time had passed than I had realised. The crowd was bigger now. People covered most of the hill. Mounted warriors had appeared, their spears glinting in the sunlight. They stood between the crowd and the area in front of the halls. Drummers started up. A gap in the crowd opened down the hill and a line of maidens in white tunics with garlands of pale flowers in their hair lined the open way.

We waited, watched as chariots went down the hill between the maidens. I had no idea who was in the chariots, and no one offered to explain what was going on. I did not see the old seer after that.

Eventually, Frida motioned me to follow her. We found our horses and headed back to Dublin. After we crossed a river, she asked me what had happened with the seer. "She helped me."

"Good," said Frida.

She looked at me with her head to one side but didn't press me. I was still thinking about what the old seer had said to me, her prediction that one of my sisters would be coming to Dublin. I felt uplifted by hope. We went on in silence, Frida smiling at me occasionally, as if she knew more than she was telling.

Later, as the two of us ate hard bread under an oak tree, sheltering from rain, our guards leaning against the other side of the tree, she told me in a soft voice that she knew I was a seer now.

No one stopped us when we re-entered Dublin. The guards at the gate seemed relaxed. She left me at the hall where Magnus and I stayed, while she went to visit the

The Power of Synne

king's half-brother, Bran. I told her to find out about any visitors to the city.

Our hall was empty, but it had not been ransacked. That was a good sign. I dug for my bag under the stone at the end of the hall and took Odo's ring and a few gold coins out and reburied the rest, deeper, listening all the while for anyone coming to take me. Being here brought back memories of Magnus and the plans we made. How stupid I had been believing in him.

Before I'd met the old seer, I'd been thinking about him, missing him. That had changed. I barely thought about him now. Coming back to Dublin would not change that.

I had what the old seer had given me, belief in myself, and my ability to weave my future the way I wanted. I would not go back to despair.

Frida returned that evening with food. I had not lit a fire or even opened the front door. She held her hand out. "You have the ring?" she said.

I gave her Odo's ring.

"Stay here, Synne," she said. "A slave will come with food for you each day."

"Where is the king?"

"Still on campaign. He won't be back until the end of summer."

"What about news of my sisters?" I asked. I would stay here hidden all summer if I had to, to find out if the seer's words were true.

"No news," she said.

I put my hands together, one wrapped over the other fist.

"Where is Ulf?" I asked.

"Not here. He is still on his mission."

"What mission?"

"Turning the seers to Christ."

Of course that was his mission. And probably reporting on what the seers were doing to the bishops, too.

Frida's face was stiff. She was hiding something. An image appeared in my mind, like a memory. Frida, weeping unconsolably. Then it was gone. I did not say anything about it. Never tell people anything bad may be on its way to them. My mother had taught me that.

After Frida left, I ate alone in the hall. The food she'd brought was good. I made my bed facing a different direction then, setting the blankets cross ways, not down, the way I'd slept with Magnus. I did not want any memories of him coming back, his spirit in my dreams. I tried to sleep but my thoughts spun like a top for a long time.

***

The Power of Synne

A slave brought food the next day, straight from the king's hall. I knew I should be grateful, but I was really still a prisoner, even if they were not making me feel like one by putting me in the hole.

Early the following morning, shouts woke me. I hurried to the door, looked outside. Three men with shields and spears stood there.

The banging started again.

"Synne the healer, open up."

I opened the door.

"Come on," the man said. "Someone wants to see you."

"Who?"

He reached for me.

I stepped back.

He pulled his axe head slowly from his belt. "Do not resist," he said. The three men with him came forward.

2

The earthy smell of burning oak filled the air. It had taken a while to get the fire going, but now it provided the warmth the three men and one woman needed.

"Tell me again, Prince Ultach, why can't we ride on to Dublin tonight?" asked Tate. They were resting together under an old but effective leather rain cover stretched between the branches above their heads.

"We want to arrive at dawn, slave," said Prince Ultach in his dismissive tone, which the two guards accompanying them always smiled at. Prince Ultach would have been a king by now, if his father hadn't lived so abstemiously, avoiding battles and always sending his sons on tasks like this.

Tate moved closer to the fire and held her hands to it. "And I will not rut with you this night either," she said loudly, so the guards would hear and snigger.

Ultach glared at her. He was probably tempted to strike her for her insolence, but he'd been explicitly warned by his father not to strike her or rut her, a warning given in her presence, and in the presence of the guards before they set out on the journey to Dublin.

A warning Prince Ultach had swallowed in glaring silence because Tate was the slave his father valued more than any other in his household. Ultach would take her to visit Dublin, to show her to her sister, as a messenger had requested them to do, and then to return as quickly as possible. She must not come back "damaged". That was the word Ultach's father, the King of Ulster had used.

"Give me your hand," said Tate, holding hers towards Ultach, the bare skin of her arm showing as she reached for him. She needed him friendly. The journey would be a nightmare any other way.

He looked at her. Her amber skin could invite any man. Clearly enraptured beyond his wit to resist, he gazed all along her arm, even though it was mostly covered by her favourite wolf skin cloak with its black fur trim. He licked his lips as he looked at her face and smiled. She knew her power, how her coal-black eyes and curly hair pulled men to her, so she didn't bother returning his smile. She stared back at him instead.

He held his hand out. She took it, pulled it towards the flames.

He was very slow to react. It wasn't until the heat became almost unbearable for her own hand that she let his go.

"What in Christ's name are you doing?" he shouted, blowing on his hand.

The other two men sniggered, looked away.

"Pain is truth and the path to purpose, my prince," said Tate. She reached for his hand again, smiling.

He almost let her take it but pulled back and winked at her instead and gripped the elaborate gold clasp of his cloak.

"Ultach, come on, give me your hand. Fire is the gateway between the earth and the gods," she said softly. She passed her hand through the low shifting flame above the burning wood. She didn't flinch when she felt its heat, as her mother had taught her, and held her warm hand out for Ultach again.

"Do you not want to touch me again?" she asked with a slight smile.

He glared, his eyes narrowing.

"It is magic like this you used on my father over the last few moons, isn't it?" he asked.

"No, it is more than this." She pushed her face forward until she was leaning towards him, her cloak open so he could see the smooth tops of her breasts. She whispered, "So much more."

The Power of Synne

She laughed, blew on her fingers as if blowing something towards him. At that, the wind picked up and the trees around them swayed and a giant raindrop hit Tate's cheek. She shivered all over and moved her back towards the old oak tree.

It appeared as if she was sleeping, resting against the tree now. The three men waited a while at the fire, while the rain pattered at the branches and leaves above them, and soon after, they lay down in a protective semi-circle around her.

Prince Ultach was the last to sleep. She wondered if he'd try his luck again this evening or if the fear of his father would stop him from doing what it was obvious he craved to do. Let him try.

By the time Tate woke, the sky was full of milky clouds streaming fast towards the sea. A light rain had passed over them, leaving the thick grass around them lush and sparkling with dew. The three men were up and sharing horse bread and drinking from water skins and whispering. She rose, shivered. She never liked sleeping in the open. She pushed her hood back and went to Ultach. All eyes were on her. He glanced at his men briefly, then broke a piece of his bread off and handed it to her. One of the guards bowed a little and handed her his waterskin.

Tate wiped the top of the waterskin and drank from it. Ultach still had his hand out with the piece of bread in it. She took it when she was finished with the waterskin. The two guards looked at each other, wide-eyed at her insolence. They said nothing.

While the two guards untied the horses from the nearby tree, Ultach took the opportunity to put his fist up to Tate's face. Something new was troubling him from the way his face had reddened.

"Do not insult me in front of the guards," he hissed. "I'll make you pay if you do that ever again. Your face will not be so pretty with scars on those cheeks."

She stepped close to him, smiling. He deserved all this. "Can I insult you in private? You do know what your father will do to you if you damage me in any way?" She said it in a mocking tone, slipped her hand out from her cloak, low down, and pressed the point of her dagger upwards between his legs.

He made a croaking noise, like a toad, and stepped back fast, his gloved hand rising to ward her off.

"You are spawn of the devil, Tate. The monks were right." He looked down at the blade disappearing back into the gap in the front of her cloak.

"I'm no devil spawn," said Tate. "The head monk said that because I wouldn't lie with him. And you are exactly the same." She slipped her dagger back into the leather sheath on her belt, a gift the king had given her before her departure.

"You will not dare harm any part of me. You know it. I know it. Your father knows it. That is why he sent you with me. You don't want to end up with your balls cut off." She glanced towards the guards, now standing behind Ultach, and then leaned closer to him. "Keep your tongue still, Ultach, if you want to stay whole."

He grunted in frustration, turned away.

They didn't speak again until they arrived at the ford of the hurdles, where the water growls over wicker mats, moving so fast they could not cross into Dublin until they got down and led their horses across one by one.

At the high wooden gate, in the muddy open area beyond the ford, she looked up at two new heads on spikes, to see if she recognised either of the faces. She didn't. One of the gate guards had a long conversation with Ultach, with many glances in her direction. Eventually, another man was called over. Other guards waited, observing. Ultach's party was allowed in only if a guard went with him and they went directly to the hall of the king.

The wind picked up from the sea as they passed through the mud-filled streets. Gulls shrieked as they vied for scraps. Tate sniffed and looked up at the dark grey clouds coming from the hills to the south.

"Something's wrong," she said. Ultach was beside her, but it was the city guard who responded.

"Every day something's wrong here." He laughed. "But your presence will brighten things up for someone, I'm sure." He winked at her.

Ultach glared at him.

Tate blew him a kiss.

The man licked his lips in reply, as if he could taste her kiss. "I can show you where to wash before you meet the king," he said, a sly smile on his face.

She grinned. "That's a fine plan," she said. "And you can help me. If you let my friend gouge out your eyes first." The guard's expression changed. Ultach's remained the same. She pointed at a pair of crows on the top of a thatched hall they were passing. "I am sure those crows like eyeballs."

The man didn't reply. He eyed Ultach as if asking how did he allow a woman to speak like this. Tate ignored him, right up to the moment when he waved for the guards at the king's hall to open the doors for them. Then she gave him a big smile as if she'd been joking all along. He beamed in reply, forgiving her.

Inside the king's hall, they were asked for their weapons. Tate shook her head, indicating she didn't have any. It was only her and Ultach now. Their guards had gone to a tavern. Ultach handed his weapons over with a sour look.

There were only a few people at the tables lined up on each side of the hall, beneath the smoke-stained thatched roof, with dead birds, quail, and cranes hanging, drying near the walls and hogs' legs hanging further along. There was no one at the top table.

"The king will be here soon," said a skinny man at the weapons check. "Enjoy the remnants of the feast we had last night for another visitor." He bowed.

He pointed at the bones of meat still on the table. They looked as if they'd been gnawed at, but not fully. There was still meat on them.

"Take what you want. I'll have bread and wine brought for you."

Tate did not like the look of the bones, but bread and wine would be good. "Do you have new cheese?" she asked.

The man bowed.

She nodded as if they were friends. "Good hard cheese." She gave him a smile.

"At once," said the man.

It was easy to get men to do what you want.

She sat and watched as Ultach made a fool of himself gnawing on the best bone he could find.

"Your father would have demanded fresh meat."

"It's too early in the day for fresh meat," said Ultach. "And…" his mouth opened.

Tate followed his gaze.

A man in a fine wool tunic with red embroidery along its edges and a soft face behind a short beard was striding towards them. He raised his arms in greeting. He and Ultach bear hugged. When the man pulled away, he looked down at Tate and nodded.

"So, this is the famous sister we've all been waiting for."

Tate rose from the bench, her head high. "My name is Tate. You are?"

"Yann, son of the King of Leinster."

"He has many sons; are you his heir, Prince Yann?"

Yann looked at Ultach and laughed. "They were right about you. Straight to the knife point," he said. "My father has yet to decide who his heir shall be. Most think it will be Murchad, but like Ultach's father, he waits for proof that he can carry on his legacy as he wants it to be carried on." He smiled as if he didn't care about such things as being the heir.

Tate bowed, but only a little. "I'm sure you are capable of many things, Yann." She pointed at the table. "Perhaps you can arrange for stew for us. I was never fond of gnawing on someone else's bones."

Yann waved for a slave with a thin iron collar around his neck. He spoke to the slave, who then hurried away.

Tate sat down. "You say I am a famous sister. Does that mean you've met Gytha?"

Yann laughed. "No, we've been blessed with your other sister, Synne, since last year. She has been looking for you."

Tate stared at him as if he'd mentioned a ghost. "Are you sure about this? My sister, Synne, was lost when London was taken by the Normans."

"You can decide for yourself if she's your sister when you meet her."

Two slaves arrived with bowls of stew and more bread, of a better quality than had been provided before. Ultach whispered something in Yann's ear. He went on whispering, while Yann stared at her, his eyes widening.

Tate finished what was in her mouth, then banged the table with the butt of the knife she'd used for cutting up the meat. "Tell me the stories you just spoke about me, Ultach."

Ultach pointed at her. "See how she is, Yann."

Yann raised a hand to stop any fighting. "This will be a good day for you, Tate," he said. "Do not spoil it."

Tate shook her head slowly, deliberately. "If my sister is here, it may not be a good day for her. I have a proper bone to pick with her."

"A bone?" asked Yann.

Tate nodded. "When is she coming?"

"Any moment."

Tate cut a piece of bread and, using the point of her knife, pushed it into her mouth.

"Is she with a man?" she asked. "Is that how she escaped the Normans?"

"She's a free woman now," said Yann.

"What's your problem with this Synne?" asked Ultach. He smiled, put his head to one side as if he'd realised something.

Tate pointed her knife at him. "If she's the sister who abandoned me and Gytha when we were captured, do not expect much sisterly…" She laughed. "Anyway, let us wait and see if she is who you say."

Yann stood. "Synne is a good woman. She has the blessing of the seers," he said, a touch of anger evident in his tone. He glowered at Tate, then strode away.

Tate and Ultach waited in the hall. Ultach started complaining to her after a pig was brought in to be roasted with an apple in its mouth.

"They are treating us like fools, keeping us waiting like this," he said.

"They're testing your patience, Ultach," said Tate. "Be quiet, go fetch some knives. Let's play a game."

The noise of seagulls hunting for scraps echoed from outside the hall. The cries from merchants selling the last of their fish ended soon after, and the hall started filling up. Ultach and Tate abandoned their knife game when a group of warriors wearing bear cloaks and looking as if they'd just come from battle arrived and sat at a nearby table.

"If your sister is here, will you need a knife to gut her?" asked Ultach, as he laid the two knives they'd been using on the table.

"The only person I'll need a knife for is you if your hands go where they shouldn't again," said Tate.

Ultach leaned towards her. "How do you get any man to like you?"

"I don't go with any man."

A hush passed through the room. Tate turned. A woman in a black cloak with its hood pulled up and the fur collar obscuring her face had arrived in the hall.

Every eye, many of which had been on Tate, now went to the woman coming up the centre aisle between the tables. Behind her came three men and behind them, another smaller woman with blonde hair and no hood or cloak. She was smiling and greeting people at some of the tables as she passed.

A shiver passed through Tate. There was something about the way the first woman walked that was so familiar.

The hush deepened until all that could be heard was hissing from the roasting pig.

The woman walked straight towards Tate, who came to her feet as the woman pushed her hood back.

It was Synne. It was her sister, but older and troubled-looking. Synne smiled in recognition and put her hands out to hug Tate.

Tate's insides twisted. It had happened and she'd never expected this moment. She stepped forward fast and raised a knife to Synne's face.

The reaction in the room was instant. A wild thrum of talk filled the air. The men behind Synne took a step forward together, but Ultach raised his hand for them not to intervene. A great clamour of voices, shouts, and laughter rose. It was so loud almost no one heard the words Tate spoke next.

"You ran off," she hissed, her anger boiling up inside her. "You could have helped us, Synne. You and Edgar just ran. You abandoned us."

The same feelings she'd had when she'd been captured, powerlessness and fear, came back in a heated rush. She hated all these feelings.

Synne had her hand up. She placed her palm in front of the knife point. Her eyes blazed. "There was nothing we could do," she said. "I watched our mother dying. We had to bury her." She spoke forcefully, a bitter tone in her voice. She paused then before continuing, slowly. "Edgar is dead. Kill me if you wish."

Tate shook her head, pulled the knife away, and narrowed her eyes. "You should have looked after him, Synne. He was our younger brother."

Synne's face hardened.

A memory came to Tate, of Synne as the girl who would always cry and run and look for sympathy from their mother. She'd expected Synne to cry now, but instead, Synne pointed towards her and spoke with an unexpected firmness to her tone. "I've spent every day since we lost you planning and saving and fighting to find you and Gytha." Synne looked around. "Where's Gytha?"

"Taken on a ship."

"Bound for where?" Synne was still angry.

"York," said Tate.

"As what?"

"A slave." Tate flicked her hand through the air. "She didn't have the luck I have." She sniffed the air. "The luck we all used to have. Who is this?" She motioned with her head towards the woman who had joined them.

The small blonde woman introduced herself as Frida.

Synne kept staring at Tate, her lips pursed as if trying to get used to who her sister had become.

Ultach pulled the guard they'd come with to one side and passed something to him, looking around as he did.

After that, he told the men he'd come with to sit at the other end of the table.

Then he came towards Synne and Tate and Frida.

"I've done what I came to do, put you two together. There is nothing else for us here. We will go back north after we eat." He said it as if it was a promise.

"Who is he to you?" whispered Synne, leaning close to Tate.

"Nothing," replied Tate. "And he's a nothing about to make a fool of himself again." She sat. So did Synne. Ultach stood over them.

"Where is Stefan?" asked Tate, looking around.

Synne spoke softly. "He is dead, Normans killed him."

Tate groaned as if she'd been struck.

"I'll go to get some ale," said Ultach. "Reminisce with your sister, Tate, and get ready to go back north." His face was hard, but Tate stuck her tongue out at him.

Tate made her tell her all about what had happened to Stefan. She kept her head all the way through as if not wanting to believe any of it.

"Do you have to go back with him?" asked Synne, nodding towards Ultach who was talking with some men nearby.

Tate shook her head. "No, I've had enough of them." She placed her outstretched hand on the table. "Ultach's father gave me my freedom. I want to take it."

"Ultach wants you too?"

Tate nodded. She was clearly well used to men wanting her. "He won't let me go easily."

Synne reached out. They hugged. It felt as if something broken, something deep inside Tate, mended in that moment. It was right they were surrounded by people, too. The reunion was better, more real, for being public. "What happened to your man?" she asked Synne.

"He ran off."

"When?"

Synne sighed, licked her lips. Her words came out haltingly. "The night before we were to wed." Her voice cracked. She coughed to regain her composure.

"So, we both have men problems," said Tate. She put her hand out and gripped Synne's arm. Synne moved closer to her on the bench.

Ultach had returned. He had two jugs of ale. He placed one on the table between them.

"We will drink together," he said with a grin.

"Ultach, go away," said Tate.

Ultach shook his head. "I say we should go back north before this feast they are planning," he said. "About as soon as this ale is finished. My father is waiting for you." He stood.

"What's the rush?" said Synne.

Ultach sneered at her.

Tate laughed. "Why don't you go find a woman you can pay to poke your wretched thing into?" she said.

"I don't pay," he said.

Tate laughed even louder. "That's what you think."

"I'd make an exception for you," said Ultach with a leer. He reached out, put his hand on Tate's arm.

Tate stared at him. Synne whispered something in her ear.

Ultach looked from one face to the other. "You too would be good together. We could all…" He stopped, lifted his hand from Tate's arm, looked over Tate's shoulder.

Tate turned. Yann was looming behind her. She put her hand over the knife lying on the table, then pulled it back.

"You'll cut yourself if you do that too often," said Yann.

Tate gave him one of her wide fake smiles. She pointed at him. "You have power in this hall, yes?"

Yann nodded.

"Tell this Prince Ultach" – she used her thumb to point at Ultach – "that if he puts a hand on me again, it will cost him in blood."

Ultach laughed. "This one is full of shit, Yann. She threw herself on me on the road here, and now she wants to distance herself in case any of my men tell my father the truth when we return."

He pointed at the two men sitting at the other end of the table. "They'll swear she's the one who's begging for it."

Tate made a scoffing noise. "Your men spit out what you tell them to spit out."

Yann looked from her to Ultach. "What is all this about?"

"His father freed me. I will not be going back with him," said Tate.

Ultach stood and walked around to where Tate was sitting. He moved quickly. Tate spun to face him.

She had the knife from the table in her hand. The noise of conversation in the hall slowed as people noticed the confrontation. Ultach stopped a pace away from her. He looked over her shoulder and nodded.

Tate spun again but it was too late. The two men they'd arrived with were on her. They grabbed her roughly and attempted to pull her to her feet. What they hadn't counted on was her ability with the knife. In the next moment, she stabbed one of the men in the upper arm; he dropped her and grunted loudly, and then she sliced the knife towards the other's face, causing him to loosen his grip too. Then, with a speed she didn't seem capable of, she slashed the tip of the knife across Ultach's cheek.

He shouted, though the injury could have been much worse. It could have been his eye out. Synne sighed loudly, waved at Tate to follow her. Blood was dripping from Ultach's cheek. His two guards had daggers in their hands now.

Yann shouted, "Stop. No fighting in this feast hall." From the doorway, three guards came running, small hand axes up and ready to cut off limbs from anyone resisting.

Tate went after Synne. She raised her hand with the knife high to warn away anyone as she walked. "Lead on, sister," she said. They walked towards the back of the hall with Synne leading fast and Tate glancing back.

Yann stood between the injured men and the retreating women. Both his hands came up in an effort to stop Ultach's wounded guards going after them. Ultach was screaming now, cursing Tate for all he was worth.

"Out of the way," he shouted, scowling at Yann, and holding his cheek.

3

Gytha held tightly to the wooden bench. The sea moved under their ship like a bucking horse. The swell grew as they came up the wide river. She prayed for a safe landing, asking Christ, Mary, and the Fates who control all destiny as the wind drove the ship fast into the mouth of the river. It was still early morning. The mist rising. They'd started on this last part of their voyage at first light. She'd been awake since before then. Her blood-filled dreams had again made sleep unbearable.

Marshes on both sides loomed with occasional ribbons of smoke rising into the air from fishermen's cottages on the riverbanks. Straight ahead, the brown smudge of London's high wooden walls grew larger with each passing wave.

The slave master, Grymmwolf, staggered towards her, bent over, his legs wide apart as the ship rocked and heaved.

When he reached her, he shouted into the wind. "Better you do the readings right this time, fortune teller, or I'll have to dump you in a mud bank on the way out, with y'rz hands tied up tight behind y'rz back."

Gytha nodded in reply and a shout came from the old man at the steerboard. She didn't understand the strange language he and the slave master spoke, but when she looked ahead, she understood his meaning.

A large Danish vessel was coming straight towards them up the central channel of the river.

The vessel bristled with shields and rode the waves like a chariot racing over sand dunes. As it passed them, and men on the other ship saw Gytha sitting in the prow, they raised their fists and shouted crude phrases at her.

Her long blonde hair, even when tied into a tail, as she had it now, often attracted that type of response. It was one of the reasons her mother had rarely ever brought her and her two sisters into town. Men's reactions were too predictable and after their father had disappeared and she and her sisters grew, the offers became increasingly hard to dismiss. She kept her face stern as the crude shouts and whistling grew weaker. She was happy they hadn't turned to come after her.

As the high wooden city dock on the north bank of the river came near, they lowered their sail and rowed to get close to it and find a space to tie up. Arriving here reminded Gytha of her sisters and made her wonder, again, where they might be and if they'd ever meet again. Such

The Power of Synne

thoughts were like a wound that never healed, one which she couldn't stop picking at.

"Pretty yourself up, girl," shouted Grymmwolf. The four men on the oars stared at her, following each of her steps as she went to the rear of the ship to find the bag with her good cloak and broach in it. Each man rowing turned his head almost all the way around as she went. She ignored them.

As they tied up at the long wooden pier, she pulled her cloak around her and put a black ribbon on her ponytail, even though it would hang down her back, attracting even more attention. It was what the slave master wanted.

Grymmwolf enjoyed parading her and charging as much as he could get for her predictions. She'd publicly predicted that the Duke of Normandy would win his great battle and take all of England, and so far, she'd been proven correct, although some argued that the north of the country was still not under his yoke. Others argued about what they'd heard coming from her mouth.

She never disputed anything such people said. She left that to others. As they prepared to go onto the pier, which was reached by jumping the narrow gap from the ship to the rough wooden planks, and risking falling to your doom, she kept her head up and her expression stiff, despite the swirling water below and the stench of an overused midden coming from it.

As she jumped, Grymmwolf made a point of catching her arm on the far side and feeling her ass after she landed. He looked around as he did, making sure as many men as possible saw that he could touch her when he wanted, something others could only dream about.

Their first stop was the old slavers hall. It had been turned into a tavern and taken over by one of Bishop Odo's liege men. They wouldn't stay there long. The slaver usually stayed at a hall not far away, but he wanted their presence in the city to be known. The appearance of a fortune teller as beautiful as Gytha usually led to the prominent locals wanting to meet her once they found out she was in the city.

"What lords and ladies are in London?" asked Grymmwolf when the woman who brought their jug of ale arrived.

"Queen Matilda is the one you want. She's not gone back to Normandy yet," said the woman. She leaned over Gytha and spoke in her ear.

"Is it true what he claimed, that you can see the future in the flames?" she asked.

Gytha shrugged.

"She's modest," said Grymmwolf. "She can see the future wherever she wants."

"If that be true, I hope you'll both come back tonight," said a voice behind Gytha. The slave master turned. An older white-haired man with a blood and beer-stained leather apron bowed to him.

"I'll send messengers to the queen's hall, on the far side of the city, if you do come back. Her fine ladies are always asking if there's anyone reliable in all of England to tell 'em their fates."

Gytha stared at the man. This was where she was supposed to agree and tell him she'd read his fortune free too and smile at him broadly. It was what the slave master told her to do in each port they stopped in to anyone important, but she hadn't the will to do it recently.

She wondered too what stopped her tongue. Was it because she'd decided she didn't care if the slave master made nothing from her readings? Perhaps then he might be dissuaded from keeping this whole charade going.

It was a charade. Gytha knew she was the least likely to have the gift of telling someone's fate. Both her sisters had more of the gift than she had, especially Synne, who her mother doted on. Gytha also knew she'd been lucky so far with a few predictions and that she wouldn't have been forced down this path if the slaver she'd been bought from hadn't doubled her price because she was not only fine to look at, but also the daughter of a seer and the eldest of three sisters, a well-known prescription for someone who could see any future.

"Send out your messengers. Tell them she reads only for gold coin," said Grymmwolf. "And…" He beckoned the older man to him and said something Gytha didn't catch.

The man stared wide-eyed at Gytha. She smiled, not for him, but at the stupidity of men. She knew she had been offered. She also knew how to give up almost nothing and yet keep men happy and wanting more, deluded that they would eventually get everything.

"Put your hood up," said Grymmwolf, shaking his finger at her. "Time to go."

As they went out into a heavy shower of cold rain, he pinched her ass. "Be proper good tonight," he hissed. "And you won't have to rut any of 'em."

Gytha shuddered. Memories of what had happened in the first port they'd been in after he'd bought her came back to her. She'd ached for days after that night, and the men in the ship had stared at her as if she was some monster they'd dragged from the sea after Grymmwolf told them she'd enjoyed it all. Lies were all he knew.

He walked beside her now as they headed up a side alley.

"Be happy tonight when you do your readings," he said angrily. "People believe anything you tell 'em."

The thought of what lay ahead, smirking and bowing for fat old men and women, made her sick deep inside.

The next house they went to was a league downriver, with only a few slaves there and one of Grymmwolf's ex-wives managing it. He seemed to have a wife in half the ports they stopped in. Each of them looked at Gytha when they met her, as if she resembled a hunk of salted meat gone bad, the same jealous twisted look on their faces.

How he'd persuaded so many women to be part of his life was a puzzle she had no answer to. Everything about him was repulsive.

They were served a meaty broth at the long table in the house. Gytha was allowed to wash and fix her hair behind a brown wool curtain in a corner, while his ex-wife cajoled him about coin and other things Gytha could not hear.

Only one guard had come with them from the ship, a giant Scot who carried a long battle axe as if it was a small dagger and fixed everyone with a look of deep sadness. If Gytha had that expression on her face every day, Grymmwolf would beat her. But on this man, it looked right, as if he was sad at all the heads he'd made roll.

They rode away as the light faded and the sun went down. Bishop Odo had ordered torches to be lit at each crossroads at night, to protect the people of the city, so it had been proclaimed, but some said he'd done it to protect his Norman followers, many of whom had been attacked in the city and robbed and some of whom had lost their lives. There were still many people in England intent on taking revenge for a family member lost in the great battle or in the many skirmishes and land takeovers that had followed.

Gytha rode behind the slave master on a white horse. Her hair was still in a tail but was adorned now with multiple ribbons, with a twisted band of black and gold silk around her forehead.

She carried no bag, but in a large pouch on her belt she kept the tightly-folded thin veil she used to hide her face when she performed a reading and a tiny bottle, which contained the oil she occasionally used.

The old slavers hall was lit with torches on the outside walls when they arrived. Horses were tied up at the side and guards with Norman-style haircuts, recently shaved high at the back, stood in a row barring the door. Some of them looked more English than Norman.

Grymmwolf glowered at Gytha as they tied up their horses. "No mistakes tonight. Give them what they want," he said.

"I always do," she replied. She fumbled as she tied up her horse. Grymmwolf went to catch the reins, but she waved him away.

"My land legs are taking a while to come back, that's all," she said. She didn't tell him she hated the sea with a passion. She'd only ever been on river craft before the slavers had taken her to Dublin and separated her from her sister. Since then, this slave master, Grymmwolf, had bought her, and she'd spent most of her time on board ship, even when they docked.

The black depths of the sea were what she hated. It seemed to call to her. Her mind filled it with the monsters too. The ones she'd heard about as a child, from her father's stories.

They entered the hall with no problem from the guards, who smiled at the sight of Gytha. The hall was only half full. Grymmwolf pointed at an empty table at the back and said, "Keep half that table for us. Tell anyone who tries to sit with you that your master will come back and cut their cocks off if they try anything."

She sat at the table, but she had no intention of saying those words to anyone. A mention of his name was usually enough to get most men to leave her alone. Only the drunk and the stupid pushed their luck.

Grymmwolf worked the room greeting people. She sat alone. Her hatred of Grymmwolf had doubled with each port they'd stopped at and with each lesson on the ways he wanted her to follow. She was just a body for him to abuse any time he wanted to, though he rarely hit her these days. She submitted to his lusts too, but never responded, about which he complained, but he still enjoyed himself.

And when he finished and pulled away, she swore each time to the Fates that she would be revenged for this time and every time, soon. This was not something she could pray to Christ about, but the Fates might listen.

Only they could help with revenge.

A few men commented as they passed her, but she ignored them. Grymmwolf wasn't far away and he'd likely be back before any man could warm the wooden bench under him, if he did sit near her. Gytha knew her worth. She knew he'd begun to rely on her.

That was the good news. And the bad news.

A grey-haired monk stared at her then, as if he knew her. She looked away. Monks were the same as all men with their appetites, she'd discovered, with only a thin cloak of prayer around them to make them seem different.

Shouts rang out from the top of the hall. All eyes turned that way. People moved towards the noise and some cheered. Gytha rose but could not see what was happening, though it was enough to guess as the screams were a woman's and the cheers from men.

She looked up as a shadow passed over her. It was the monk.

The Power of Synne

"You are brave to sit here alone as a Saxon woman is defiled," said the monk.

Gytha did not reply.

"Has your slave master cut out your tongue?" asked the monk.

"No."

"I'm glad to hear that," said the monk. "I suppose you are right to be wary." He sat opposite her.

"I am Ulf," said the monk. "If you need a prayer said for you or for another, ask me."

"I do not need prayers," said Gytha. She looked around for Grymmwolf. "You had better go before my master sees you."

"I'm not afraid of slave masters," said Ulf.

"What's going on over there?" She pointed at the crowd gathered around the top of the room.

"A Saxon woman is being molested as we speak," said Ulf. He stared at her as if wanting to see her reaction.

"That is a shame on everyone in this hall," said Gytha. Her blood was running faster now. In halls that permitted shows of violence, anything could happen. Once a crowd had their blood up, they could turn on anyone.

"It is," said Ulf. "But who will stand against the Normans and stop them?"

"Do they need stopping?" She gave him an innocent smile. She'd been warned often enough not to claim any allegiance to those still fighting the Normans.

"I'm not here to spy on you," said Ulf. Grymmwolf was across the hall and staring at them. Ulf nodded in his direction. Grymmwolf went back to his conversation.

"I'm just wondering what you think about all this." Ulf pointed with his thumb at where the crowd was now dissipating, and a woman could be seen fixing her tunic, wiping tears away, bent over, hiding herself. "This is a common sight in London since the Normans took over. Many women who lost husbands and land have no one to protect them. Their men are dead and Bishop Odo, who is supposed to control this part of the city, does nothing to stop his men doing whatever they like." He wrung his hands.

"I fear for the future of every family in this land." His words hung heavy in the air.

Gytha was wary of getting involved. "I'm sorry for her," she said. "But what can I do?" She stared at the woman who'd been attacked, thought about going to help her, but as she rose, Ulf put a hand on her arm to stop her. He shook his head.

"No, don't. They might think you are with her and turn on you. It'll be easier for her if you let her slip away."

The Power of Synne

The woman slinked towards the back of the hall. Gytha pulled her hand away from Ulf's. Everything about being here sickened her. If women weren't safe in a hall such as this with dozens of onlookers, there would be no safety anywhere in London.

A feeling of vulnerability, which she hated, had come back. She looked around to see if she could identify the men who'd led the attack. She could. It was obvious who he was. A small man, swaying from ale or wine, was receiving slaps on his back from men at a far table.

She knew what often came next after such vulnerability was exposed, assault, violation and worse. And a realisation that any sense of order and peace could be taken away at a moment's notice.

The monk leaned towards her. "I heard you'll read the fortunes of some Norman ladies here tonight. Is that true?"

"Maybe." She wasn't going to say much about all that. Some monks disapproved of fortune telling, expecting people to use prayer for such things.

"If it is true, I hope you'll send them a message."

Gytha had heard a similar plea before. Someone had tried to sow dissension in a lord's hall in one of the ports they'd called into. Grymmwolf had heard the man and had threatened him with a knife across his throat.

It would be better if she did not tell Grymmwolf what this monk was asking. She'd deal with this herself.

Arranging for a monk to get a blade against his throat was not a good idea.

She kept staring at Ulf until he answered her with a smile.

"You agree?" said Ulf. "So, you're with us." He glanced around.

"What message do you want sent?" she asked. She was a little curious now. Perhaps it would be better to simply play along with him.

"They should be afraid," said Ulf. He was whispering now. His eyebrows shot up as he spoke.

"I'm sure they're afraid already, coming here."

"We want them afraid of being in this city, so they all go back to where they came from, and get their men to follow them," said Ulf.

Gytha groaned. "That is a lot more than I can do."

"You can do more than you think. Norman ladies love fortune tellers. They talk about the Fates and their destiny all the time." He smiled knowingly. "You can warn them the water here is poison, that the air has sickening qualities, and that any children born here will be deformed if they stay here. And…" He put his face close to hers. "Tell them that the women in this city all want to take their men to save their skins." He slapped the table and grinned at her.

That part would not be hard to get across. It was probably half true. She spotted Grymmwolf loping towards them.

"I'll do what I can, Brother." She doubted that would be much.

"That is all I—" Ulf's final words were cut off as Grymmwolf pulled him up from the bench by one shoulder of his dirty woollen tunic.

"You stay a long time with my slave, for a monk under a vow of chastity," said Grymmwolf. He made an angry face into Ulf's but let him go. Ulf scurried off without a backwards glance.

All this was forgotten moments later, as horns blew to announce someone important arriving. It had to be the Norman ladies they were expecting. Half the hall were on their feet looking towards the entrance. The barking of dogs and the neighing and stamping of horses came pouring in through the open doors. It was gloomy, almost dark outside, so when the party came in, with torchbearers around them, they were framed by a golden light, as if they were coming straight from heaven.

Gytha's curiosity pushed her to her feet and onto her toes.

The first part of the arriving group were guards in clean leather tunics with shiny breastplates and helmets. They must be expecting trouble, she thought. Behind those first six guardsmen came a man in a black monk's habit with a gold chain around his neck.

"Bishop Odo himself. Your fame has spread further than I thought," said Grymmwolf into her ear, as applause and shouts of approval echoed all around them.

Behind Bishop Odo came three ladies dressed in long silk gowns with white veils over their faces. Two were large women. One was thin and had a gold band around her headdress. They all walked slowly, nodding at the people in the hall as if they knew everyone. When they reached Grymmwolf's table, he bowed low and pulled Gytha by the arm to do the same.

Gytha did, but rose quickly from the bow. The women had their heads together as they passed and seemed not to notice them, but Gytha was sure they had.

The ladies headed for the top table. As they arrived there, a minstrel struck up a tune on a small travelling harp, set up to the side of the main table. The minstrel had on a gold silk headband, which complemented his red tunic with its shiny gold thread embroidery along all the seams. For a few moments, Gytha wasn't sure if the minstrel was a man or a woman. Then she spotted a light beard.

The crowd muttered as unfamiliar notes filled the hall. The minstrel began a song, a lament in the Norman tongue. Gytha didn't understand much of it, but from the few words she'd picked up and the mood of the song, it was a lament for a lost lover.

Food arrived then on large wooden trays carried by pairs of slaves. Other servants scurried around. Gytha wasn't hungry, but she ate a little of the steaming stew and thick bread that appeared. She hoped the food might calm the tightness in her stomach and cure the feeling of trepidation that hung over her.

The minstrel sang another song, then bowed and scraped his way across the room, heading for Gytha and Grymmwolf. Grymmwolf stood as the man approached.

"We do not need your songs, minstrel." He waved the minstrel away.

The minstrel laughed. "I'm not here to play for you, Master Grymmwolf."

"What then? The lady is not for sale." Grymmwolf had his hand up to stop the minstrel coming closer.

"I heard your ship will be leaving the dock on the tide in the morning."

"So?" Grymmwolf's tone was becoming angrier by the word. He hadn't told Gytha they were leaving in the morning.

"I wish to pay for passage to Barfleur. I am told you will take passengers, if the price is right."

Grymmwolf stared at the man, his expression changing, lips curling into what looked like avarice. "We have no plan to sail to Normandy. Do you have coin to pay us to take you there? It is out of our way."

The minstrel bowed. He pulled something small from his sleeve and passed it to Grymmwolf, who put it up to his eye.

"What is this?" He bit what Gytha now saw was a coin. It glistened like gold. She knew Grymmwolf would want it. Who wouldn't?

"It is real," said the minstrel. "A good gold coin from the mint at Pavia."

Gytha hadn't seen a gold coin in a long time. Recently they'd only seen silver ones, purses of them sometimes.

"You have many of these?" said Grymmwolf, his eyes widening.

"No, not on me." The minstrel held his hand out for the coin. "But if you agree to take me, and my baggage, away from here in the morning, you will get two more from my associates at Barfleur when we arrive there. Or should I find another captain?"

Grymmwolf took the coin. "We'll take you," he said. "Be at the dock near here at dawn or you'll lose this one." He waved dismissively at the minstrel.

The minstrel didn't go. He walked around the table and sat down on the bench near Gytha, who smiled at him.

Grymmwolf leaned on the table, his hands flat out. "Keep your eyes off her."

Gytha laughed to herself. It was too easy to make Grymmwolf jealous.

The minstrel waved his hands in the air. "Is she your personal slave?" he asked.

Grymmwolf nodded.

"Is she as good as she looks?" The minstrel stuck his tongue out at her.

Grymmwolf nodded, laughed, picked up the giant mug of ale he'd been drinking from and upended it into his mouth. Some of it overflowed into his thick beard.

"Have no fear. I will not take her from you," said the minstrel. "I prefer something different."

"I am not afraid of the likes of you," said Grymmwolf. He pointed at Gytha. "Stay here," he said, then he belched and headed up to the main table.

Gytha kept her eye on him. Two guards at either end of the top table came forward as he approached them, blocking his path. They each had axes on their belts as well as long Norman daggers in elaborate sheaths, with their hands close to the smooth handles. Grymmwolf had only a dagger, which he used mostly for transferring meat to his mouth.

The guards protecting the ladies at the top table did not let him pass. He waved at them to move but they didn't. They stared at him, their expressions hard, ready for him to try anything. Grymmwolf put his hand up and waved for the ladies at the table to come see him, and after waiting some long moments, one of the older ladies stood and came to speak to him. The guards opened a gap between them so she could speak, but they were still ready for anything Grymmwolf might try.

He pointed back towards Gytha and waved his hands as he spoke. He was too far away for her to hear what was going on, but she could guess.

"Your master tells everyone about you. Word of your beauty and your powers has been passed to many," said the minstrel, moving a little along the bench to get closer to Gytha.

She looked at him, then down at bench at the distance between them. It wasn't unknown for men to claim they liked something else to get close to a woman.

The minstrel put his hands up. "No, my lady, I am not after you. I was just thinking there might be better ways to get you an audience with Queen Matilda."

Gytha smiled. This was a good trick. "With the queen? Surely not? Where is she?" He was unlikely to know the answer to that question.

"Who do you think those guards are here to protect?" He nodded at the men guarding the top table.

Gytha breathed deep. She should have known. Everything was so strange here, not like when she was here when Harold was king. There were so many Normans

The Power of Synne

everywhere for a start. She could hear their laughter amid the shouts in the hall. And then there was the matter of the queen. Meeting her was something few women ever expected to achieve. To tell her fortune was something far beyond all expectations.

So far beyond, it was likely to be dangerous. Did Grymmwolf know who was at the top table?

"You didn't know?" said the minstrel.

Gytha didn't reply.

She was still trying to work out what was really happening. The thought of running away also crossed her mind again. Then she remembered what Ulf had told her. This was not the time to run. Everything might change again.

"You have a good skill at this fortune telling?" asked the minstrel.

"Enough," Gytha replied. She hoped she'd not have to read his future.

But what would she tell a famous queen she did know a little about? She would not be able to refuse her.

Gytha's mind almost froze at the thought. She could barely remember the form of words she used to predict even the most mundane future, which was what she read for most people. How would she do this for a queen? She'd be found out, she was sure of that. Then she'd have her tongue cut out on the spot, the punishment for those who made false predictions.

Grymmwolf came back to their table shaking his head.

"She barely speaks our tongue at all," he said, sitting down, then picking up and banging his mug on the table.

"They don't want me to read their fortunes?" She was usually happy when Grymmwolf was thwarted, but she'd been looking forward to meeting the queen, even if the prospect was daunting.

"Go away, was all she said to me. Can you believe it? We've wasted our time coming here. There are other halls we could be in tonight. Bah!"

A servant filled his ale cup. A piper had started playing. The guards in front of the top table had moved a little away. The piper was in the centre of the hall, all eyes on him.

"Let's go," said Grymmwolf, getting to his feet.

The minstrel rose as well. He put his hand out towards Grymmwolf. "Wait one more song, master," he said. "I'll see if the ladies know that it is Lady Gytha who might read for them."

Grymmwolf stared at him, then nodded, and the minstrel was gone.

"He thinks you're a lady," he said angrily. "Where did he get that idea?"

The Power of Synne

"Not from me," said Gytha. But she smiled at the thought. It was flattery, she knew that, but an attempt to annoy Grymmwolf, which she enjoyed.

"He'd better be quick," said Grymmwolf.

They were both watching the minstrel closely. The guards at the top table nodded at him as he passed them, as if he was a trusted member of their entourage. He headed for the thin woman in the centre of the table, going around the back to reach her. He bowed low for her, and when she turned to him, he pointed toward Gytha and spoke at length while waving his arms.

The woman shook her head, seemed to be saying no to him. The minstrel pulled away and came to stand in front of Gytha. He put both his hands out in a pleading gesture as he spoke.

"It is only Lady Gytha that the queen, in all her glory, wishes to speak with tonight."

Grymmwolf nodded. "That's a special request. I'll have to make sure the price is set right."

The minstrel threw a red leather purse at him.

Grymmwolf caught it, looked inside. He smiled, waved at Gytha.

"Make it quick," he said.

"The queen will decide how quick this will be," said the minstrel. He motioned with his fingers for Gytha to follow him.

A quick burst of excitement and anticipation made Gytha's hands tremble. She licked her lips as a fluttery sensation filled her up. She, a slave, would meet the queen, wife of the new King William, the most powerful Norman in the land. She wondered was she dreaming.

The minstrel led her to the side of the hall then along it until they reached a door. As she went through it, Gytha turned. Grymmwolf was on his feet staring after them. He looked down at the leather purse in his hand.

The minstrel grabbed her hand as they passed outside and pulled Gytha close to him. Gytha didn't know whether to be afraid or happy.

"My name is Robert," said the minstrel. "You must trust me. We will be going to a ship tied up at the next dock. A royal ship. There you will meet the queen. She is not here." He nodded towards the hall, then squeezed Gytha's hand. She wanted to laugh. Of course the queen wasn't in a slavers' hall, but she held her amusement inside herself, and nodded.

She was happy and she didn't care if she was being kidnapped. If Robert didn't bring her back here, Grymmwolf would be spitting anger everywhere, but she would have a good excuse if she saw him again, and with luck that would be a long time from now.

"Get up, my lady," said Robert. "You can ride, yes?"

"Yes," said Gytha.

The Power of Synne

A guard in a grey wool cloak held his hand out to help her mount one of the four horses standing quietly at the side of the hall. Robert mounted another and led the way. Two guards in grey cloaks followed on horseback with her between them.

She kept looking back, wondering with mounting anxiety if Grymmwolf would appear. She'd imagined Queen Matilda was one of the women in the hall, but she realised now that was a mistake.

They rode along the river road, heading upstream in the fading evening light. The smell of shit from a stream running into the river made her wrinkle her nose as they passed near it. London was as smelly as she'd been warned. Her gaze darted and she clutched her cloak tight as she wondered about what lay ahead. She'd never expected a royal audience for her fortune telling powers. She'd never wanted one.

She wondered if her sadly limited abilities would be enough or if the queen would laugh. Knots multiplied inside her as they rode. There was also the possibility she would never see Grymmwolf again.

But could she convince the queen she had real powers? The ability to talk a good game did not mean you could see the future. Though sometimes her guesses spooked herself, especially when people cried out or shouted in amazement at her predictions.

"You're a good learner," was what her mother had said when she caught Gytha doing a telling like this for a local child. "It's a pity you have half the gift of your sister Synne."

That had cut her to the bone. She'd never forgotten those words. They showed how little faith her mother had in her, but now she was going to meet the new Queen of England. Her mother would have been proud.

Another voice spoke up inside her. Maybe her mother was wrong. Maybe she had more of a gift than Synne. Didn't the old stories say that when there were three sisters, each had a different gift. It was possible, especially when she thought about all the women she'd done readings for in the last few weeks. Many had been surprised. Some had even been fearful of her skill. She mustn't doubt herself.

They reached a lane with torchbearers and a wooden gate on the river side of the road. There was building work going on nearby, the beginning of a wall, and beside the river a dock with a derelict-looking trading vessel and beyond it a barge with torches along its side illuminating it.

They were stopped three times, by increasingly intrusive guards as they went towards the barge. Finally, one suggested Gytha should pull up her long tunic to show she was hiding no weapons. Gytha flung her hands in the air.

"I will not be sport for all your lewd intentions. Is that what the queen demands? Does she know this?" She was pushing her luck, she knew, but she could not accept this demand.

Robert, the minstrel, walked up to the guard and even though the man was a head taller than him, struck him across the face with a slap that echoed.

"The queen will have your head on a spike if you suggest that again," he said. "I am a trusted adviser to your king and to your queen. I suggest, if you enjoy breathing and being alive, you apologise to the lady and let us pass."

The man stared at Robert with barely disguised contempt, but then he was nudged by one of the other guards, who whispered something to him. His eyes widened and he apologised.

"I am sorry, my lady. You may proceed." The guards stepped aside.

Gytha let her breath out. She hadn't realised she'd been holding it. What intrigued her, though, was that Robert was an adviser to King William and his queen. But if this was true, why did he want to leave the city on the next tide in a slaver's boat?

Had his promise to take passage with Grymmwolf been a ruse?

They reached long planks that led onto the barge. The guards here were more richly dressed, more like palace servants. One was got up almost like a woman. This one led them onto the barge and through a door part covered in gold leaf and into a long low-roofed cabin with couches along the walls and braziers heating it. These gave off a pungent aroma, similar to the incense she'd sniffed once at Christ Mass, but stronger and it caught in her throat. She enjoyed the smell.

The couches on each side were empty. At the far end, two women sat, staring at her and Robert. They were both holding round embroidery holders and had needles in their hands.

"Bow for Queen Matilda," said the man who'd led them in. He had a high-pitched voice.

Robert and Gytha bowed low. Robert stayed that way. Gytha looked up sooner, to see one of the women approaching her.

"So, the famous fortune teller is a peasant." The woman laughed, held her hand out with a heavy gold ring on it for Gytha to kiss. It had a red stone at its centre.

Gytha kissed the stone.

The hand pulled away and the woman pointed at her. "Tell us lies and you will be punished, Gytha the teller, for I am your queen." She pointed at Robert. "And you, wait outside, minstrel. This is not for your ears."

The Power of Synne

Robert walked backwards, bowing, and disappeared.

"Sit with us," the queen called out as she went to the couch where the other woman was sitting and sat down, then patting the place beside her.

"Did you eat at that feast?" said Queen Matilda. "The one they are having in my name at that cursed hall."

"A little, your majesty," said Gytha. She almost couldn't get the words out, so strange it felt, like a dream, to be here, talking to the most important woman in the land. She was fascinated by the high-fronted dark green gown the queen wore. It had a pair of facing lions, their forelegs high, embroidered on it with thick gold thread. It was the finest gown and embroidery Gytha had ever seen.

"Good, we can talk about why I wanted to see you. But first, you must swear to never speak about what I tell you." She paused, motioned Gytha to lean forward, then reached for a loose lock of hair and yanked it.

Gytha muffled her alarm and pain into a slight groan.

"I would hate to see your pretty head on a spike, all your great beauty wasted."

Gytha nodded. This was not an idle threat. "My lips will be sealed forever, my queen." She meant it too. She knew not to tell a woman's secrets. "My mother taught me never to speak about what is shared with us or what we share in a telling."

"Where is your mother?"

"Dead. I was taken by the slavers after that." She wasn't going to tell her a long story. The queen released her hair.

Near silence descended. The slap of waves and the creaking of the barge were the only sounds. The other woman whispered something in the queen's ear. Then she stood and came around to the other side of Gytha. This woman also wore a green gown, though hers was not embroidered in the same intricate way. Both she and the queen wore thin veils, pushed back from their heads. Gytha felt out of place with her bare head, but female slaves never wore such head coverings, reserved only for high-born women.

"My name is Anand. I will tell you a story," said the other woman. She was not Norman. Her accent, all highs and lows, was from somewhere in the deep south of England. Gytha had heard similar accents in some of the ports they'd passed through on the way here.

Anand looked deep into Gytha's eyes as if assessing her.

"This woman has a terrible dream. It comes to her every night, and for more than a week, always the same. Echoes of it reach even into her daylight hours." She paused, leaned towards Gytha. "Have you ever heard of something like this? Does it foretell the future, what this woman dreams?" Her frown was matched by the queen's.

The Power of Synne

Gytha's mind raced. She knew about terrible dreams, how bloody sights you'd seen could reappear every night, haunting you endlessly. Such things were not easy to deal with. Nightmares are about the weave of your fate.

"What's in this dream?" Gytha looked towards Anand, but occasionally glanced at the queen to see her reaction. The queen gestured with her hand for Anand to keep going, to say more.

Anand moved closer to Gytha. She took her arm. Her grip was tight through Gytha's rough wool tunic. Words came as whispers close to her ear.

"A man and a child appear at her bedside, looking down. They are grief-stricken, holding something in their hands. Slowly they lift it, show it. It's a woman's head. Their hands are bloody from holding it. The woman's face is twisted in pain. The man and the child raise their eyes. The dreamer wakes with their faces fading in front of her. What does it mean?"

Gytha's jaw clenched. It felt as if this dream had happened in reality, and not too long ago. The queen gave Gytha a searching look, then looked down at Gytha's hands, which were gripped together, and raised, one wrapped tight around the other, as if the answer was there.

"Is that the whole dream?"

Anand nodded.

"Did the dreamer know these people in her dream?"

The queen nodded.

Gytha knew such a dream could be a curse. How to break the curse was the question.

The queen coughed.

"Does the king know about this dream?" Gytha asked.

The queen shook her head. No.

Gytha reached for her wrist. Anand moved back, apparently afraid that Gytha might pull a weapon out.

"Do not fear me," said Gytha.

"We do not," said Anand, brusquely.

Gytha pushed a thread bracelet from her wrist, a red one, with wool threads snaking around each other. She held it out.

"The queen will wear this. If the dream wakes her again, she will turn it on her wrist twelve times, once for each apostle, forcing all night spirits away. She will sleep better if she does this." It was a simple remedy her mother had taught her when Gytha had bad dreams, a trick to turn the mind to something else.

Anand whispered. "We've tried such things. None of it helps. Is that all you can do?" There was dismissal in her tone, as if she wanted Gytha gone. Was she jealous that the queen had asked for someone else's help?

The queen leaned forward. "I need to know what my dream means." She spoke slowly. Her eyes had hollow circles around them, which Gytha could see clearly now.

The Power of Synne

Anand put her head to one side. This would be Gytha's last chance.

Gytha held her hand out. "Give me your hand, my queen," she said.

Anand had a shocked look on her face. Had she gone too far?

The queen held out her hand. Gytha took it, turned it, and rubbed her palm in small circles until her fingers warmed. "I will touch your forehead," she said. "Close your eyes."

The queen's eyes closed. Gytha put the tip of her now warm middle finger to the queen's forehead and massaged it near the centre in small circles. Such circles could help people agitated in their minds.

"Did you witness a woman and child being killed?" she asked.

The queen nodded.

"Here in England?"

Another nod.

"You must go back to Normandy. You will lose all your fears there," said Gytha.

"Do you work for Odo?" said the queen with a half-smile.

Gytha shook her head.

She was still doing the circling motions with her hands. She could smell stale sweat now.

"The dream sits in my head just there, where you are rubbing," said the queen hesitantly.

"You can ask the king to stop the innocents suffering," said Gytha.

"He will not stop," said the queen, while shaking her head. "It is who he is."

"I know," said Gytha. "But he can become more than this."

Gytha moved her fingers until she was circling at the side of the queen's temple. She put her other hand on the other temple and circled with her fingers there as well.

"You have more power than you think, my queen," she said. The words were meant to encourage. She often said similar things to women suffering because of their men.

The queen put a hand up and grabbed at Gytha's wrist. Gytha stopped rubbing the queen's skin.

"This king's plans can never be undone," said the queen.

A wave of apprehension rose fast inside Gytha as she felt the queen's grip tighten. Her lips felt suddenly dry.

"Do you know who that minstrel really is?" asked the queen.

Gytha shook her head.

"He is a messenger from the pope. A sly man who fixes things and knows dirty secrets. You didn't know about that?"

"No."

"Did he tell you that I must go back to Normandy?"

"No," said Gytha. "He said you might want a fortune telling, that is all."

"That minstrel is a snake," said Anand.

The queen put her hand towards Anand, waved at her to cease talking.

Gytha went back to doing the circular motions. After a few moments, the sound of neighing horses came to them. The queen raised her hand.

"Stop it all, someone is coming." She waved her hand high in the air. Two guards in mail shirts appeared out of the shadows at the far end of the room. One came up beside the queen.

Gytha heard what the queen said to him. "I'm not well enough to meet any guests."

The guards hurried away. "Now you'll see how this kingdom causes so much trouble, Gytha," said the queen.

The guard returned. "Bishop Odo begs an audience, my queen. I told him you are not well. He insisted I tell you he is here."

The queen sighed, looked at the deeply stained wooden floor. "Let him in," she said.

A few moments later, a giant of a man in a fine black monk's cloak with a giant gold cross on a thick gold chain around his neck appeared.

He looked around until his gaze stopped on Gytha. A look crossed his face as if he recognised her.

"Queen Matilda," said Bishop Odo. "I am here to warn you about a highly dangerous man on the loose nearby, and to ask you if you have seen him or if anyone else has."

He stared at each of the women.

"Who is this dangerous man?" said the queen.

"A minstrel."

"What has this minstrel done, Bishop, insulted you?"

The bishop's face reddened. He looked like the kind of man who would normally strike a woman who answered him this way.

"He's a thief," said Odo, spitting the words out.

"That may be, but he is not here," replied Queen Matilda. She waved with a hand towards the empty seats around her.

"If he does come here, Queen Matilda," said Odo, "he must be held. He cannot be allowed to leave London."

"What did he steal?" There was a hint of mockery in the queen's tone.

"Something belonging to the king."

The Power of Synne

The queen leaned forward. "The king is back in London?"

"No, he is still a long way to the west. He has not come back, and he has no plans to do so."

"But you have come to grace us with your presence." The queen smiled.

"Rumours reached us that this shapeshifter, this agent of the devil, is abroad in London, causing fear, sending people out of the city in fear. Some city guildsmen even had to close their businesses. Inns and markets have been closed."

"This shapeshifter did all this?" The queen had a look of concern on her face.

"We do not know, not yet," said Odo. "My men are tracking him this very night. This part of the city is one of the few where inns are still open. I hope to hear word about him soon."

Gytha noticed he was staring at her. It made her uncomfortable. Men who stared at her usually wanted something.

"Who are you?" he asked Gytha. "I have a strange feeling I met you before."

"We have not met, my lord."

"Who are you and where are you from?"

"I am Gytha, from near York."

He put his head a little to one side, his eyes widening. "I knew a healer from near York. That is it, you remind me of her."

For a long moment, Gytha wondered if it was wise to say anything about her sister Synne, but then it came to her that this man might be able to tell her where her sister was.

"I have a sister named Synne. She is a healer. Do you know where she is, my lord?"

Odo's eyes widened further. He raised his fist.

It looked as if he was going to say something, but the baying of dogs made them all look around. A horn sounded. Bishop Odo waved in the air, dismissing the conversation.

"That will be my men," he said. "Forgive me, my queen. I must see what is happening." He headed for the door.

The queen was whispering to Anand.

Gytha was wondering if she could get up and go and see what was happening; perhaps she could ask Odo again about Synne.

The bishop turned back at the door out. "Come, my queen. You may see the rogue, if they captured him." He waved at the queen to follow, turned on his heel, and was gone.

They all followed him out and up and along to the stern of the barge, where the bishop was already shouting down at people on the dock.

They reached a low wooden railing in the stern together. Gytha looked over.

A body was being pulled from the river. It was too dark to see who it was, but it could easily have been Robert, the minstrel. The body shape and size and his dark hair looked right. But this man's throat had been cut from ear to ear. A gaping hole like a wide second mouth filled his neck, sending a shiver of disgust through her.

The sight reminded Gytha of a dream she'd never spoken about, which had come to her a few times since she'd been captured by the slavers. She'd always imagined it was her own neck that had been cut, so in that moment, looking down, she felt a wave of relief. It is strange to feel relief at someone else's death, she knew that. But these were strange times.

4

I stood by the mast, holding it as tight as a lover, wrapping myself all around it. We'd been at sea for three days.

We'd seen land the day before, and had spent the night in a cove, the captain of the ship unwilling to let us sleep ashore, because of outlaws, he said, but probably because he didn't want us slipping away without paying him the rest of what we owed. Since then, we'd been following the shoreline.

Tate was at the back of the small boat, talking to Yann. Tate had taken a great interest in him since he'd helped us find a boat in Dublin. He'd volunteered to go with us during our hasty departure from the city after Tate injured Ultach. She'd caused a big commotion with accusations flying all around. We'd been allowed to leave only because Ultach was still alive.

Mostly it was his pride that had been injured. I wondered was that what Tate had intended. If so, it showed her skill with a knife.

A face scar was nothing for a warrior to complain about, Tate claimed and that it would improve his appearance. She was right. I told her we should leave the city at once to avoid any further disputes. Ultach would be looking for revenge. This way we could look for our missing sister, Gytha, now that we had a clue as to where she might be.

Tate claimed loudly to Yann that she could calm waves, to persuade him to come with us, and then she laughed in his face when it looked like he believed her after we'd left shore and her prayers for a calm sea went unanswered. That told me a lot about how she'd changed since our mother had died. It also told me how her powers of persuasion had grown.

I wondered if I'd made a mistake allowing Yann to come with us. Wouldn't it have been better to have him waiting for me in Dublin than having his choice of sister presented to him every day?

Yann insisted on telling Tate the long version of how I'd saved the King of England's son, Magnus, which everyone in Dublin seemed to know, and how I'd been rewarded with broken promises. He also said that stopping Ultach coming after us on the night of the fight in the hall was a big favour he'd done us. No doubt he was looking for some reward. Maybe Tate would give it to him.

That thought irritated me. Why is it, when you get what you want, it turns out to be different than you imagined, and not as good?

A mist clung to the low hills beyond the rocky shoreline we were sailing past. We hadn't seen any fishing boats for half the morning and no curls of smoke since we'd passed a village with a half-finished wicker wall and rows of drying fishing nets between poles by the shore.

The captain wanted us to land at Palehaven, a small port he knew, which sat between the often-warring kingdoms of the Scottish Kings and northern English tribes. It was too dangerous to come ashore further south, he claimed, as spies for the new Norman king were in every port further south.

Tate waved at me, motioning me to sit beside her on the plank we all slept under, curled together like lice.

"You don't mind me flirting with Yann, do you?" Tate whispered in my ear in her half-joking tone. Yann was on the other side of Tate, staring at the shoreline.

I grunted as if I didn't care.

"It's just you look upset, ready to kill me sometimes," said Tate.

I whispered in her ear, "You can have him." If he was so easily distracted, I'd be better off without him wanting me.

The Power of Synne

But I had to admit to myself at least that a part of me resented what she was doing.

Tate sucked in her breath. "I might just take him then."

"Did Gytha know she was going to York?" I asked, changing the subject.

"All I know is what I told you. That's where her slave master was heading."

"So, they could be anywhere?"

"We have to start somewhere, Synne."

"Look," said Yann excitedly, pointing at the shore.

We'd reached a rocky headland and were being pushed fast by the wind. Three columns of smoke had come into view as we rounded it.

"Palehaven," shouted the captain. "See, I told you, a fine landing place, with Danes still holding it. See the white banner on the shore."

I blinked. He had good eyesight. I could see a banner fluttering but making out its colour was beyond me.

As we came close to the short wooden dock, we all stopped talking. Two Danish-style fighting vessels were pulled up on a pebble beach before the dock. The ships were supported by wooden trusses. They were being repaired. The dock beyond lay at the centre of a bay, protected by the headland.

Men were working on the vessels, both outside and some men could be seen on top of one of the vessels. As our ship approached, men moved towards the dock. Many carried axes. Some carried hammers or cudgels. They were ready for a raiding party.

There was no room for us at the dock, so we pulled close by, rowing alongside a fishing vessel. I wondered what sort of reception we would receive. Newcomers were treated with suspicion in most villages I'd ever been to.

"This is my cousin's ship," said the captain as we came alongside the smaller fishing vessel.

A shout came from the other ship. Two men with shaggy blond hair and beards appeared. One of them was doing the shouting.

"I hope you brought something useful this time, cousin." The man bowed towards me and Tate.

"Are these ladies for sale?" he shouted.

Yann put a fist up. "No, and they're with me, under my protection."

"That is sure disappointing," said the man, as he put a plank across between the boats. "They're a fine pair." He made a gesture as if he was grabbing two breasts.

"Keep your dirty hands away," said Yann.

Both men laughed.

I gripped Yann's arm. "We can't go ashore until we're sure it's safe," I said softly.

As I spoke, Tate jumped up onto the plank and walked across it, with her hands out wide, swaying confidently, as if she did this every day.

"Do you always greet strangers this way?" she said, pointing at the man. "Or is it because you grew up with a grudge, 'cause your mother tried to throw you in the sea when she saw your ugly face."

The man laughed, put both his hands up in shock at her tongue.

"She did throw me in the sea," he said. "But I crawled out with a giant crab in my mouth. What's your name, stranger?" He had a wide smile on his face.

"Tate, the healer's sister." She pointed at me. "This is the sister you want. She healed a son of the great King Harold. He fights even now to free your country."

"Not my country," said the man. He spat overboard. "But anyone who helps in the fight against the Norman bastards is welcome here."

He bowed towards me, his hand waving down. The gesture was a mockery.

On the dock beyond his boat, a small group had gathered. Some of them were women. One came closer and called out.

"Don't mind our Olaf. You're all welcome here. We are cousins here, all of us fighting to stay free." A ragged cheer went up from some in the crowd. Then they dispersed, as if the woman's greeting had taken away their concerns.

Olaf and his half-brother helped us ashore. We were taken to the main hall, half buried in the side of a low grass-covered hill. The hall had a grass roof.

We were given warm milk and hard bread and told there was a feast planned for that evening. It was the end of their three-day festival, which ushered in the season of light, longer days, easier hunting, fishing, and gathering, and tending to the crops they'd sown.

A time of settling disputes, too.

People slowly filled up the hall as the sun waned. Most came to look at the strangers and ask us questions. What had happened to the King of Leinster? Was he still fighting to unify Ireland? And what had we heard about William the bastard's plans for his new English kingdom?

At the centre of the hall stood a giant hearth with two iron spits on which two boars were roasting above low glowing flames. Young boys turned these boars occasionally and kept the fire fed with driftwood. The smoke drifted, darkening the air above us. A sticky smell of roasting meat set my mouth watering.

Olaf and some other men joined us at our table as more candles were lit in the fading light.

The Power of Synne

"How do you always know to come here at feast time?" he asked our captain, slapping the man's shoulders as he pushed us along the bench.

"Don't thank me," said the captain. "Thank Tate here. She's the one who decided when we would depart Dublin." He nodded towards Tate.

I was annoyed instantly. He'd turned our unfortunate and speedy departure from Dublin into a story favouring my sister, but I would not denounce her in front of everyone, so I smiled and went along, though I guessed what his game was.

The hall was almost full. There seemed to be more people here than expected for such a village. Some must have come in from surrounding areas. Olaf moved closer to me.

He nudged my side. "I hear you were at the great battle, the one where the old king died?"

I nodded.

"What was it like?"

"Madness and blood."

He opened his hands. "That's it?"

"I don't talk about it."

Olaf stared at me. Perhaps he thought I was lying about being at Hastings when King Harold fell. I didn't care. I wasn't going to brag about it the way some warriors love to make the most of every injury and death they caused.

A shout echoed around us. Then another. A fiery buzz of conversation passed through the room. Everyone stood and headed for the door. We followed, with Olaf behind us. I asked him what was happening.

"You'll see. The queen of the night will be here soon," he said softly, his eyes wide.

Outside the hall, the sky was starlit with a crescent moon riding high and clouds racing. People were standing, spread out in a half circle in front of the hall, with the open side facing a wide path leading inland. Many of the men held burning torches now.

The path was muddy near the hall. Beyond the open gate in the wicker fence around the village, it rose towards low dark, tree-covered hills in the distance, a narrowing pale track heading towards a dip between the hills.

That was where everyone was looking. Some were pointing towards it. At first, I wasn't sure what they were pointing at. Then I noticed a faint glow on the horizon, which could not be the setting sun. It was the wrong direction for that.

Something was coming towards us. The glow grew. A hunting horn sounded far off. The baying of hounds responded to it.

Whatever was coming, it was part of a hunt.

The Power of Synne

Tate was by my side now. Yann stood beyond her. At the horizon, pinpricks of light appeared, followed by others. All noise around us fell away as time seemed to stop. We stared as the pinpricks became a row of torches glowing and ebbing in the light wind coming from the sea, all heading towards us.

The wind picked up then, as if it knew something was happening. I sniffed. I could smell the torches. And then a splattering of warm raindrops fell on us, as if the gods had brought summer early, just for us.

The procession of lights oozed closer. Low, soft drumming came to me. I could see women in long pale tunics, and a giant of a man at the back dressed in green, with a wide crown of leaves on his head. Noise filled the air, people hooting, whistling, and pipers playing a rousing tune, as if they were all off to battle.

At the head of the procession came a tall woman on a low golden chariot pulled by neighing horses. The smell of burning torches made me sniff and cough. As she neared the village, a premonition made my eyes widen. She would pick me out, make me suffer for some transgression.

"Step back," I whispered to Tate as the procession entered the village, and I could make out faces.

But it was too late. The tall woman's gaze was on me.

As she neared the entrance to the hall, where we were standing, her chariot slowed, and, to my dismay, she pointed at us. Yann was at my side. Tate on my other side. Our captain was no longer beside us.

Had he guessed what would happen? Had he led us here for this? *I'm a warrior; I know that now so I can fight Loki's tricksters.* The world is full of tricksters, my mother used to say.

My mouth dried as the woman pointed now at Tate, then at me, but her bony, pale finger kept pointing until it stopped at Yann. The torchbearers gathered around her, chanting. I did not understand most of their words, but I did understand one: fight.

I felt a gaze up on me, turned.

Olaf was behind us. With him were men from his ship. They had their arms crossed. This all felt wrong, dangerous, but I knew not to show any hesitation.

I put my hand up and towards him. "Is this how you welcome guests?" I said.

He pointed towards the woman leading the procession, indicating it wasn't up to him what was happening.

The woman had disappeared among her followers, but a moment later she reappeared, leading the giant towards us, her milk-pale hand on his thick arm. Was someone expected to fight this man?

The Power of Synne

Tate was whispering in Yann's ear. I stood close to his other side. Everyone moved away from us as if we had the plague.

"You don't have to fight," I said to Yann. I did not want him to fight.

His eyes were on the giant, assessing him.

"No, I do," he said. "This is what I trained for every day since I was a child. I was born a fighter. I'm no merchant or farmer or fisherman, Synne. If I don't do this, my name will be a laughing stock as will my father's, and he will find out by the time I get back to Dublin. It will be worse for me if he finds out I ran from a fight."

"He's twice your size."

Yann grinned. "He's a big oaf ripe for puncturing," he said. He stood straight, reached for the dagger on his belt.

The tall woman shouted something I did not understand. Her women followers swarmed towards Yann. I stepped forward. This was not fair, but Tate stood forward to stop me, pulling me to the side.

"I've seen fights like this in Ulster. They'll get Yann ready. I'm sure he can win." She shouted, "Cut him deep, Yann. He has a lot of fat."

Yann's fist rose in the air as the women around him pulled off his tunic. I knew what this would be now. A naked fight, with each drawing of blood visible to all. The fight could only be stopped by a man who'd suffered a cut if he dropped his weapon, but it went on if he didn't. No grappling or touching allowed, just the touch of the cold blade, thrusting or swinging.

It was a dangerous game for proud men. I hated all such games. They showed men's stupidity when they refused to stop when they could or were mutilated or died. In my mind, I chanted the winning charm for Yann, then a prayer to the Mother of Heaven. He had to win.

"Fight time is here. Blood will flow that we may learn the ways of the night," shouted Olaf.

"Praise Holda," came a shout from another throat, then it came from every throat around us.

The tall woman screamed, raised her fists. "Holda."

A worrying thought came to me. I'd heard that some in the borderlands ate human flesh. Were these followers of Holda looking for humans to eat?

I looked towards Olaf. His eyes had widened and his tongue was out, licking his lips as if he could taste something on them. Both Yann and the giant were naked now. Each had black soot swirls painted on them. The giant was bigger in every way and brazen with it, raising his arms and legs to show himself while people in the crowd made admiring noises.

That was not what Olaf was staring at. The followers of Holda had slipped out of their tunics too. A circle of naked women swayed now around the fighters, who had not even swung a blade yet. The women were dancing slowly, shadows from the torches, held by onlookers, illuminating their bodies with darkness and light. Streaks of red ran over their skin, blood from some sacrificed animal, most likely.

Tate screamed at Yann. "Cut him deep, Yann."

With a tremble in my voice, I echoed her shout, but my voice was drowned out by horn blowing, the signal for a hunt to begin.

The drumming intensified. The giant took a wide swing at Yann, laughing as he did, but he missed. The two men circled, the giant's knife swinging through the air from side to side, Yann's down.

My heart thumped in my throat. My mouth went dry. I was afraid both for Yann, but also for myself and Tate. I'd been so stupidly confident we could get to York with Yann's help. Without him, we'd be prey.

Tate gripped my arm. "Help him, Synne," she hissed in my ear. "Use your powers."

I whispered the chant the old seer had taught me and as I did so, I wished for Yann to survive, bending forward as I tried to set my desire upon the outcome.

"Grant my soul's desire.

Grant my soul's desire, for Yann to win this fight."

Tate gripped my arm tight. She'd heard me.

Yann blinked, stepped forward lightly, swaying from side to side as if dancing. He looked at me. The giant did too.

Yann swung.

His blade nicked the belly of the giant, who also swung at Yann, missing his chest by a hair's width. I didn't want to watch anymore. But I couldn't stop. Hope and despair were all mixed up inside me. I wanted to vomit.

"You will all be my slaves," shouted the giant. "I will have this man's balls to eat for my dinner. Then I will shaft the women," he shouted.

Yann grunted angrily.

That was what I feared. That he would lose his reason. I recited the chant again, louder this time. Tate repeated it, then screamed it. People looked at her. The giant did. Yann swung, leaning forward to the edge of his reach, his blade almost touching the giant's neck.

The giant swung into the blade, as if he didn't realise the danger. A red mouth opened across his neck.

But that didn't stop him.

His blade came up fast. Yann was too near. He couldn't stop it. A line of blood sprung across Yann's face, heading for his eye.

Cheers rang out.

"Yann," I shouted, warning him.

He swung wildly with his blade. They were both dripping blood now. The giant did not seem to notice the blood coming from his neck. Had he that much muscle that a neck wound didn't stop him?

He advanced on Yann, pulled his knife back. It would all be over in a moment. Yann's face was a blood mask. He might not even see anymore. One stab from the giant and he'd be felled.

The drumming stopped. The blasts on the horn too. The crowd went quiet.

The giant's gaze met Holda's. She nodded. A message passed between them.

5

Gytha shivered, looked away. The sight of the wound had sickened her. She'd seen too many injuries like that. Too many wide-open wounds pulsing with blood. Something touched her shoulder.

"Your friend is waiting for you," said a whispered voice.

Gytha turned. Anand was so close she could smell her oniony breath.

"Which friend?" She did not want to see Grymmwolf.

"Robert, the minstrel."

He was alive. Gytha wanted to kiss Anand but restrained herself.

"Where?"

"Back along the path. Board the first of the other vessels."

For a moment, Gytha wondered if she was being deceived. But to what purpose?

"Go," hissed Anand. She released Gytha.

"God be with you," said Gytha loudly.

Bishop Odo turned to her. "Do you need an escort?" he asked.

She shook her head. "No, no, I have friends waiting for me."

Odo looked her up and down. "A husband?"

Gytha bowed. "I am to meet the one promised me soon. I must rush away now, as it's late." She put her hand out. "Do you know where my sister Synne is?"

Odo's eyes narrowed. "I do not." He stared at her with a pensive look.

Queen Matilda was watching her guards pull the body from the mud. She turned as Gytha walked away and waved to her.

"Thank you for your gift," she called out. Then she waved again in a friendly manner at Gytha, who proceeded back along the dock as fast as she could walk.

She'd been sickened by the sight of the body, and by wondering who it was. She did not want to get in any other vessel without being sure of who was waiting for her, but she could not stay with Odo and Matilda either. If they discovered she'd run from Grymmwolf, they might pass her back to him. His anger at her defying him could push him to do something unspeakable as soon as he got her out to sea. He liked to do cruel things, to warn his other slaves who might get ideas.

A plank had been laid from the dock, leading to the other ship, resting low in the muddy water, waiting for the tide to come in. She glanced over her shoulder as she approached it, anxiety blooming again inside her. Neither Odo nor the queen was even looking in her direction. She walked down the plank fast without looking back and went to the leather-covered storage area at the front of the ship. It was the only place Robert could be hiding. She pulled aside the opening and looked into pure darkness. Were those eyes looking at her?

"Come in, quick," a voice whispered. Robert's voice.

She went in, let the flap close, bringing darkness, and a moment later, a hand on her arm.

"Sit down and be quiet," said Robert. "We sail with the tide."

She sat, immediately relieved. It looked like she'd escaped Grymmwolf. She sniffed. The stink of bodies was unmistakable now.

"Are we all prepared to sail?" she asked. Grymmwolf usually had his men running all over his ship, fixing ropes and tying things down before he left any port.

"We're ready. The tide is turning. It won't be long; we just have to wait until the water lifts us."

She sat in the darkness, put her hands out wide, felt warm bodies, pulled her hands back. Who was with him?

"How many people are here?"

"Be quiet," said a different voice. "You'll put us to the sword."

She felt around the wooden planks beneath her and discovered there was just enough room for her to lie down. Everyone seemed to be draped in a blanket. A light thud sounded beside her.

"For you," another voice whispered. It was a coarse blanket. She held it tight to her for a long moment. Tiredness and fear were all mixed up inside her.

It took her a long time to sleep, listening to snuffling, muted coughs, groans, and snores all around her. She was woken by the chatter of people passing above them along the dock, and then she rested some more until a voice whispered in her ear.

"We leave England now, are you ready?"

"Who are you all?"

"We are those who run from the new rulers of this cursed land," said a woman's voice in a strange accent. The grey light of dawn was seeping in through the thinner parts of the leather covering over them and through cracks and holes, so Gytha could see the woman who spoke was high-born, wearing a fine green tunic and with silver bracelets that no low-born women would have.

Everyone was sitting up now, but no one even put a finger outside the leather covering normally used for protecting goods. The boat rocked under her then and creaked and lurched violently, first one way, then the other, so much she thought the ship would tip over and she wondered how she'd swim in mud and what it would be like to drown in it, but then the loud creak of the ship settling and water sloshing reassured her. They could float on water.

Voices crying out from the shore sent a tiny shiver through her. She heard the word "dues." The shouts died. Had they paid the taxes that the dock stewards would have demanded? They kept swaying, first slowly, from oarsmen probably propelling them out into the main channel, then faster after the whoosh of a sail being raised.

Seagulls shrieked, followed by distant shouts, perhaps from another vessel. The smells changed soon after, from the city smell of middens and sweat to the smell of salt.

"I have to empty myself," she said.

"Hold it or piss on the floor," came Robert's voice. "We are not away yet. If someone reports people appearing on deck, they might send ships after us. They don't give up easy on people they want."

Gytha waited, holding herself, rocking back and forth. After a long time had passed and only the slick sound of moving water could be heard she asked him. "What are you running from? That Bishop Odo said you'd stolen something."

The Power of Synne

Someone laughed. Robert sighed.

"Taking back what a man's due is not stealing," he said. "But before I answer questions, how about you tell me about this skill of reading dreams you have? My master is interested in such things."

"Your master? Who is that?"

No reply came. They sat in near silence as the ship passed fast down the river. Soon rain battered on the leather above their heads and seeped through to drip on them everywhere in giant drops.

"Where are your sisters?" said the voice. "I would like to meet them."

"I do not know. They may be dead." She had an idea Tate had gone back to their home village, but she had no intention of telling him anything he might use against her.

Her hand was picked up and a wineskin pressed into it. "Drink a little to warm you," said Robert. "You can piss soon."

Gytha drank. It was sweet wine, the likes of which she'd never tasted before. She spluttered as it went down and some flowed over her chin. "Where is this from?"

"The Holy Father's vineyards. It is blessed wine. Do not waste it because you are not used to such quality."

"You stole his ship?" she asked.

"No," came the exasperated reply.

That made her wonder how wine from the pope's vineyards had come here. She'd never had wine from that far away, but as she didn't get to ever taste the wines lords and ladies drank, that probably didn't mean a lot.

"It came in with the ship," said Robert. "They sell wine. I sing. You read dreams. We go to their home."

"With extra passengers."

"We help all our brothers and sisters." He said it in a tone that made it clear Gytha should not argue. And he was right. What business was it of hers?

"Where is home?

"Florence."

Gytha sat still, stunned into silence. She'd heard of Florence, a city where traders went for spices and silks. A city so far away it took all summer to reach, and on the way, you'd encounter many strange tongues and marvels. She did want to go there.

The ship picked up speed as the wind took them. She was allowed to go outside and relieve herself over the side into the rushing water, her tunic barely covering her. The minstrel was not the only one staring at her as she did her business. A dark-skinned captain, his face burnt from too many days in the sun, had his eyes on her too. She held onto the ropes set into the side as she went, which helped make sure she didn't fall overboard.

Most of the other people stayed put under the leather covering. Gytha sat low in the stern afterwards and watched the coast of England grow more distant with each passing swell. So much had changed, so fast. Robert had helped her escape, and for that she was grateful, but did it mean she was bound to him, to go where he said? Had she no chance of finding her sisters?

A waterskin appeared in front of her. Robert pushed it towards her face.

"You have to drink water," he said. "We'll be out of sight of land soon. If you get sick, you'll need water inside you to stop the humors drying."

She sipped a little water as they both sat watching a distant fog roll towards them. "We could go all the way to Florence in this ship?" she asked.

"No, we'll sail to Francia, then go overland."

"Is Florence where you come from?"

He nodded. "Yes, and you will come with me. You'll be valuable there. Maybe you find a rich husband, dream reader from the north with flaxen hair." He smiled, put his hand up to brush some hair from her forehead.

She knew what he wanted.

"The Holy Father in Rome can free you from any claim on you by a slaver. His word is law. He helps many slaves gain their freedom."

"I have no coin to pay anyone."

"I will pay for all this. The Holy Father might even do it for me without a fee, if you tell him what's happening in England under this new king." His eyes bore into her. What did he want her to say?

"There will be many ways you can make coin in Florence," he said. "For someone with the telling gift, it will be easy. Telling people what their dreams mean is a good type of magic."

"Anyone can read dreams."

"No, they can't. Not properly."

Gytha stared at the still-distant fog. She did not want to set up as a dream reader anywhere. Dream readers were people who spun packs of lies, just because they could get paid for them.

"There are other games you might play there too," he said, a smile coming slowly to his face. "What did you do to keep the wolves from your door before?"

She was wondering how to answer when they saw the prow of a vessel appearing from the fog.

"I learned how to run," she said. She pointed at the other ship.

Robert let out a shout in some tongue she could not understand, but their captain did, as he barked a series of orders and crewmen ran about pulling on ropes and getting oars out.

The Power of Synne

But the other ship was soon closing on them fast and she could see warriors with shields and spears waiting on its deck.

Robert stood beside her as they closed in, even with every oar straining.

"They're looking for me," he said. "Do not fear them. You will be safe." He pulled a short sword from the leather scabbard on his belt. The other ship was still too far away for the fighting to start anytime soon, but Robert kissed his blade, then held it forward for her to kiss.

"If I die, let it be with the kiss of a beautiful woman on my sword."

She kissed the blade. He kissed it again where she had kissed it.

They were heading for the fog now. Shouts echoed from the other vessel. "Put down your sail," was the distant order she just about heard. She squinted, trying to make out who was on the other vessel. Then she saw. There were four men with weapons on their ship and ten or more on the other vessel. They would have to surrender or expect to die.

She looked around. The wall of fog was close.

They might make it.

"May I ask for one more favour," said Robert.

He went on one knee, his head bowed. "If you survive, and I do not, will you send a message to the Holy

Father about how I fought and died and that I prayed for him before I passed?" His eyes closed.

He began mumbling strange words she could barely hear. From across the swells came laughter and shouts. There was something vaguely familiar about Robert's mutterings. The words stirred a memory from across a gulf of years, bringing back the scene of her father's departure from their home. He'd whispered in this way back then too, as if sharing a secret prayer. She put her hand out and touched Robert's shoulder.

He reached up, took her hand. They held onto each other, her heart beating fast with a mixture of fear, bittersweet memories, and hope, as the fog bank neared so slowly and their pursuers closed on them.

She had to survive. She wanted Robert to survive, too. She pointed at the fog.

"We'll be hard to catch if we make it," she said, hope swelling with the billows of damp fog that seemed to be reaching out for them.

The whistle of arrows filled the air, followed by thuds as some hit their ship.

"Row faster," our captain roared. More arrows thudded in hard around them.

Robert stood, moved between her and the other ship, protecting Gytha. Her relief was followed moments later

The Power of Synne

by the distinctive soft thud of an arrow punching into flesh and then a groan from his lips.

"No," whispered Gytha. She grabbed Robert as he fell. An arrow had pierced his side. The wound was bad. Blood oozed. The thud of other arrows landing followed. Then the fog enveloped them. It was so thick and so wet she could barely make out Robert, who'd fallen beneath her.

Another thud sent strong reverberations passing through their ship and water streaming in on one side. They'd been rammed. Her mouth opened in horror at the thought of being dumped into a fog-shrouded sea.

A groan came unbidden from her lips. They would all die.

Triumphant shouts echoed.

The prow of the other ship, a giant wolf head, slid along their side with a great tearing sound as carbuncles in giant dirty fists slid along their side and water came sloshing onto their feet.

Had they been holed?

A grinning bearded man came jumping down from the other ship. She wanted to cry out, but her voice had stopped working. As he landed, he was speared, she did not see by who, and more loud creaking noises came, the agonies of wood, the prow of the other ship sliding past, and then it was gone into the fog with curses and shouts dying behind them.

The man who'd jumped onboard was twisting and groaning loudly in the water in the bottom of their ship. Their men, with axes and staves up high, had surrounded him; with fog clinging around them, it was a scene from a nightmare.

"He's not praying," said someone with a laugh as the man's head fell back and he started shaking.

"Quiet," hissed the captain.

A hush fell, broken only by the dying man's groans.

A gap opened between the men around him.

Gytha recognised the man. He was one of Grymmwolf's men. But that hadn't been his ship. How was he here?

She stepped forward, put her hand to his now clutching his chest. Immediately he gripped her the way soon-to-be-dead men do.

"Pray. For. Me." Despair filled his voice.

"Where's Grymmwolf?" Gytha whispered, bending low over him.

The man smiled a little.

Then his eyes dimmed.

"Search him, throw him over for the crabs," said the captain. The man was stripped almost bare. He went over the side with a slight splash and a gurgle.

They sailed on, with no swell or wind now, not rowing and moving with the current.

It was almost dark when the fog lifted and there was no land to be seen in any direction. Gytha looked back at the fog bank, a fading grey darkness. The wolf head ship was emerging from it.

6

The air felt icy stiff in my throat. Winter still held us in its grip. Yann had been left behind, while Tate and I were led, our hands bound tight together by a rough rope, led like slaves towards the hills. We were both shaking, not just from the cold, but what we knew lay ahead.

In front of us strode the tall woman who'd pointed out Yann for the fight. I'd asked Olaf that one of us be left behind in the village to tend to Yann's wounds, but he shook his head angrily. The fight had not gone the way they'd expected.

Around us walked other women in long pale tunics, all streaked with dirt and ashes, their heads bowed in mourning. At the front of this bleak procession, men from the village were carrying the dead giant on a wooden litter. It took six of them, and at times they swayed, struggling with the weight.

We veered off the path into pine woods at a place where it forked and the climb became steep. We walked for a while across a scrubby grass landscape and then into woods and onto a deer track. The moon was high but its light was thin. A veil of clouds obscured it. Only a few torches up ahead gave us any confidence of where we were heading.

The sweet odour of pine trees mingled with the sweat of the people around us to make a heady brew. A low mourning chant had begun from those ahead of us as we went into the woods. I knew keening songs like it from my time in Dublin. It had echoes, too, of keening songs from my childhood. Many Danes still lived in York and the surrounding villages.

That was when I saw the ancient stones ahead, most likely from the time of the first people, in a bare, treeless opening in the woods. That had to be where we were heading. A flat rock in the centre of the open area was held high by other giant grey stones at such an angle that you could bend down and get under it.

The giant had already been laid near the rock when we arrived. The women formed a circle around him. Most of them had branches in their hands, windfall from the woods. I watched as a layer of branches was laid down and the giant's body moved onto them, and more branches placed all around him.

I knew what was coming. I'd seen bodies been burnt before. We'd visited York when I was young after the

Danes had been defeated and they were still burning bodies near the city that day; Danes who'd been executed.

The smell of human flesh burning is similar to that of other flesh, the types we gorge on. It sets mouths watering and then the revulsion sets in, as we recognise its sweetness.

These women were not Christians or perhaps, like many, they made a show of being seen in the church in their village but practised old ways at night when together. That meant they might also perform other night-time practices, the ones banned long ago by abbots and bishops.

Night revels while wearing masks went on around York too, a few times a year, with women roaming together looking for young men to go with. Was that what this was about? Was that what had been planned for the giant? A night of rutting after victory?

Tate stood beside me. We still had the rope around our wrists. The other end was held by an old, tough-looking woman with long greasy grey plaits and an unblinking expression. She had her eyes on the giant as his body slowly caught fire.

I leaned toward Tate. "Our spell saved Yann," I said.

"He heard my words. That's all that matters with a spell, what is heard."

I sighed. I had an idea this was the way she would go, taking credit where she could, and giving blame out where

The Power of Synne

it suited her. It was the way she'd always been and one of the reasons our mother favoured me.

"If you offer them your powers, perhaps they'll let us go," Tate hissed. She watched me. I knew what this meant. If I was useful, she'd be my friend. No change there.

I muttered the chant the seer in Ireland had given me. This time I wished for me and Tate to survive. That was all.

"Look," said Tate; her hand covered her mouth as she spoke. "It begins."

A woman had appeared carrying a red earthen bowl. She was holding it carefully, as if it was full. I knew what Tate meant. This was a blood bowl, used to gather and drink blood from cows and sheep, oftentimes without killing them. The old stories spoke about how such bowls had been used in the past to gather human blood before a festival. We should be able to survive this if they didn't try to drown us in blood.

This bowl was passed from mouth to mouth. All the women drank from it. I was reminded of what the followers of Christ thought about such rituals. They were not permitted anymore in any place where a priest or a monk held sway.

Our turn was coming.

The stench and smoke from the giant's burning body blew into our faces. Even the wind knew my fear and disgust. Tate put her tied hands out in front of her when her turn with the blood bowl came. They shook as she opened her upturned mouth and swallowed the blood poured into her with a loud slurping noise, then licked her lips when she was finished as all the others had done.

It was my turn.

Every part of me trembled as the woman holding the bowl came closer. The hot-iron smell of blood filled my nostrils and throat as they raised it to my lips. My stomach tightened with revulsion and my mouth closed tight. I'd had blood before, but the smell had been different; perhaps it had not been this fresh.

A chant started up because of my hesitation.

"Drink, drink, drink." Hand drums took up the beat. There would be no shying away from this. I'd have my mouth opened forcefully if I refused.

I opened up, gulped at the stickiness. It went down badly. I coughed, bent over. Hoots of laughter echoed, but the chant stopped. A wave of disgust filled me, distressing me. The blood I'd drank felt like a wet stone in the pit of my stomach. Tate looked at me. Her eyes widened. What more had they waiting for us her face said.

I pulled gently at the rope binding me and binding us together, trying to touch the knot, to loosen it. The old woman who held the other end saw me or maybe felt me moving. She motioned me to stop. Tate was smiling now in a way that said she knew what I was trying to do and had already done it.

That, at last, was a moment of hope. We might survive this. I was glad she was with me. No matter what, we were bound together by blood and life.

The bowl continued around the circle while dark shadows danced on the ground and light from the blazing torches stuttered in the wind. The drinking chant started again. All eyes were now fixed on a child on the far side of the circle, a young girl whose arms were shaking as she faced the bowl. Her eyes were wide too and innocent. Her gaze flickered around the circle. Her skin was pale and her hair raven black. She looked unlike anyone else in the circle. The daughter of a slave most likely, given an opportunity to join the group and perhaps freedom later, if she did what they wanted.

The drink chant came faster, like a war chant.

The girl shook her head. A hush descended.

All I could hear was the wind, whistling an admonition as it moved through the trees, speaking in the ancient tongue, words that my mother said we'd all lost the meaning of.

Two older women stood beside the girl. They lifted her under the arms and walked with her to the edge of the woods. The hush continued as they pulled away her tunic, tore it from her until finally, they pushed her into the trees, naked. What period of being an outcast she faced I did not know. Being left in the woods for a night was a harsh punishment given to young disobedient children, longer periods for older children. There is no room for soft hearts when work has to be done to keep a household alive.

The girl's chin lay down on her neck as she stood at the edge of the trees.

Perhaps she was crying, but I could not hear her. She was too far away. I guessed it from the movement of her shoulders. Tears were unlikely to sway these people.

A soft drumming began as a woman moved to the centre of the open area. She was beautiful, her hands thin, unmarked by hard labour, likely high-born, her face sombre, the line of her mouth turned down, as if in regret. Her hair was tied back with a long knotted red-wool rope that swung behind her as she walked. She stood still and our eyes met, as if she'd been waiting for me to see her, and then she began swaying, dancing, her legs kicking higher and higher as the drums beat louder.

Heaviness filled my chest.

The woman moved with the drumming, her dance a lamentation. It spoke of suffering, ill treatment, a throwing down and rising up again, what all women know because of the men who surround us.

The Power of Synne

New gestures came. She touched her hair, held her breast, her ear, all lightly, quickly, as if remembering someone and distracted by it.

A memory of Magnus came to me. The shape of his neck, his arm, his hand reaching for me. I'd forced myself not to think about him since Dublin, or his treachery, as such thoughts made me want to go to the other side. Such thoughts, once lit, were a fire I could barely control. I had to push them away. They brought only pain. And hate.

But there was another side to him I could not forget. His passion, liveliness, pride. We'd danced to drums just like this in Dublin, a rising desire within him visible on his face, a bare naked look of wanting in his eyes. That memory was too hot, too pleasurable; it awoke desire and a wanting for him that mixed up with the hate and sharpened it.

The dancer moved close to me.

Had something else been mixed in with that blood? A heavy warmth had spread through me. The dancer stared into my eyes, hers wide, before her head turned. I felt fixed to the spot, waiting to see if she would look at me again when she came around the circle again. That was a moment of both fear and hope. If such a dancer wanted something where I come from, it would be hard to resist her.

I realised Tate wasn't beside me anymore. Gone to relieve herself, perhaps. Warm blood can loosen the bowels. You can shit yourself if you didn't move fast enough. But how had she been released from the rope?

The dancer was in front of another woman, on the far side of the circle. I was waiting, impatient for her gaze. Eventually, as my patience almost ended, she looked at me again and then moved sinuously towards me, like a snake rearing up for its prey. She'd been trying to make me jealous by dancing for that other woman.

Which means she wanted me. That was a scary thought.

Noises made me look towards the trees. A neighing sound came, as if a horse was trapped in the woods. I squinted into the trees. A movement caught my eye. A horse was coming out of the woods. Two people were riding it. The bridle was held by the man at the front.

The person behind him looked like Tate. I squinted into the darkness.

It was Tate.

And the man with her was Yann.

7

The hall of the King of Dublin was quiet except for the soft hissing of the logs on the fire. It was late morning, which would normally have been a busy time in the hall, but almost everyone had been ordered out. An important visitor had arrived by longship and only the personal guard of Murchad, the King of Dublin, was present.

His guard that day was six armed, mean-looking men all leaning on their axes, three on each side of the long table at the top of the hall, where Murchad sat alone eating hard bread and drinking the light Wexford ale he enjoyed.

The door of the hall burst open and Erlend, a Jarl of the Orkneys walked in, alone, his guards still grumbling loudly outside the door. Erlend had no visible weapon but was tall and well-built enough to kill with his bare hands. His greasy blond hair flowed onto his shoulders.

He walked slowly up the centre aisle of the hall, raising both his hands as he came, showing he came in peace.

"My, my, Murchad, you have done well since we last met. I expect the wenches might like you now." He smiled.

Murchad rose and extended his hand.

"You are still a bad liar, Erlend. That woman you thought favoured you was a spy who begged me to get away from you."

They laughed, clasped arms.

"What brings you so far south?" asked Murchad.

"I will tell, after I get some of that fine ale into me." He pointed at Murchad's engraved silver goblet.

"Join me," said Murchad, pointing to an elaborately carved chair near him.

Erlend sat, drank his fill, grabbed at the slave girl who brought the ale and laughed at a few jokes Murchad made. Then he pulled out a small knife that had been hidden in his high sealskin boots and put it near his own throat. He waited until all the guards were staring at him, their hands tight on their axes before explaining.

"I am honour bound on a search, King Murchad. I have sworn to cut my own throat if I do not succeed."

"What search?" said Murchad. He leaned back, sipped at his ale.

Erlend put the knife down. "We have an ugly bastard who claims to be our brother. He took up arms against us."

Murchad nodded. "I heard you lost some men," he said.

"Good men. My best. I trust you, Murchad, is why I tell you this. I've sworn to find this evil spawn of the devil and kill him in the most painful way and that his offspring will all become slaves, each separate from the other, no matter their seeming innocence. They have dark powers, that family, which must never be joined together." He crossed himself. "You know well, if anyone does, we cannot allow such a beast of a man or his blood to roam around us stirring dissent, claiming any right by blood to the earldom of the Orkneys and seeking to pull us back to the old dark and evil ways."

Murchad nodded. "You are right. But why do you come here?" he asked. "I have not met these people."

Erlend banged the butt end of his knife on the table so hard the wood shook all the way along. "I believe two of this man's daughters are here, Murchad. One is named Synne. The other Tate."

8

There was nothing they could do. To repel a larger ship, especially at night, required weather that could assist and men willing to fight. But men who are willing to fight usually only do so when they believe they can win.

As the other ship approached, Gytha could see twenty men onboard it now, all brandishing weapons. And their ship still had more men rowing. Gytha's ship had ten men in total, and their captain looked as if he was ready for defeat. Gytha knew her fate could be decided in moments.

If one of the men leading men on the other vessel wanted her, he would claim her as a spoil of victory. She would have to put up with, and appear to enjoy, whatever he wanted to do. If she didn't comply, she would be shared among all of them. That would be a fate far worse than death.

Robert was sitting in the bottom of the boat, blinking, as if he didn't believe what had happened. He'd be aware that if he said one word against the men from the other ship, they might finish him quickly or perhaps slowly and dump him overboard whenever they'd stopped toying with him.

The harsh scraping sound as the two ships came together sounded like a death-hag's warning. It spoke of pain, punishment, and a watery oblivion.

Their captain was not so brave in those moments. He waved his axe, then threw it in the bottom of their ship and motioned for the other men with him to do the same. The men that boarded them all had axes up. They all looked Danish, as if they'd come from a raid up the coast. The first two to jump onboard grunted in the faces of the men on the ship and laughed when none of them responded. One of them stuck his face in Gytha's and smiled, showing yellow teeth and a puckered red scar that ran from his lip to his ear.

A shout from the other ship sent the man stepping back from Gytha.

"What is a fair lady doing running from London in this weather?" called a stern voice.

Gytha looked across to the other ship. A tall man wearing the crested iron helmet of a lord was gazing down at her.

She bowed. "What is a lord doing stopping simple traders?" she asked, a slight tremble in her voice. She had her hands on her hips as she stood over Robert. She was afraid, every muscle tight, but was not going to show it.

Men were jumping down onto their vessel. She kept her eyes on the man who'd spoken to her but could see at the edge of her vision that the men on her ship were being pushed around. Shouts and a splash sounded. Laughter and more shouts followed. Someone had been pushed overboard, probably after being knifed. Most likely someone, it seemed, who was going to cause trouble.

She kept her eyes on the leader from the other vessel. Her mouth was like dead leaves and a trembling inside her came and went in waves.

The man didn't reply to her. He said something in rough Danish to the men near her. One man went to grab at her.

She slipped from his grasp, strode to the point where their two ships swayed together, and jumped up and across into the other ship. She was afraid for a moment that she wouldn't make it, and slip between the chaffing vessels and die a cold death, but she would not be manhandled in front of all these men. Better to die quick.

But she was lucky with her jump. She made it onto the other ship as if she'd been doing this all her life.

A cheer went up from the men around.

The lord took his helmet off, smiled, and bowed a little, but kept his gaze on her.

"We collect proper taxes for the true King of England, my lady," he said. "We stop all ships who can make recompense for the evil alive in our great land."

"We're on the same side then," she said. "I'm freeborn English from near York." She bowed for him.

"Name?"

"Gytha, the dream reader."

He laughed. "You're more a dream maker than a reader. I expect." He looked beyond her. "Which of these lowly men is with you? One of them your husband or a suitor?"

"I came on board with Robert the minstrel in London. We were both in danger from Norman treachery."

"Well, now you are well free of them. There are no Normans where we are going."

"Where are we going?"

"Dorestad."

"Frisia?"

He nodded. "By the mouth of the greatest river in the world."

"What will you do at Dorestad?" she asked, her mind racing.

He pointed down along his ship. At the far end, under a leather skin stretching from side to side, a huddle of women and children stared out with vacant eyes. They all looked worn out, dirty, and beaten down.

Her stomach flipped, like a fish leaping. "You're a slaver?" she asked.

This was bad news. He'd want to sell her, and everyone else. Slavers were not known for their generosity of spirit or for overlooking any opportunity to make coin. She stuck her chin out.

"Yes, my lord?"

He hesitated, as if considering whether to answer her. "I am Edmund, a son of King Harold, the last rightful King of England."

She blinked in astonishment. A son of King Harold should not be out at sea capturing slaves. Was he lying?

He pointed down the ship to where the slaves sat. "You, my lady, go sit with the others."

"I'm no slave," she said.

"There is nowhere else to sit, lady." He wore a crooked smile, as if he didn't expect her to believe him.

Gytha reached her hand to him. "Brave Edmund, the minstrel Robert, who lies injured on our vessel, is an envoy from the pope. His life will be worth far, far more than the ship you just captured." She smiled. Her hope was that he would want to save Robert, not put him over the side as too much trouble. Robert might then offer enough to persuade Edmund not to sell her to the highest bidder.

His eyes narrowed and he waved her to go away. She sat with the slaves and watched as Robert was carried on board. She went to him when he was dropped near her.

Edmund's men had murdered two of the crew from the other ship. Two men who had argued with them. They roped the rest of the crew together and put some of their own men on board the ship. Both ships then sailed towards the coast of Francia and, within sight of the coast, went north to Frisia to its capital, Dorestad, some way up the estuary of the great river.

***

It took them all of three days to reach Dorestad. The stink from the slaves around her was as bad as anything she'd experienced by the time they reached the long dock beneath the high, double palisade wall of the city.

Godwin ordered all the slaves to stand after they tied up, their ship leaning up against the next, like loaves pushed up against each other on a baker's tray.

Edmund stood in front of each of them and checked teeth and looked them up and down. She did not turn away when it was her turn. She'd been appraised many times since slavers had murdered her mother.

Edmund smiled at the man beside him, who nodded.

They were going to sell her. They thought they'd get a good price for her. Fear twisted inside her like a worm.

She'd been sold before, so she knew what men wanted. The fear was about not knowing who would get her, what type of man.

A deeper dread was to be taken to the lands of the Saracens and sold into some house where other women might poison you or cut your throat if they thought their master had turned you against them.

Many women died on the journey south to the land of the Saracens. Slave drivers could be unbelievably cruel. They fed their charges just enough to keep them alive. Sickness often travelled with slavers too, spreading fast among their slaves, and leading to bodies being discarded among trees or down ravines for the wolves and bears.

That was not a fate she wanted to think about. There were better things to think about.

All through her many journeys, no matter the storms and grasping men and the cold or heat, she'd kept memories of her sisters alive, memories that helped her pass the time and made her feel she was only dreaming her current life as a slave and that her real one was back with her sisters in those memories. And every day, when she remembered them, she prayed they were safe.

Two high halls with steep, angled roofs and banners fluttering at the top stood along the shore beyond the quay. Further off, a scrubby treeline could be seen. Many people moved about in front of the halls while some waited in lines. They were too far away to make out faces clearly, but she saw ropes and neck rings. It looked as if half the town were slaves.

She'd heard that slave trading was big in Frisia but had not expected it to be like this. Then Edmund let out a series of commands she did not understand.

She understood, though, when his crew approached the slaves with ropes. One by one, the crew tied up the men, women, and children. You'd likely not die from a blow from one of their crews' clubs, but the pain would be real and it would last a long time.

Gytha held back, deluding herself that she was not to be roped up, but she was not that lucky. A swarthy crewman grabbed her wrist and yanked her forward. She could have fought him but decided not to.

She knew what slavers did to the reluctant. She also knew she'd fetch a multiple of what any male slave would sell for.

A wide plank had been set between the ship and the dock. Gytha stared at the man pushing her towards the plank, stepped away from him, and went across to the next ship and then onto the dock beyond with her head up. She did not look around for Edmund. She would not give him the pleasure of dismissing her appeal for clemency.

There were crewmen on the dock already. They had the other slaves tied up all in a line. This was the moment she'd dreaded. To have your hands tied by rope to other slaves meant you were debased, subject to the whim of whoever claimed to own you and to be alive only if your owner wanted. She should have felt humiliated, but all she felt was a shuddering anger.

Most of the men on the dock were looking at her. Many had an expectant look, as if they were hoping she would rebel and be debased further in front of them. But she would rebel only if she had a possibility of winning. She held her hands out. A skinny crew member, he looked pleased, tied a rope around her wrists, pulled it tight and attached the other end to the rope the slaves were all connected to.

Thankfully, they didn't have iron collars for them too. She'd worn one once, after shouting at Grymmwolf, and had hated it not just because of the weight and the chaffing, but because everyone knew you'd rebelled and had been beaten or worse.

The slave line was led along the road past two ancient-looking dark halls with low eaves. They had lines of slaves outside them and men with axes and cudgels pushing them around. They stopped at the third hall, the largest, which had two strands of smoke rising from its dark, almost black, thatched roof. Edmund appeared from inside the hall. He glanced at Gytha, smiled, then went back into the hall, leaving his slaves standing in the mud.

The Power of Synne

Something made her turn. Perhaps it was a change in the wind or a band of rain coming in their direction.

Others had sensed the clouds approaching, too. Some of their guards moved under the overhanging eaves of the hall. When the rain came, not long after, driven by a bitter wind slapping at her face, one of the guards motioned them all to shelter too.

That gave her hope. Not all these men were cruel.

She prayed then to be free of all this and to find her sisters. Was there any hope of that now? She knew the slave trade from Frisia extended south into the lands of the infidel and east to the lands of the Rus and beyond.

What had the Fates in store for her?

A muttering had started up among the slaves. She turned her head. She hadn't seen the horses coming along the path towards them. The jangle of armoured men and the clop of their horses grew as she watched them approach, assuming they would pass by. But the lead horsemen stopped near her and stared down at her, looking from her feet upwards.

He had a pale scar on his cheek, which ran into his lip, and wore a dirty wolf skin cloak with a white streak down it. Beside him rode two other riders carrying banners wilting in the rain. The man sniffed as he looked at her, as if he might smell her.

He laughed to himself, mumbled something. His outriders laughed. They were enjoying a joke at her expense. He said more, louder, in a language she did not understand. She stared up at the men one by one. They laughed, moved on, and further along got down from their horses and most of them went into the hall. She was glad they moved away and hoped never to see them again.

A little while later, after the rain ceased, one of the men from the ship came outside, undid her from the rope of slaves, and pulled her towards the hall. She did not want to be taken inside looking like this, mud-splattered, her hands still tied, her tunic dirty, but when she went through the door, she changed her mind. There was heat in here. She could feel the warmth immediately. But better than that, was the smell of roasting meat and fresh, warm bread. Her mouth instantly watered. She looked around.

A serving woman, probably a slave, was walking among the tables with a tray of thick dark horsebread slices. She wanted one of them. She would eat it in two bites if she could get one.

She'd barely noticed the men at the tables, but as a hush descended and laughter broke out, the men at the tables came into view. There must have been fifty of them all staring at her. She saw only eyes for one long moment and hated every pair of them. Then she heard the laugh again and looked up at the top table. Edmund was sitting there, as was the man with the scarred lip.

And he was pointing at her and talking to Edmund, who was shaking his head. She knew what was going on. They were arguing about her price.

She looked around. Perhaps someone else would bid for her, someone she might be able to stomach.

In an instant, she knew who she wanted. A tall Dane with a thick head of hair and a smile on his face was looking at her with his head to one side. She smiled back at him. He laughed, stood, and came towards her.

Before he arrived, the man holding the other end of her rope pulled Gytha after him. He wanted her to go to the open space in front of the top table. She took a step as if she was complying, then stopped abruptly and jerked the rope back. The man holding it, caught in mid-step, fell backwards.

More laughter broke out. He stumbled again in the dirty straw as he got up.

She stared at the Dane. His dark tunic had red threaded runes embroidered in the neckband to make clear where he came from, though only those who knew how to read the runes would be able to tell you exactly where.

She waited while the man holding her rope made a growling sound and pulled his hand back as if to strike her. She kept still. The blow did not fall. The Dane was standing beside her now. He'd caught the hand aimed for her face. She nodded her thanks. A shout went up from the top table.

The Dane smiled at her. "How much they want for you?" he asked.

"You must ask him the price," she said. She pointed with her thumb at Edmund, then widened her eyes in that way men like, which tells them you will enjoy being with them. Men are easy creatures to lure to the hook.

The Dane looked at the top table. Edmund was banging his red goblet hard on the wood.

"Stay away from her, Dane," he shouted. "She's already sold."

The Dane shrugged, bowed, came close to her, and whispered in her ear.

"If you ever get free of him, ask for Erik the boatbuilder, third of his name. I will set my wife aside for you." He swayed. He was drunk.

She'd hoped he might try harder, but it was not to be. She was pulled to the front table, had the indignity of scar lip coming up and touching her, before she watched as a bag of coins was passed and she was pulled by the same rope to a corner of the hall, where the other men scar lip was with were waiting.

Scar lip did not rush to her either. He waited as other picks from the slave line were brought in. He paid for a young girl, probably soon to start bleeding, and a boy even younger.

Gytha waited, tormented, for scar lip to drag her to some quiet corner, but it was not to be. The man who watched over her and the other slaves simply sneered when he was asked anything and shouted at some serving girls who brought bread, cheese, and a gristly stew for them. Gytha ate only a little while sitting on the floor and finally, exhausted, fell asleep in the rushes when the noise in the hall died down a little.

It seemed scar lip would bide his time.

***

The following day, another man appeared. He spoke an English tongue and explained to Gytha that she'd been bought by an official of King Henry of Germania, fourth of his name, and would be taken to him for his use or the use of his household.

The news dismayed her.

If she was to be abused here, at least she had some hope of escape and finding a vessel to return to England. If she was taken upriver to Germania, a land she'd only heard about, she'd not even be able to speak their tongue. How could she find people to help her there? Runaway slaves were objects of derision and punishment everywhere. No one wanted the possibility of an accusation and fine if you helped one. In some places, she'd heard, you could forfeit your freedom for helping a slave.

She did not want to eat now and it was only after the coaxing of a young girl that she managed to eat some of the hard bread before they set off again, after the rain stopped.

They left the town through the east gate and headed towards the distant line of the forest, along with a straggly line of traders all taking advantage of the clear skies. The only people on horseback in their procession were scar lip, his two bannermen, and two other mounted men at arms at the back. Otherwise, they all walked. Gytha, used to sailing in short hops and wintering in halls with Grymmwolf, was not ready for the lengthy fast walking that started that day.

Her boots gave up after two days and when she held them up in complaint, the soles flapping, new wider boots were given to her and hers were taken away. The new boots chaffed but did not break.

They sheltered each night at long cabins set back from the road and guarded by representatives of the local lord in the area. She wasn't sure if scar lip was charged much for this service and for the slaves with him, but she did see him pass something each night before they all went in and were fed from the communal pot.

The Power of Synne

It took over a month for them to reach the city on a river they called Augsburg, which was supposed to be the mightiest city in the Kingdom of Germania. Gytha was not impressed. London had been much larger, both its houses and halls and its population. London teemed with people. Augsburg did not.

She did not say that. She'd seen how proud the men of Augsburg who were with them were, all puffed up as they spoke to each other.

The hall of the king here was better than any other she'd seen on the journey. It was near to the river, but still only as big as the smaller halls in London.

She'd been pleased at least not to have to fight off men looking to enjoy her on the journey, but she expected this would end when she was taken to see the king here. But that did not happen immediately.

The new slaves were all taken to the side of the main hall, where two slave houses sat side by side. One was for house slaves, which they were put in. The other was for field slaves, all men. They were fed separately too, early that evening. The weather was warm and the fresh scent of the river gave that part of the city a cleaner feel than the road from the main gate, which stank.

A large pot and bowls were brought into the slave hut, and they were joined by four other young house slaves as they ate. Gytha understood none of them. When they were all finished, the four slaves fussed around the three new slaves, giving them clean tunics and dabbing at their faces with a wet cloth to remove stains from the road. They were also given new shoes, smaller pointed boots.

A great noise could be heard from the main hall, as if a thousand people had crowded into it. That was how it seemed too, when Gytha was led inside by the hand by a similarly aged young woman, in a similar tunic to hers. Gytha noticed that her tunic style, in a pale green with darker green edges, was also worn by other slaves carrying food and wine and ale pots.

Some of the slaves also wore belts of different types. She was not able to work out what the different designs and widths all meant, but she expected they indicated a rank in the king's household.

The people at the tables were mostly men, warriors who kept daggers with them, which they used to hack at hunks of meat and loaves of bread placed in front of them. Many of the men had hair as black as ravens' wings. They wore it in a variety of styles, the most unusual of which was shaved at the front and left long at the back, the opposite of how Normans wore it.

Some of the men stared at her as she was led up the room, but it was only as they approached the main table that she felt under real scrutiny. A line of women sitting on one side of the top table stared at her as if she was a horse they'd captured.

Scar lip was sitting near the middle of the table, whispering to the man at the centre, who was younger than him and fresh-faced. Beside him sat an older woman who could have been his mother. They both wore tunics embroidered with gold thread. The young man was looking Gytha up and down.

Gytha knew this was a moment that could change her life. The young man was most likely the king and the woman beside him his mother or guardian. Where his wife was, she could not guess, as the women to his mother's side were all too old to be the king's wife. Gytha kept her face still, hoping not to show any weakness, which she expected would be despised.

Scar lip waved at the woman holding Gytha's hand. The woman turned to Gytha. The look on her face was apologetic. She was going to do something that Gytha would not like.

9

It was the next full moon before I was taken back to the clearing where Tate and Yann had escaped. I'd spent the past month working in the kitchens in a fishing village. No man had yet tried to force himself on me, probably because of what had happened, the death Yann had caused, and the ill fortune it might mean for any man who went with me. They made me collect seaweed too, and I skipped stones from the pebble beach as I did, remembering the games Stefan and I used to play when we were young, firing stones at birds to see who could down one.

I found out that the people here spent a lot of time worrying about their luck. Some people, I discovered, had even been speculating about whether the incident at the ceremony had brought bad luck on the whole town. A fishing boat had floundered and all three on board had died during a storm a week before, including a much-loved man from this village, and some now whispered these deaths could be laid at my door.

I dreamt on two nights about a ship sailing into the small harbour and Magnus being on board and coming ashore. I wanted this to be a premonition. I wanted him to find me. And I wanted to yell at him for leaving me and to slap his ugly face.

Our life in Dublin had been so much better than this life. I prayed each night and each morning to Mary, then to the old gods, to be released from this unfair and unjust bondage. But my prayers had not worked. Yet.

I thought many times about running away, but without a horse and with the whole countryside dotted with farmsteads who would report my movements and bind me and carry me back if they found me, my chances would be slim. A warning that I'd be branded on the cheek and a metal collar fitted to me permanently, which could never be taken off if I ran, had also discouraged me. I needed some other way to escape this trap I'd fallen into.

Magnus would provide that if he came. But he hadn't.

So, as I walked at the back of the procession towards the woods, I was unhappy, my head down. Not even the nudges of one of the other slave girls could stop that. My life had gone from being a partner of a prince to being a despised slave with the passing of a few moons. Everything had gone wrong. My sister had betrayed me, and Magnus too.

There was nothing that could console me. A curse seemed to have been placed on me.

The procession moved fast through the woods. Someone claimed to smell rain on the air. It was midsummer now, with lots of work in the fields.

"Move faster," someone hissed behind me.

I turned. It was the old woman who dried fish. There was a smell of fish around her, always, which was probably why she was at the back, a near-outcast like me.

I didn't bother to argue with her.

When we reached the opening in the woods, we took our places in the circle. I guessed this ceremony was to do with encouraging the crops and the fishing. We had similar in our village near York. Every effort had to be made to ensure the village prospered in summer. From what I'd seen, the people here believed as much in the old ways as in praying to Christ. Christ in the day, the all-father at night, I'd heard a few people say.

On the far side of the ring of people sat the old woman who'd put Yann into the fight. Around her were women in the same long tunics with long faces and beyond them two young men, with matted brown hair. I hadn't seen them before. The drumming started up, pulling us into the coming ceremony. I kept my face stiff like the others.

The young men stepped forward and the drumming stopped. They walked towards me. One of them spoke as

The Power of Synne

he came. His accent was strange, but his tongue was the same as ours.

"Come with us." One of them had a rope in his hands. I'd been sold.

I kept my face stiff. One of them had a small wooden cross hanging from a leather string around his neck. He felt for the cross as I looked at him and smiled, showing half-broken teeth. The other one raised the rope higher as if he was about to use it on me.

I had little choice, but it was a consolation that they were followers of Christ, who were well known to go easy on slaves. Being with them might give me opportunities to escape. I'd recited the chant the old seer had taught me every night before sleeping since I'd been separated from my sister and every morning too after I awoke. Was this how the gods answered me? It had to be.

"Come," said the man who'd spoken. "We have horses and will be back at our farm before first light."

He was as good as his word. We rode in the moonlight and before the first sign of dawn, we rode off the track and down a thin overgrown trail that rarely saw a cart. Finally, we stopped at a large farm. There was no light coming from under the door. I asked where the women of the house were.

"Our mother died this past winter. We have no sisters or wives, yet." He smiled at me.

I had all sorts of fears that first night. I imagined both of them wanting to share me or to fight over me.

***

In the morning, after sleeping in the rushes near the door, I was shown the hearth and discovered they had a store of food anyone would be proud of. We ate honey cakes, sausage, and warm milk for breakfast.

"You must keep the house right and keep the food coming," said the same man after stuffing his face. His brother seemed not to want to talk to me.

I watched them both heading out and across the fields after breakfast.

The day passed quickly. No other woman came to the house and the two young men were like lap dogs around me. I wondered whether this was all leading towards something, but after a few opportunities for them to jump on me came and went, I began to trust them and make plans.

One thing that still bothered me was the lack of women. It was explained to me the next morning that their mother had a feud with the next nearest landholder, who had one daughter. Apparently, there was no one else in the valley who was interested in the boys. But it still felt strange to me, as most young men would have local women lined up and waiting for them from their circle of acquaintances.

But perhaps I was wrong to question all this too much and anyway, things began to change as the more talkative brother came to visit me in the kitchen that afternoon.

That was when I found out what I hadn't been told before. Each of these men had a wife. Both wives had died. After that, they'd sworn not to take another woman for at least a year.

And they were nearly through the time period for their promise.

***

The following Sunday, the two brothers went off without telling me where they were going. I followed them at a distance and saw them lying on two grassy mounds that looked like graves. I did not wait to see what happened next.

That night, I had a strange dream. I was calling to Tate from a boat at sea. I did not know if she could hear me, but I kept calling. I did not care that she and Magnus had abandoned me. I needed her. She had to come. But instead of a reply, all I heard were distant hounds barking. The next day, I woke full of hope that the dream might have been a premonition, but it was not to be.

That day, the two brothers, I still did not know their names, seemed to be preparing for something. The talkative one told me to prepare a feast.

Then he told me I should pick which one of them I wanted.

"I do not want either of you," I replied sharply.

"Then we must share you."

"I cannot agree to that."

He put down the bowl of pottage he'd been eating.

I stared at him. "So I choose you," I said. I smiled at him. He was the obvious choice.

He smiled back, a radiant smile. "It is as I expected," he said. He motioned to his brother, who looked glum, to go outside with him. When they came back, the smiling one spoke again.

"My brother will sleep by the door from tonight and you will sleep with me at the back," he said, pointing at where they had slept every night since I'd been here.

"We need a priest to bless our marriage first," I said. That would delay things.

"No, we do not need a priest. We'll have a test marriage first, to see if you are fit to be my wife."

I shook my head. "No, I have changed my mind," I said. "I prefer your brother. He does not talk as much as you."

The Power of Synne

A whoop sounded from the door. The other brother had been listening. He marched into us, pushed his brother out of the way and stood in front of me smiling. His hand out reached for me. I made a kissing motion with my lips.

At that, the two of them started fighting.

I waited, watching. It started with a push, then one of them threw the other. Then a stool was picked up.

As the more talkative one appeared to be about to win, he had his brother in a headlock among the dirty rushes on the floor, I pressed a hunting knife to the quiet one's hand. He pushed the knife aside. I let it fall.

He was not going to kill his brother for me.

But he did get a burst of energy and threw his brother to the floor and his brother did not rise. He was too winded. He just lay on the floor, wheezing. Then he came towards me. The knife had landed near me. I picked it up. He laughed. I expect he imagined a woman would not be able to use it. He did not know my skills with a knife.

I pointed the knife towards him, as if offering it to him, my head bowed. When his hand reached for it, I did what I had to do. I stabbed at his side, slashing the knife up, not deep. It was a wound that was not likely to kill but he'd be in no fit state to come after me.

A noise filled the cottage. The other brother had recovered from his beating. He came toward me. I had no choice. Despair and fear of ending up a slave for both these men filled me with rage. I stepped back, as if afraid, waited until he was on me, then stabbed at his groin, and then his neck when his hands went down to defend himself. A fountain of his hot blood poured over us. My heart raced and my breath shuddered from me and a strange feeling of not being there came over me, as if someone else had done what I had just done. I remembered my father's halting words about going berserk, killing everyone in your path, how Hel, the goddess of death, enjoyed having bodies laid out for her and how he'd complied with her wishes. I'd wondered when I was young if that was why he'd left us, to serve Hel again.

Was I now serving her too?

The wounded brother watched all this, his hands holding his side. They had thought a woman would be easy.

"You have someone for the third grave," I said.

The brother shrugged. And then he spoke for the first and last time I heard his voice. "I warn him he talk too much."

I kept the hunting knife in my belt as I gathered food, took their best cloak and their other knife, and went out the back to fetch one of the horses hobbled there. I was still shaking a little from what I'd done. I am not a bad person, giving bodies to Hel. I just have to be free. Is that such a bad thing?

The Power of Synne

A shout from the house made me jump. When I went around to the front, two horses were tied up there. I sighed. I could not escape with two people riding after me. And I could not fight again so soon.

I pushed open the door, expecting to be jumped, tied up. What I saw made my mouth open.

In all my time as the daughter of a seer, I'd not believed in my powers, but in that single moment, my belief came to me.

Standing in that small room, with the injured brother on the floor still clutching himself, were the last people I'd ever expected to see again.

Tate and Yann.

I blinked, disbelieving my eyes. Was this a dream?

Tate rushed to me. She wrapped her arms around me. "I am so sorry we had to leave you," she whispered. A shuddering wave of relief rose and passed through me. I'd not been abandoned.

It was the strongest feeling ever.

"How did you find me?" I whispered, still hugging Tate.

"We found out who you'd been sold to and travelled at night to get here."

"I am so happy to see you."

"Did you call me? I heard your voice in my mind, Synne," she said.

I nodded. So, it was true. I had powers from my mother.

Yann gripped my arm then. "We did not mean to wait so long, but we had great difficulty finding a way to get three horses." He moved his hand to cover Tate's.

"I told you we would rescue her," he said. There was something about the way they looked at each other that made me sure they were a couple.

"We cannot stay here," he said. He had a sad look when he turned back to me.

"We stole these horses, and the owners are tracking us. They are no more than half a day behind."

"How many?"

"We saw five or six men on horseback yesterday at the other end of a valley."

"Did they see you?"

"They didn't need to. They have hounds with them."

"I heard hounds in my dream."

Tate smiled. She knew what it meant.

Yann pointed at the quiet brother holding his side and looking up at us.

"Shall I finish him?" he asked.

"No," I said. I went to the brother and bent down. "I've helped you escape from the prison your brother placed around you. Enjoy your freedom but make sure you tell no one what happened here." I paused, put my hand against his arm, and pushed him.

He winced.

"If you give witness against us, one of us will come back and slit your throat the way your brother's throat was slit. Do you want that?"

He shook his head.

We ate some hard bread, quickly, then prepared the horses. Soon after, we were cantering away. We headed north and west, with the goal of changing directions after we'd lost sight of the house. We'd then head south to the city of York. With good fortune, Gytha would be there and our struggles to reunite would be over.

Wishful thinking and delusions are what keep us all going.

***

They kept us going for two days. We should not have slept at night. They found us on a bright and sunny morning, the type reserved for happy days, but it was not a happy day for us.

They saw us the evening before, I expect, as we crossed a river at a stony ford and were visible briefly all the way along its course. They were seven men, the right number for a hunt like this, and they all had axes and daggers, and one had a sword. They all wore leather helmets too and looked as if they practised every week with weapons.

"Lay down your weapons or we'll kill you all," boomed a voice as they appeared all around us at first light, leaving no obvious escape path. We'd been sleeping in a hollow under a fallen tree with thick brambles behind us. Foolishly, we'd imagined the tree provided protection. It trapped us.

Yann groaned, stood. "I stole the lady away," he said bravely. "Blame me and punish me as you will but do nothing to these two sisters or the wrath of the true King of England will be upon your heads." He dropped his axe and bowed his head, waiting for the death blow.

"I'm promised to the son of the King of Leinster," I said, my voice shaking a little as I stepped forward. "If you let us all go, you will be rewarded." I would not let them hand out death to Yann without offering an inducement.

The oldest of the men, a tall, scrawny creature, did not bother to respond with words. Instead, he came forward, leered at me, then sideswiped me, knocking me to the ground, loosening my teeth.

"Put your right hand on that tree," he said to Yann.

"Don't," I said.

"If you don't, I will take the hand of one of these ladies instead."

"No need," said Yann.

He held his hand on the tree trunk and looked away.

Without hesitation, the man slammed his axe blade into Yann's outstretched wrist. Yann groaned, then screamed, then pulled his hand away. Blood pumped. His right hand, the one he used for fighting and riding, was gone.

"Light a fire, women, if you want to save your friend from the blood sickness."

He pointed at Yann. "Losing a hand is the penalty for stealing slaves, for the first time we catch someone. If you steal again, you will lose two more limbs. And it is hard to survive with both feet cut off. Most die at that point." He went close to Yann, whose face was purple from the pain and the effort of not whimpering and crying.

"I know this to be true, because I had a clever man like you last winter, who stole a woman from me, and he told me, after I took both his feet off, that he would have preferred to lose both his hands, as his life had become that of a worm." He laughed at Yann. "But you are luckier than him. I cut his cock off too." He turned to us. "The only reason I won't do that just yet is because you brought a second young woman for us to enjoy."

He came in front of me and licked his lips, showing his ugly purple tongue. "I'll enjoy you more than the other one. I had her kind many times, but not a tall skinny one like you in a way long time."

"I am to be wed to one of King Harold's sons," I said. "I advise you to be careful. If he finds out you defiled me, I would not wish his punishment on anyone."

The man laughed. "You are a might spirited one, that is for sure." He stuck his tongue out again. "But we have no allegiance to the dead King Harold. He never came to visit us, and we never went to visit him. So, who you are promised to is nothing to do with me."

Yann let out a long moan. Blood was still pumping from his wound.

"Now tie this man's wound tight so he doesn't die on us," said the man. "I will blame you if he does." He pointed at the belt Yann wore. "Use that," he said. "Your friend has no use any more for somewhere to hang an axe or a dagger."

I undid the belt that kept Yann's tunic tight and tied it just below his elbow. Blood still came from his wound, but the more I tightened the belt, to his heavy groans, the more the blood slowed.

He fainted too and my hands were slippery with blood by then. Tate was building a fire near us.

When Yann came around, he shuddered, groaned, and whispered to me, "Escape as soon as you can. Do not care about me. Slip away at night. Promise me." He looked at me with pleading eyes. But I would not promise such a thing.

The Power of Synne

He shook his head. I guessed why Yann had his hand taken now. They assumed if we were his friends, we'd stay and look after him. And we would not cause problems.

***

And so it came to be. Four days later, we entered a dun, a circle of mud and wicker huts in a clearing with mud wicker walls, the home of our captors, a home for slave traders.

I'd heard of such slave traders' villages before, where captives are forced to work before being sold. Such tales always spoke about the grisly punishments handed out to anyone who dared question the slave trader. Both myself and Tate said not one word against our captors on those first days. They didn't expect us to speak anyway. We were no more than animals to the free men there. A few asked Yann some questions, but he was still suffering from his injury, barely able to speak beyond a groan. I thought he might die, he asked twice to be abandoned on the side of the road, but I told him he'd make it, that I'd seen him in a dream, even though that had been a long time ago.

And every night since it had happened, I whispered a chant of strength into his ear. The words hold power to distract the darkest thoughts and make us see that all things pass, the good and the bad, for the kingly treasure owner as much as for the injured wanderer.

I hated the place then and the men who took pleasure in the suffering of others. When will the day come, I wondered, when people cannot be sold or bartered into slavery and all the wicked punishments be stopped, no matter what the provocation?

One thing I was grateful for though, was that we weren't branded or nocked as some of the slaves were, with nostrils cut and earlobes off so the owner could be known and the slave's status beyond doubt to all.

Not every slave owner does this, but I don't think it was a sense of right and wrong that stopped them doing it to us. It was more likely they wanted us as a whole as possible, so that any new owner could brand or nock us as they wished.

We talked little in the following days and were set to helping with preparations for the harvest. I was called on at night twice those days and made my heart a stone each time, closing my eyes and cursing his seed as the scrawny one pumped away into me until he released and let me go. Both Tate and I were lucky they did not share us more widely. It would diminish our value, Yann said.

He kept pressing us to run away at night, but both Tate and I agreed we would not leave without him. And he was still too weak to live off the land.

We slept in the slaves' hut, which was jammed with people all resting close to each other. The scrawny bastard had been busy this past year buying slaves from raiders and sending his own sons out to villages down the coast and taking hostages.

Yann was put to work tending to cows. He was not allowed to sleep near us, so the longest time in his company we had was on a Sunday, when we rested.

It was a Sunday that we found out that the scrawny bastard's wife, Maurein, was ailing. She was heavily pregnant and bawling so loud the whole village was on edge.

Another woman had heard I was a healer from talk in the village, so she called for me.

The sight in their hut was sickening. Maurein was in the middle of the floor with men all around her. The first thing I did was order them all out. Men make things worse at times like this, with their glib answers and stupid questions.

We saved her and the child. I do not take responsibility for that. I follow what my mother would have done, and hers before her.

***

The next day, early, Tate and I were taken by one of the slave trader's wives to the orchard at the end of the low valley. The orchard needed tending, branch fall piled for carting away for the winter, and the weeds growing on and around the trunks cut away. It was light work. Yann was not allowed to come with me but Tate was and she was happy. It was a fine mid-summer's day.

A day that gave me time to think.

I'd been dreaming too much that summer, pining for my mother and the life we'd once had. I still did not know why we'd been attacked and my mother murdered. That made me angry whenever I thought about it. Tate said what happened to our family was some random attack. I wondered was it something to do with my father. He'd been so closed-mouthed about his family. Could that explain what had happened? Most people I'd met since I'd been on the road talked about their lineage. That made me think he'd been hiding something.

I'd felt guilty for a long time about surviving the attack my mother had died in, and I knew that was part of what drove me on to seek my sisters. I felt for Tate too those days. She was far harder than she'd been before, shaped no doubt by what she'd been through, though she did not share much of that with me, but I guessed how hard it had been for her from the haunted look in her eyes sometimes.

She also made fun of my chants too, claiming they did not work because they did not bring a lightning bolt down on our enemies, but I'd seen our fate twisting in a good way, which I was sure the chant was making happen. How else could things be getting better? But my certainty was not enough for Tate. She wanted irrefutable proof. I didn't have it yet. A bead and a chant were not enough for Tate. I had to concede they were a thin argument.

Stupidly, I pinned for Magnus too, despite all he had done to me, and still I made excuses for him when someone asked me. Those moments were when I felt most stupid. I explained he'd gone away before our marriage to save me from becoming a widow.

Tate sensed my spinning thoughts. She always could. It was one of her powers. She lay down under one of the apple trees near me in a slight hollow so she would not be seen taking a rest. The apple trees around us here looked like witches, watchful, with wrinkled grey skin and knots like eyes.

"Did you dream about Gytha again?" Tate asked.

I kept collecting dead branches, moving slowly around her.

"How do you know I dream about her?"

She didn't reply.

A few moments later, after listening to the bees humming, I told her, "You are right, Tate. I did dream of Gytha. I saw her in a city with a mighty church by a river."

"That will be York," said Tate. "She's waiting for us."

"It did not look like York."

"No city looks the same in a dream."

It was my turn not to reply.

"And anyway, your dreams are not premonitions, are they?" she said.

"No."

"Just the few that come true." She came to her feet and started picking up branches again. "And how often does that happen? Once a year?"

She enjoyed taking me down a peg or two.

"It would be better if you had real powers to change things, Synne, wouldn't it? We wouldn't be stuck here."

I did my best to hide my disappointment and anguish at being stuck here. It might elicit derision, which I did not need to remind her about.

"You can run away any night, Synne. I've seen the guards. They're half asleep most nights. And a few guards should not be able to stop you."

I spoke quickly and sharply. "You know they'll punish Yann if we run away. I will not have his blood on my hands."

Tate scoffed. "You want Yann."

I laughed. "No, I do not, you foolish woman." I pointed a thin stick at her. "Yann will be able to make a journey in a month. Let's talk about it more then."

※※※

The Power of Synne

But it was not even a month when we received an opportunity to escape. The fighting men of the valley had been called to arms by a local lord, because a Norman army was approaching up the coast from the south. That meant the only men left were men like Yann, the injured, or old men and boys.

That gave us slaves hope.

Tate and I could have left Yann around harvest time, so few were the precautions taken, but the women of the valley, who were running everything at this time, were so lenient with all the slaves, sharing everything as if they were family, we decided to collect and hide apples and the honey cakes one of the women made. Going hungry on the road was the main reason escaped slaves ended up being recaptured. If each of us had a bundle with stolen food, we had a chance at least to get beyond the valley into the hills and the lakes between us and slopes down to York.

I'd wondered from the beginning if any other slaves might want to escape, too. I found out that some had hopes of finding their families, but few had the courage to head off as runaways.

A local monk had taken to coming to the farm and blessing all the slaves, making it clear to me that the church approved of what was going on here.

Soon after, we heard the slave trader and most of his men had been killed in a battle.

For me, that meant the time had come to leave this place. The end of harvest night passed with the usual revelries, dancing with masks and the young men rutting anything that walked on legs and drinking all the mead they could get into their bellies. It was the perfect time to go, as most of the compound would be nursing mead heads. I'd warned Yann the day before not to drink too much and Tate and I had watered down everything we drank to the point that all we drank was water, even if we did face the risk of becoming ill from it.

Tate had asked an old man, barely able to walk, he must have seen fifty summers, about what the people living beyond the valley were like, pretending she was interested in finding a man to buy her, in the hope of also finding out what the land beyond the line of hills like broken grey teeth to the east, was like.

He waxed about lakes and heather and fairy rings, where Roman gold was buried. He claimed the Pendragon family ruled all the land to the west, kins of Jarl Erlend, and that Tate would be lucky to have any of those men. He'd leered at her then and she'd walked off.

But what he'd said gave us hope that the Pendragons might help us if we found them and told them our tale. It gave Tate more hope than me. I was not inclined to put my fate in the hands of strangers. We did a last search for food

The Power of Synne

and, as the sun rose with a misty light, we slipped from the compound.

I'd been wound tight, as if in a deer trap, for the days leading up to this, so the moment we reached the woods I wanted to shout in relief. We headed to the south this time where a ridge with a high gap marked the way into the land of lakes beyond.

Yann had a leather cover over his wrist. It was battered strips of leather, not one single piece, but I admired the way he'd stitched it together with one hand and an elbow and never complained. He'd taken his injury as a penance for something he said he would not share with me and said he prayed to Christ every day to offer up his suffering to God.

He'd also become proficient in most tasks and refused all offers of help.

When we reached the gap in the high ridge and looked back, we saw no smoke rising from the compound. No one was up yet.

We did not steal horses this time, as the only ones left in the compound were broken-down hags, which would need as much food as we ate.

I also did not expect a chase party to come after us. Who would they send? Wars have a way of changing things when the strongest men are all gone from a village. It was probably why the slave traders' wives had started treating the slaves well, too. They knew they would not be able to control the slaves the way they had in the past. And beaten slaves sometimes slit the throats of evil masters.

The sight that greeted us beyond the gap lifted all our spirits. Lush ferns extended all down the gently sloping hill towards a long finger of a lake the colour of a summer sky. Beyond, a humpbacked ridge had trees all along its lower reaches and a bank of brambles at one edge.

We kept to the stony path, and when it branched, we changed direction and headed north.

This was the second time I was on the run this year. But I was more hopeful this time. The pack of food we each carried gave me that hope. We could skirt compounds and get far away before our food ran out.

The old man had told Tate stories about the fair ones who lived in the land of the lakes. They could enchant you and set you to sleep for years if they wished, or show you a druid's treasure, hidden from the Romans.

He'd also warned that we could be turned to stone if we talked with the fairies. He said the proof of that could be seen all over these valleys as the stones standing in fields marked where a traveller or farmer had been turned.

I tried not to believe such things but when we saw a circle of grey stones, I was reminded of what he'd said and a shiver ran through me.

The Power of Synne

We moved fast as we passed them. I could feel their presence like a shadow on me. My mother told us such places were ripe with power, which required careful handling if you did not want ill fortune.

When we stopped to rest in a glade by a brook, Yann congratulated us on sending the slave trader and his men to their deaths.

"I take no credit for killing," I said.

Tate shook her head. "You must take the credit. You cursed them," she said. "That marked them."

Yann nodded. "I'll remember never to get on the wrong side of you two."

"They've probably had a hundred people or more putting curses on them," I said.

Tate sighed. "But you have the power, Synne. When will you accept that?"

I sighed. "Perhaps sometimes I do, but why did Magnus leave me, and why did Yann lose his hand? I wasn't able to stop either of those things." There was bitterness to my tone, which I regretted, but every word I said was true.

"Perhaps good will yet come from those things," said Yann. He reminded me of Gytha, always looking for the good in people. I missed her.

"Yann is right. He might already have been sold and taken far away, if he was able-bodied," said Tate. "His injury may have been a blessing."

I did not want to argue with them, so I sat there, listening to the babble of the brook and a rustling in the trees around us as a breeze passed over.

Then something moved in the trees.

"Someone is watching us," I whispered. "Head downstream, pretend you're going to relieve yourself, Yann, and come around the trees, slowly."

Yann stood. "I have to piss," he said. He walked downstream.

After a long wait, a yelp came from the trees. Yann appeared with a grey-haired woman's arm in his grip.

"This one was watching us," he said.

The woman slapped at Yann's hand. "Is this the way you treat old people where you come from?" she asked. She kicked at Yann's ankles.

"It is when they spy on us," he said. He pushed her towards us.

"Let her go," I said as she came close.

Yann released her. I held my hand up in her direction. The healer's greeting. Many old women who lived alone were healers, often outcasts for saving one life but failing to save another. My mother told us all about such women, and I'd seen such women calling to our house and being fed by her.

This old woman's bright blue eyes glared at me. Her grey hair was matted like a bird's nest and her tunic was more patches than tunic.

"You ain't no healer," she said, leaning towards me, then flicking her hand through the air.

"I'm learning," I said. It was the way most healers I'd heard describe themselves.

"Why was his hand removed?" The woman nodded toward Yann. She had a disdainful look on her face, as if she could escape from us if she wanted.

"For fighting a slave trader."

She put her head to one side. "The one in hardwater valley?"

"I don't know what the valley is called."

"The one back the way you came."

I nodded.

She hooted like an owl. "I thought they all be dead by now," she said.

"The men are."

She leaned towards me, put her hand out, slowly, to stroke my cheek. "You were brought up to the healing path, yes?"

I nodded. Her fingers were ice-cold.

"Then you must come with me."

"Where to?"

"Not far, fretful one."

As she turned, a premonition came to me. I'd seen this woman before or someone like her. I'd listened to her riddles.

10

Gytha reached towards the roof and spread her arms wide. She knew what was coming. The woman behind pulled Gytha's tunic down. It wouldn't come off because Gytha had her arms wide.

"I'll slit the tunic from you," hissed the woman.

"I'll take it off myself," replied Gytha. She slipped her arms out of the tunic and let it drop around her. There'd been a lot of noise in the hall, but it quietened abruptly. She was naked, her breasts prominent. She stood proud with her feet apart. A wild cheer erupted as she turned slowly so that everyone could see her.

It was a routine she'd been taught in England. It never failed.

The young German king came to his feet. He raised his golden cup towards Gytha. She nodded in reply. The old woman near the king began talking fast to a servant, a man who was bending down to her. Gytha had completed one more full turn and the shouts were louder when that man came and stood in front of her, his hands on his hips.

"Show's over," he said.

Gytha finished her turn, grabbed her tunic from the outstretched hand of the woman behind her, and strode down the middle of the hall, naked, her tunic trailing. She was proud of her effect on men.

A woman at the door pointed at her tunic, stabbing her finger towards it. Gytha slipped her tunic back on to groans from men at a nearby table. Two of them made fist gestures at her. The woman pointed at Gytha's face. Two stony-faced guards grabbed her.

The woman spoke fast in some tongue Gytha had never heard. The guards both nodded and pulled Gytha out of the hall between them. Her abrupt departure from the hall was accompanied by groans of displeasure from men all around, as if they knew they would not be seeing Gytha again that night.

Gytha didn't resist, hoping and assuming this was a temporary banishment and that she'd be fending off men, if not the king himself, later that night or the next day.

As they moved from the glow at the wide-open door of the hall and made their way across the muddy open area towards darkness beyond, it crossed her mind that something else might be in store for her.

"Where are we going?" she shrieked. Perhaps these men could be turned from their task.

They didn't reply. They just kept moving. That worried Gytha. They turned a corner. For one bad moment, Gytha thought she was about to be raped. A slippery fear stirred inside her. But then, up ahead, in the deepening gloom, she saw two torches on spikes, lighting up the entrance to a jetty with long barges attached to it.

Were they taking her to a barge?

She'd seen lots of barges and rafts sailing downriver or being pulled upstream by ropes and horses. Did someone want her locked away on some barge? Then she heard the crying and not just from one person and she knew with a feeling of nausea where she was being taken.

To a slave barge.

A place where slaves were held and sometimes sold from. And the crying at this hour meant that some slaves had been punished recently or mothers and children separated.

It was a curse of slavery that natural human bonds could be ignored, families split apart, and minds twisted, just for the sake of a bag of silver coins.

A lamp on deck signalled that there were people awake on the barge. As they came close, two giant guards, men with shaved heads and blue tattoos, came into view. They were sitting at the front of the barge, near where a plank went down to the jetty. Beyond them stood a long cage made of thick wooden poles. Inside it, between the poles, despairing faces peered in her direction.

There were too many faces for such a small space.

A gnawing fear ate at her inside. She took a deep breath. She could break free, run, jump in the river, swim away. She was a good swimmer. But, as if sensing her plan, the men holding her tightened their grip.

A flood of regret passed through her. That must have been the king's mother who ordered her here. She'd seen the effect Gytha had on the king. Perhaps she did not permit the king to pick his own women. Whatever the reason was, Gytha's fate was sliding in a bad direction.

Female slaves sold downriver could end up under a string of old men until they got pregnant and were sold off, with each following master worse than the last.

The cage was opened and she was pushed inside, while begging hands reached out appealing for food and water. She knew what this meant. The slave master who owned this barge kept his slaves hungry and thirsty to weaken them and ensure their compliance with whatever he wished.

And so it came to be.

***

The next ten days were among the worst she'd ever experienced. She ended up gnawing at pieces of wood she was so hungry, while a sick shroud of fear hung over her, forcing her head down. Luckily, she was raped only once, probably because there were so many women for the slavers to pick from. The man who did it, the slave master she assumed, forced her to look at his face too.

All that time, in her mind, she cursed him over and over, willing the pox on him and for him to die in the worst torment. He seemed to think she was enjoying it, as he took her from the cage again that evening as they rounded a bend in the river and gave her a cup of water. On each side of the wide, swift river, there'd been endless forests with occasional small palisade-walled forts on the banks, but now, up ahead, a large fort stood on a bluff overlooking the river.

Streams of smoke rose from the rooftops and a jetty ran into the river. It had what looked like a Roman galley tied up to it, with long shields in a row along its side. The slave master spoke enough of the English tongue for her to understand him. He was a large man with deep scars and black hair shaved at the front.

"You'll be sold here, girl. This is the fortress of Baba Vida. If you act right, perhaps even the commander of the fort might take you. They say he'll head back to Constantinople soon. You could go there with him."

"Constantinople has a fort here?" She'd heard of the fabled city, where games and races were still held, as in ancient times.

The man nodded. "We are near the edge of their empire. We do good business with them. Many boys become eunuchs right here because of us, and many women learn how to do their work."

She knew what he meant. Women were taught here to be used by men for coin. Boys were changed by a hot knife.

"You'll bow and smile and show yourself as they tell me you did after we picked you up. Understood?"

She nodded.

"If you cause any problems, you can stay with me to be shared with our crew first and then anyone else with a coin to spare."

She stared at the fort. It felt as if she'd reached her worst point. She'd been contemplating throwing herself in the river for a few days and breathing in the water to end it all, and that thought came back again now. The torments she'd experienced since leaving England had been beyond what she'd imagined anyone would have to endure without dying soon after.

As she watched the trading post, they tied up at a second jetty, attaching their barge to a row of three others taking up just one place at the jetty. The border post was obviously busy. Guards in shiny conical iron helmets stood all along the jetty, and a double-headed eagle banner flapped in the breeze as they tied up.

Torches lit the gate into the fort, though it was still only mid-evening. A row of torches lit the path beyond, too. They made it almost seem as if night might be banished. Gytha had never seen so many torches. Then she glimpsed a marble column in the distance and a fountain spewing water. What a waste, she thought.

At that moment, the slave master appeared beside her. He pointed at Gytha.

"You and me are going to an imperial trading post. Do not create trouble, no matter what happens. Keep your mouth shut." He pointed at her face.

She gave him a nod and a half-smile in reply. That she was being taken with him gave her reassurance that she would not end up like most of the other slaves.

She whispered a prayer to the great mother then, Mary, to protect her and give her a chance of finding a master who was not pure evil or even to escape all this.

The streets were wide and paved with stone and had a rut for carts down the middle. On each side, a colonnade provided a covered area where tradespeople displayed their wares. Pottery was on show as well as wicker baskets, dark blankets, and lots of weapons. Many of the traders were closing their stalls, and as they reached a crossroads, a crowd had gathered at it.

A sudden urge to run, head down through the crowd, get away as fast as she could, came to her. As if he read her mind, the slave trader grabbed her arm and held it tight.

"Slaves who run here get their noses sliced, and any man who wants is allowed to rut them all the next day," he said. He half-dragged her through the crowd at the crossroads. They were mostly men and some serving women moving around with cups of ale and trays of bread. Gytha felt hungry at the sight of the bread.

"Can we eat," she hissed at her tormentor.

"I'm not wasting coin on your belly," he replied.

Then they were through the crowd and in a square of colonnaded two-storey buildings with a marble column in the centre.

On the far side, a building with a row of marble columns had oil lamps outside it. They gave a golden glow to the paved area in front of it. Red-cloaked guards with shiny helmets stood to attention by the oil lamps. As they approached, two of the guards left their post, put a hand near their short swords, and came towards them.

One of the guards barked words in a language Gytha had never heard. It sounded like singing to her. The slave trader responded, then put his fist to his chest. She had no idea what had happened, but one of the guards nodded and gave him a similar salute. Had the slave trader served with the empire? He was certainly old enough and grizzly-looking enough.

The guards stood aside. Gytha and the slaver went into the building. Three men in pristine yellow tunics were putting document rolls into leather cases at the far end of a large hall with gaily painted walls and a high ceiling. A brazier glowed near the men. Oil lamps hanging from pillars kept the darkness away.

A man wearing a red military cloak had his back to them as they came up the room. Gytha was being half-dragged to move faster.

The man must have heard them approaching as he turned. When he saw who was coming, he threw his arms wide and shouted a greeting. His gaze then moved to Gytha, sliding down her body, appraising her.

As they came close, her tormentor released her and stood away from her, bowing as if to present her.

Gytha looked around. Was there any other way out? No, both doors, the one at the front and a smaller one at the back, had guards by them. And the windows were too high up to be of any use.

The man in the cloak moved around her as if she was an animal that might leap at him at any moment. The slave trader was speaking fast now, describing her, she assumed. She heard the word England. The man in the cloak smiled at that. Then he stepped towards her and raised a hand towards her face. She knew what he wanted, to check her teeth.

She stood still. The man didn't bother with her mouth. He took a handful of breast and felt her, as if he was kneading bread. She didn't move, didn't smile. Waited.

From the door they'd come in through, a shout echoed. All eyes went to the doorway. A man in a short green tunic was trying to get past the guards. He shouted something and Gytha realised she knew him. He'd been at the German king's hall before she'd been bundled out. Had he come to inflict another indignity on her? She kept her face still, despite a sinking feeling adding to her woes.

The man appraising her shouted something. The guards at the door let the man through.

The trader grabbed Gytha's arm. "Look at me," he said. His face was red, his eyes wide, as if something had happened Gytha hadn't noticed.

"This man here beside me is Romanus Diogenes, the commander of this fortress. Soon he will be heading back to Constantinople. He will buy you and you will go with him. You will be his house slave and perform every woman's duty as he wishes." He paused, let Gytha's arm drop. "Smile and bow now for him."

Gytha let a curl of a smile reach her lips. If she was being told all this, there was a reason. So, instead of

The Power of Synne

turning to Romanus, she turned to the man who'd just arrived. He bowed low to her. When he rose, he spoke in words she understood.

"My king has ordered that you return with me to Augsburg. He wishes to free you from this trader." He nodded towards the slaver.

This all brought a low growl from the slaver's lips. A moment later, a dagger appeared in his hand. It wasn't a fancy one with jewels. It was dark and scratched and looked like the type that had taken many lives already.

A shout echoed.

Gytha wasn't sure where it came from, but Romanus Diogenes also had a dagger out.

"Put your weapon away," he shouted at the slaver. "There will be no brawling and no killing in this hall."

Before he had finished speaking, the slaver lunged at the newcomer, swinging wildly as if he knew he only had moments before he'd be disarmed. Gytha wasn't shocked. She'd seen other knife fights, and some had been about her too, as one man tried to get another to step aside from her.

A tingle of excitement pulsed through her. They were fighting over her. Muscles tensed all over her. She had no idea which of these men would prevail, but by ancient custom, it would be the strongest and he would have a say over her.

The trader's blade hissed like a bee as it flew through the air. It missed its mark. That gave an opportunity for the newcomer to pull a small dagger and slice it fast towards the trader's neck.

That missed too, but it gave warning that this fight would likely not end in anything but death.

Romanus was fixed to the spot, watching all this. He'd know that intervening at the wrong moment could see the sharp part of a blade across your own throat.

The trader lurched to the right, then back again as his assailant's knife sliced the air back, then forward. At the last swing, a knife drew blood from a bare arm. But the newcomer didn't flinch. He came in close and grabbed with his other hand at the slaver's arm, making him step back and stumble.

The slaver fell. He held the stone floor like a downed oak. The hall went quiet, except for a gust of wind that battered at the windows. A flush of warmth came to Gytha. This was the deadly moment. Bloodlust was up. You could have flesh sliced into for any reason now and fountains of blood soon after.

11

We reached the cave at midday. The sky was clear and bright blue, as if it had been washed. The mouth of the cave was bright and filled with light. Tate stood at the entrance as I went in.

"No, I'm not going in there," she said.

The old woman went marching towards a large rock near the back of the cave.

"What's to fear?" I asked. "She's just an old lady."

"You were always the stupid one," said Tate. Then she made a scoffing noise and folded her arms.

I stopped, sighed. Yann had already stopped. The old woman turned and smiled at us all. I wanted to follow her. There was a promise in her smile, and warmth. There was something about all this that reminded me of our home too, of my mother. A wall of yellow catkins grew on each side of the cave entrance. Was it them? They were like a cloak hiding the entrance unless you were right in front of it. The floor of the cave was a mulch of dead leaves, ancient grey acorns, and broken blackened hazelnuts.

The old woman came to me.

"Your real power will come when you're all together with your sisters, not just you alone," she whispered to me.

"How do you know I have sisters?"

A trace of a smile flickered over her face. "That is when you will do all the things you can only dream about now."

"What things?" I said flippantly. How could she know what I wanted?

Yann was snorting like an animal. It was clear he wanted no part in all this.

"Come back, Synne. We'll keep going. There's a bad smell here." There was a note of fear in Tate's tone. That wasn't like her. Was she right? I sniffed. I couldn't smell anything bad. The old woman had her hand out.

"They're jealous because I speak direct with you," she whispered. "Because you're the one your mother favoured." She pushed her face forward. "Your sister does not want you favoured again. Make your choice, Synne. The old path of jealousy, darkness, and despair or a new path with light and hope."

She bent her head towards the back of the cave and flickered her eyes there. She must have lit a fire there as a golden glow emanated from the back of the cave.

I had to see what was there.

"We won't be long," I said. I followed the old woman.

The Power of Synne

A slit in the rock at the back of the cave led through a short tunnel with a low roof to another, smaller cave with a hole in the roof and a beam of golden light illuminating a central area with lots of white bone pieces scattered about. What animals they were from, I could not tell.

The old woman hugged me.

"Only the chosen make it this far; women with no fear who step into light," she said.

I hugged her back.

"Do not listen to the sorry voices. Let them wail into the ear of Frige. She will spit their words out like ice-mites."

I blinked. Was it a trick of the light? The old woman looked younger, her skin smoother, hair darker in the half light. I remembered a story my mother had told me about a witch luring children away. They stayed with her for a night while years passed in their villages.

A bird cried. One of those high-pitched calls that blackcaps or wrens use to warn the woodland of the approach of humans.

"Be quick," said the woman. "Repeat these words. *I am the holder of the triple keys. I eat the nuts of destiny. I train for every dawn.*" Her words came fast, tripping over each other as her gaze swivelled. She thought we were going to be disturbed.

I repeated the words.

She leaned towards me. "What is it you wish for? Revenge?" She smiled brightly, as if she knew my heart.

My mouth was dry. "No, not for me," I said.

"For him?"

I couldn't stop myself. I nodded. She must be guessing this, I knew, but there was something in her eyes and in her voice that made me want to believe that she could read my heart. And how could she have known my mother favoured me?

A noise from under the hill, a rumbling, sounded.

"Can you feel the spirits of the land around you?" she said, urgency in her voice, her eyes wide.

"Yes."

"Will you drink to their health?"

I nodded.

She bent over, cupped her hand, moved some bones, picked up one shaped like the top of a human skull, went to the wall behind her, and held it against a spot where the wall glistened. A moment later, she was back beside me. A sliver of golden liquid lay in the skull cup. She held it out to me.

I stared into it. She took it back, sipped from it, held it forward again.

A shout echoed.

"Synne, come." Tate's voice, a warning in it.

The Power of Synne

"Do you have dreams that turn out to be true?" asked the woman.

I nodded.

"Have you saved people from death?"

I nodded.

"Have you paid the price of knowledge?"

I nodded.

She held the cup close to me. "Drink now and all you wish for will come true."

I drank, breathed in, waited, all my hopes running through me. My fears too. Someone was looking for me, I'd realised. I could feel it the way you feel someone looking at you with a tingle at the side of your head. But who was looking for me? Magnus or someone else? Someone we'd crossed?

The skull cup was still in my hands when they came into the inner cave. I turned as the flash of light from a torch chased the shadows away.

"What are you doing, maiden?" The words were filled with shock and anger.

"Synne, put on your tunic," shouted Tate. She was behind the man with the torch.

I looked down. I was naked. My skin was as white as the bones beneath my feet. My tunic lay beneath me. I looked around. The woman who'd led me here was gone.

Tate was beside me in a moment, pulling my tunic up to cover me with hurried hands. More men were coming fast into the cave, warriors with grins and swirl-patterned swords in their hands reflecting the glow of torches. Each man had his weapon ready, as if they were expecting a horde of warriors to be waiting for them.

Tate tightened my tunic at the neck and whispered in my ear.

"They fight for the Normans, looking for rebels."

They looked like men of Northumbria, where I grew up. We'd heard men from every corner of England had joined the Norman cause.

"There are no warriors here," I said loudly. "Only women. You will not need your weapons."

One of the men came towards me. He reached to his groin and grabbed it through his tunic. "Maybe there are other weapons we can use here," he said. He leered at me, stuck his tongue out, and made a licking gesture.

I stood my ground. If they were planning to rape us there would be no escape, but I might just be able to stop them before they crossed that line. Lust, once raised, is hard to quell, my mother had said. Slap it down, hard.

"We could be your younger sisters," I said. "There is no need for that talk."

"I have a need for what I saw," he said.

The Power of Synne

"Stand back," called a voice. "Or I'll have your ears off." It was the man who'd come into the cave first. His hair was cut in the distinctive Norman style, shaved at the back, though that was growing out. It looked as if it had been at least a moon since he'd had it cut.

He bowed to me. "Forgive my men. They probably never saw a lady as beautiful as you unclothed."

"What is the meaning of this intrusion?" I asked, my tone as haughty as the daughters of the King of Leinster. I'd learned a few things watching them. Their pride could make strong men stop whatever they were doing.

"We were told we'd find rebels in these parts." He spoke softly, looked towards my feet.

I looked down. The skull cup was there.

"You've been drinking from the heads of the ancestors," he said, a note of wonder in his voice.

He bent, picked up the cup. It glistened inside with moisture.

"It is a healing cup," I said. "There is no harm in it." I'd heard the Normans wanted to suppress a lot of the old traditions.

"You are a healer?"

I nodded. I often thought of denying my skills in the past, but I'd grown more confident now that I was back on English soil and all that I had been through.

A smile grew on his face, like a dawn. "You must come with me then," he said, as if happy to discover something useful about me.

"Why? I've done nothing wrong."

"I do not have to give you a reason. I act under the new king's seal." He left me, went to the back of the cave. "Have you checked that hole?" he shouted at his men.

"Too small for anything but a fox," a man replied.

He came back to where Tate and I were standing.

"Let's go," he said.

"How long will this take?" I asked.

"You'll find out." His voice rose. "And if you're clever, you will not ask too many questions, lady. Be like a good Norman woman."

I spoke then, quicker than I should have, but it too was so hard to resist. "Is this the way you treat all the women you meet?" I pointed at him. "No wonder there are rebels if you force us to your wishes with no explanation."

He laughed, raised his fist, shook it at me. "You need a lesson in Norman manners, lady. They've changed the rules in this land and it's a good thing. You will do as I say and be grateful. Remember, we don't sell Christians into slavery as if they were cattle like those we drove from this land. And we won't be branding or cutting the ears or noses of wayward slaves. If you're on the side of the old

The Power of Synne

ways, the slavers, do not expect an easy time when you meet our commander."

"Who is your commander?"

"The king's brother. Be warned. He does not suffer fools or foolishness."

I blinked. "You mean Odo, the bishop?" For all this man's talk of opposing slavery, Bishop Odo could have us slaughtered if he was told we'd encouraged rebellion. His last words to me had been a warning against sedition.

"What do you know of the king's brother?"

"We have met." The other men were staring at us, as was Tate.

"So, you will meet again. We shall see if he knows you." He had a sly look on his face, as if he didn't believe I'd ever met King William's brother.

It came to me then why I was being taken to meet him. "Is Odo ailing?"

"Speak nothing about that." He raised his fist. "Or I may have to close your mouth with bruises."

Tate stepped close and spoke. "Will you let me and my companion outside get on our way while you take my sister?"

The man laughed, as if she'd told a good joke.

"If you mean that Irish ruffian, no, you will both be coming with us. And if any of you refuse to do as we ask, one of you will suffer. We would not want the healer to be harmed, not even a hair on her head, but there is no law against making rebels suffer." He unsheathed a dagger from his belt and pointed the tip at Tate.

"Now stop asking stupid questions."

When we were all outside, he ordered a fire to be set at the entrance to the second cave.

It took them a while to gather enough firewood for the size of the blaze he wanted. I did not ask why he was doing this. I knew why. He wanted to see if anyone emerged coughing from anywhere on the hill. No one did.

***

It took two days to reach their camp. It was on the other side of a large lake, near a crossroads, though the roads were more like paths across the windswept heath with grey hills all around it. The camp had no wall but had sentries at intervals all along each side. The camp was not as big as the Norman ones I'd seen in the south, but there were still many rows of leather tents and large groups of men practising at their weapons.

We were taken straight to the largest tent, which had pennants on it, both a green Norman pennant with a cross, and a red-and-yellow striped Northumbrian pennant.

I expected someone to be inside the tent, but it was empty when the three of us were pushed into it.

The guards ordered us to wait on a bench inside the entrance. This tent was not as well equipped and had no long table with stools the way Odo's tent had been set up when I'd met him the year before. It had one single large chair at the far end and a few benches in front of it.

We waited all that afternoon before anyone came to greet us. Finally, a young monk hurried into the tent. It was raining now, a light rain, but he was not very wet so had not come far.

"You are Synne, the healer," said the monk, pointing at me.

I nodded. We'd given our names when we'd arrived. Yann sighed. Again, no one seemed interested in him, even though he was a son of the King of Leinster.

"Come," said the monk, motioning me to follow him.

"Get him to release us," said Tate sharply, as if I had a way to get them to do anything. I was hoping nothing would happen to my sister or Yann for being with me.

The monk led me across the open area in the centre of the camp to another larger tent. It reminded me of the tent for injured men I'd worked in down south.

Men lay on straw mattresses down both sides of this tent. Women with their hair bound up moved between the men, giving out water or applying ointments and changing bandages. At the far end, a large mattress with patterned wool blankets over it had a figure lying on it. That was where we headed.

Bishop Odo was lying lifeless on the mattress. The monk bent down to him and whispered. Odo's eyes opened. He gave me a thin smile.

"I wondered if I'd ever see you again," he said. His voice was little more than a croak.

I bowed. "Greetings, Bishop. I shall pray for your swift recovery."

He smiled briefly. I took my change. "I am hoping, Bishop, you might allow my sister and her companion to be released," I said. My heart was beating fast. I could feel it in my chest. This man could order our death or tortures, and there'd be no one to appeal to.

But if there was half a chance for Tate and Yann to be freed, I had to try.

I bowed. "I will do what you wish, if you free them." I gave him the benefit of my most willing tone.

He laughed for a moment, then coughed.

"Always looking to trade, Synne. You've not changed."

"What ails you, my lord?" It was time to seek a different path.

"I have the flux. It robs me of all will." He pressed his lips together.

"When did it come on you?"

"A week ago."

I stepped towards him. The monk put his hand up to stop my approach, but Odo waved him away. "This woman is the only Saxon healer I know who can heal well," he said. "Go, monk. We have prayed enough today."

The monk eyed me enviously, then backed away to stand by the entrance, out of Odo's sight.

I put my hand to Odo's brow. He was warm. The balance inside him had been disturbed.

"Do I have your permission to make a potion and fetch whatever herbs I need?" I asked.

I might be able to get him to release us all if I healed him, even though it would be a gamble. Potions could cure, but they didn't cure everyone.

Odo nodded. "Yes," he said.

"Can I take your monk with me?"

He nodded. I wasn't likely to be allowed in and out of the camp on my own, but if the monk was with me, I could probably go anywhere.

I went to the entrance, explained what I wanted to do to the monk.

"I have to gather fresh herbs in the woods," I said. "You'll come with me."

"Prayer will be a quicker way to heal him," he said.

"We will pray as we go."

"There will be questions asked about what we are up to," he said.

"I'm sure they'll all imagine what we're doing together." I smiled. "But please have no thoughts of rutting; my herb knife can cut your parts just as easily as any other twig."

He opened his mouth, then clamped it shut. I couldn't work out if he was angry or disappointed.

It took until nearly nightfall to gather the herbs I needed. On our way back, we passed the tent where Tate and Yann were, and I was both pleased and envious to hear that they'd been fed already, admittedly with only bowls of pottage.

"We need to eat too," I said to the monk as we headed for Odo.

"Start making your potion. I'll get food," he said.

"I need boiled water."

"Follow me."

The kitchen tent was a similar size to the tent for the injured. It had two hearths, one at either end. I found a small black pot and rinsed it with wine. A cook nearby laughed when I did that, but the monk ordered anyone away who asked what I was doing, so dirty looks and laughter were all I got while I worked.

It took until the camp was dark and quiet for the triple-boiled and triple-filtered potion to be ready. It takes time for the goodness to come out of some plants. The real goodness.

The monk escorted me back to Odo. I touched Odo's forehead. It was hot now. He needed help. I pulled the sheepskin blanket off him. The monk shook his head, tried to put the blanket back.

I slapped at his hand.

"You'll kill him if you make him too hot." I stabbed my finger towards his face. The monk reeled back, wide-eyed.

"Hold his head up. I need him to drink this." I'd put the potion in a cracked red bowl I'd found and covered it with muslin. I pulled the muslin half off. The monk smiled.

"It smells sweet. Is that how the devil smells when he entices us to sin?" he asked.

"This is not the devil's work. Where did you get that notion?"

"The men say you were found at the devil's cave." He smiled. "You were naked, they say." He blinked, twice. "There's a lot of talk of it. One man said you were coupling with a horned beast when they found you."

I laughed. "Say a prayer for him, monk. It'll help you keep your mind off his stories. Now come on. Raise the bishop's head or I will set the horned beast on you."

He looked at me with his wide, scared eyes, then raised Odo's head. I put the bowl to Odo's cracked lips. I managed to get him to drink half the potion, between some spluttering and coughing. It was enough. I put the rest aside, covered it, and slept under a sheepskin after ordering the monk to watch over Odo until first light, and then to swap places with me.

It was long before first light when the monk shook me awake. I'd been in a strange dream back in Dublin, hiding in a hall because someone was searching for me, someone calling me spawn of the devil.

"He's fading. His breathing has stopped," hissed the monk. "You've poisoned him; get up, get up."

I went to Odo. The fire of his sickness was raging inside him. While I was asleep, someone had put a heavy wolf skin on him. I dragged it away. A wild wind, like a wolf pack, was battering at the tent wall nearby as if the spirits of his ancestors were trying to get in.

"Who did this?" I said, holding up the sheepskin and looking around.

Almost everyone was sleeping. One woman, tending a man nearby, glanced at me, then looked away. The monk stared straight ahead, then put his hands together in prayer and started whimpering, eyeing me occasionally as if I had grown horns.

"They will punish you," he hissed in my direction, as if he looked forward to watching me being tortured.

I went to the edge of the tent and pulled a section up from where it was pegged down. The wind rushed in like a wolf. After a few moments, Odo's chest went up in the air and then it dropped and he gasped. His face was white as bone now. I went to him, put my ear to his chest, and listened.

I couldn't hear anything.

12

"Stop, or I'll have you both impaled, right slowly, and the stakes with you impaled on them put outside the river gate as a warning to others to do as they are told in this fort," shouted Romanus.

The trader and the man in the green tunic both paused at the same moment. They both groaned, dropped their weapons.

"Who gets the girl?" said the trader.

"The Holy Roman Emperor, the King of the Germans, is someone whose wishes we respect, always," said Romanus with a slight bow. "But the owner of this slave must be paid a good price for his trouble, double what such a young woman usually fetches in this fort." He smiled broadly.

"Triple," shouted the trader.

"We will pay what Romanus suggested," said the man who was about to get what he'd come for.

And so, Gytha's journey back to Augsburg began. They went by horse with an escort of two outriders. They rode fast most of the way, except when it rained, which was often during that late summer, when the rain usually came down like a waterfall. The dark rolling forests had been filled with bandits from the east for the past few years, they told Gytha, which was why they moved fast even though the road was little more than a mud path in places.

They slept at night in the long halls set aside for traders and changed some of their horses when they could at hamlets that provided that service.

It was mid-afternoon when they arrived back in Augsburg. Gytha had been wondering what the king's mother would say when she saw her. She hoped the woman had time to get used to the idea of Gytha coming back.

As their horses were being taken from them, Gytha asked the king's man if many of his family lived with him. The man laughed, leaned close to her.

"If you mean his mother, she has been sent to Rome to take a message to the pope. She cannot send you away again."

It felt as if a rock had been lifted from her chest. She still had the prospect of the king forcing himself on her, but the prospect of immediate banishment afterwards had now receded.

"I must clean myself up before I see the king," she said.

"Come with me," he replied.

He led the way to a long house near the main feast hall. Two women there helped her bath, gave her a fine green tunic, and helped her braid her hair. It seemed as if they'd done this before, many times, but they answered no questions and simply provided everything she asked for. She could barely remember what the king looked like too, except for his wide smile as he'd stared at her.

She'd been the centre of attention before, so it didn't bother her. What did bother her was the idea that she'd been sold, again. Would she ever be free? Would she ever see her sisters again?

***

It was the following morning, early, when she was summoned to see the king. Two young slave girls in bright green tunics arrived at the straw mattress where she was sleeping and nudged her awake. They pushed her to get dressed quick and said nothing about where they were taking her, but she knew. Early morning summonses as a female slave often meant one thing.

So why hadn't he satisfied himself with either of these young slaves, both younger than her? That was a question that stayed with her as she was taken to a smaller, but

The Power of Synne

elaborately decorated hall with round shields all along the front wall.

Inside, a row of candles lit the square room. Old rushes covered the floor and a collection of spears and axes leant against the walls on both sides. Outside, it was rapidly getting bright, but the front door was closed behind her, so it was difficult to see to the other end of the room. She waited to be summoned, while inside she alternated between raging that once again a man would do what he wanted with fear of what that would soon mean.

"Come, slave," shouted a voice.

She stepped forward slowly and as she went, the back of the room came into view. A large low bed covered with wolf skins stood by the back wall. Someone was in it. A dark head of hair poked up. As she approached, she noticed wineskins and beakers strewn about and finally, as she neared the bed, she saw another head of hair lying on the chest of the king. That head moved as she came near and a handsome face smiled at her, teeth flashing.

It was the man who'd brought her back, and he had a bare arm around the king.

"Undress," he said in a tone as smooth as a flowing stream, while he leaned up from the king. "His Majesty wants to see what he has purchased." He sat up now. "I know you have no weapons, sweet Gytha, except your body, that is, and you must know slaves are punished for any transgressions in this kingdom, but let me warn you again properly. Any disrespect, disagreement, or failure to act quickly on the king's wishes will be dealt with by a punishment starting at branding on the forehead and followed by the losing of an ear or the tip of that sweet nose, at which point you will no longer be of interest to the king and will be sent to service his men. Understood?"

She nodded.

She was trembling but tried hard not to let him see it. She knew his threats were real. She'd seen mutilated slaves in markets, men and women, and how beaten they appeared, their eyes hollow. Was that her future?

She slipped her tunic off while trying to steady herself. She had nothing on underneath. It was how she'd been prepared. She stood still, waiting for the next command. The king opened his eyes wide and smiled while staring at her, then motioned her forward with his head.

She took one step nearer and saw a golden cup of wine near his hand. She pointed at it. The king nodded. She drank from it. He touched her thigh, then wrapped an arm around her and pulled her to him. She managed to down the rest of the wine; it was sweet and good, before they enveloped her between their bodies.

13

I slapped Odo's face to get him to wake up, to not slip away to join his ancestors, but he didn't wake. I whispered in his ear, first a prayer charm I'd learned at Mother's knee. That didn't rouse him, either.

But he was cold now, his forehead icy. The heat had left him, so I hugged him, leaning tight into him, to gift him my warmth. The monk was still nearby and mumbling, probably hoping his prayers would make the difference, but at least he left me to do what I could do, and for that I was grateful.

I thought Odo might die soon and wondered how I would be punished. Powerful men like to blame others for their misfortune, especially any woman who was nearby when that misfortune occurred.

That thought kept me hugging him on and on until eventually I tried to get him to drink some more of the potion I'd made. His jaw opened when I lifted his head; a bad sign. I waited for a moment before I poured the potion in, wondering if this was when I would discover that he was dead. Sleeping people gag when something is poured into their mouth.

So, I dripped the potion into his mouth and thought he was dead, and my heart fluttered with trepidation for what was to come.

Then he coughed and the monk strode towards me and raised a fist high.

"The bishop is alive," he hissed. He waved his fist at me. "Do not kill him now."

Bishop Odo's fever had passed. He would live. I hoped I'd be blamed for that, too. Relieved, I pulled the wolf skin over him and kept watch as long as I could until I fell asleep, dreaming about my sisters around me, smiling, holding hands and the world spinning around us. I woke with a start with a hand on my shoulder. It was the monk.

"Rest with your friends," he said. "My prayers have been answered, thank Christ."

I stood and straightened my bones. Monks always claim any improvement in someone is because of their prayers. I knew not to argue with them.

"It is good to see you here, Synne," came a weak voice. I looked down at the bishop. His eyes were open.

"Thank you, my lord bishop. Stay warm until you get your strength back."

He stared up at me.

The Power of Synne

"Your arrival is an answer to our prayers," he said.

I thought he meant me helping with his illness. I found out later he meant something else.

Yann and Tate took great heart from my story about me helping heal the bishop. They liked his final comment too.

"You must ask him for a favour," said Tate, directing me as she used to when we were young.

I didn't bother arguing with her. I was too tired.

Yann was quiet. He said nothing about Odo or if I should ask him for a favour. He knew who Bishop Odo was and the power he had and that the bishop would decide his fate and our fate. That is not a position anyone would enjoy. But especially men who are brought up to believe power is theirs by birthright.

It was night before they brought bowls of stew and a wineskin for us. After we'd eaten, I was again summoned to attend the bishop. The monk came for me. He motioned me to come and barely said a word as I went with him.

I imagined he was jealous of the impact I'd had on the bishop's health. Perhaps the bishop had indicated he would reward me. My hopes were so high as I was brought into the tent where Bishop Odo lay still on the mattress at the far end I had to suppress a smile.

When I came near the bishop, the monk ordered me to kneel before him and recite the Lord's Prayer aloud.

I did this, loudly.

When I was finished, Bishop Odo was half sitting up, looking at me.

"You're lucky we do not have your head on a spike already," he said, a blade-sharp edge to his tone.

"B… but, why, my lord bishop?" I was truly shocked.

"You could have killed me last night with that deadly potion you made me drink. It was lucky my colleague was here to force water into me."

I shook my head slowly and felt my mouth open wide. That was not how I remembered the night before. I turned to the monk. He had a satisfied smirk on his face.

"There was no watering down, my lord bishop. I was with you until your fever broke."

Odo glanced at the monk, who was shaking his head. "There is a different reason I'm not going to watch your head come off," he said. "Do you want to know what it is?"

I was all jumbled up inside. The sickly pull of disappointment had followed his words, but there was anger too, and a sprinkle of terror at what was to come.

I nodded. What had he planned for me?

Odo spoke slowly now. "You have spent time this year with one of the sons of King Harold, yes?"

I nodded. He was well-informed. But where was this going?

He smiled. "So, you will come with me, Synne the healer, as we march to York."

***

The next day, we marched with them along a narrow path by the side of a lake, heading for a distant pass in the surrounding hills, which we passed through before nightfall. We made camp soon afterwards, and Yann, Tate, and I were all given tasks appropriate to slaves: brushing down horses and wiping away shit that clung to them.

We were told to sleep near the horses too, under a leather canopy protecting their feed. There were guards posted by the horses, which was probably why we were told to sleep there. They wouldn't need extra guards to watch over us.

The weather was better then, with long sunny periods and showers that passed over us quickly. The smell of the crowds of unwashed men and horses around us almost made me sick though, after the fresh air we'd experienced recently, but I'd smelled worse, and what choice did we have? The food was mostly tasteless pottage far too watery for my liking.

We crossed a road heading east and Yann wondered why we didn't take it if we were going to York.

The following night, our whole camp was woken by the screams of injured guards and our horses neighing wildly at the commotion and the smell of blood. They knew what that meant: battle and death.

But there was no battle. It was a night raid to harass us. Who had done it, no one speculated. It seemed as if everyone marching with us was used to such night raids and barely paid any attention to what happened the next morning. The injured men were put in a wagon and the following night the number of guards on the horses was doubled.

It was after the second night raid, a bold attack on our flank where our camp was near a wood, that I first heard a name given to whoever was harassing us.

They were traitors, rebels against the rightful King of England, King William.

I wanted to say something when I heard that, to deny that anyone attacking a column supporting William was a traitor, but Yann put a finger to his lips just as my mouth opened. I bit my lip.

The man who went on and on about traitors in league with the devil kept talking that way for half that day and into the following night. But then he stopped, and laughter could be heard from around the campfires as people revelled in the fact that they'd encountered so little resistance that day, as it had been rumoured there would be fierce resistance to any Normans and their local supporters this far north every day, but that was not to be.

Some of the men spoke about these being their last days.

I did not know what to say to that. It felt wrong to reassure them when their prospects of staying alive were low if we did come to battle with the rebel forces.

"If I don't make it, send word to my father that I died a warrior's death," Yann said to me.

"You will not die," I said as convincingly as I could.

Yann shrugged.

"You do not know what will happen," said Tate. She laughed, put a hand on Yann's arm. They exchanged glances. There was something about that which made me realise they had a secret. And then it came to me. They were rutting when I wasn't looking or when I was asleep. I had whispered a chant that none of us would fall out a few days before after seeing them arguing, so this meant one of my recent chants had worked. I was still waiting for others to work, like getting us our freedom.

"Too right," I said. I leaned closer to her. "Do you have a baby coming? Is that why you're angry?"

"I'm not stupid," she said. "I wouldn't get far as a pregnant slave. And we have neither weapons nor kin nor gold to help us become free again." Her words had turned angry. She pointed at me. "I was hoping one of your chants, those prayers to the old gods, was going to work and get us out of here."

As the laughter from the fire nearest us, which we weren't allowed to sit by, rolled over me, a wave of determination rose inside me.

"I prayed for good things, things that have happened, Tate. I prayed to find you. I prayed to get away from Ireland. I prayed for Yann to survive. I am sure more of what I've prayed for will happen, too."

Yann spoke then. "Thank you for your prayers. I needed them."

Tate went quiet for a few moments. Then she leaned towards Yann. "What will happen if you go back to Dublin like this?"

Yann stared at her, unblinkingly, as if he was a wooden statue.

Then he shook his fist in the air. "I will demand respect. My father will die some day and I will claim my inheritance. Nothing will stop me. I am sure word has gone to him already that I've been captured. I'm sure he'll pay whatever is needed to free me and you too."

Tate stared at him as if she didn't believe him.

We were woken in the middle of that night by screams. It wasn't the first time that had happened, but I always hated it. My dreams were bad enough without adding screams to them. We found out a watchman had taken an arrow to the stomach. From his screams, the arrowhead had hit something tender.

I was taken to him. He was in the same tent Odo had been in, but Odo was nowhere to be seen. There were two other men looking after a few other wounded men in the tent. They all looked surprised when I arrived. One man held his hand out to me as if he knew me. From his half-dead eyes, I guessed he was in a bad way and craved some care.

I stumbled, the sleepiness of the night still not out of me, and I was looking around to see if Odo was still here, in some corner. I was both relieved and concerned that he wasn't. Relieved that I would not be subject to his attentions but concerned as to where he had gone.

The wounded man was groaning softly and thrashing about on some straw. The end of the arrow was still in him. Someone had broken the shaft trying to pull it out. Perhaps the arrow had also been deliberately weakened in the middle to give a better chance that it would break inside a body, and not come out cleanly.

It was a trick that archers like to play.

As I came near to the man, his eyes widened as if he was looking at a ghost.

"You can save me. Come on, come save me, lady of the night, lady of the woods, healer, come save me." He kept whispering those words, jumbled in various ways, as

I leaned over him, checked his wound and turning him slowly further forward – he'd been on his side – so I could see the point of the arrow coming out of his back.

A ring of men were staring down at me. I waved them away. "Be gone," I shouted. Prayers and chants don't work with so many faces around. I noticed Odo was among the faces. He didn't step back as the others did. Soon it was just him watching me.

I put out my hand in his direction. "Give me your dagger," I said.

He looked me in the eye but handed his jewelled dagger over.

I straightened, went to one of the rush lamps lighting the tent with their yellow glow, and put the tip of the blade into the spluttering oily flame. I waited until the heat reached my fingers holding the other end, then took the blade quickly back to the injured man. I'd seen a cloth beside him. I picked it up and put it in his mouth.

"Bite," I said.

The man bit the cloth.

I turned him so the end of the arrow was visible poking out of his back.

"Hold him," I shouted.

Odo and another two men put their hands on him. I pressed the knife point fast into the man's skin. Blood erupted, as if it had been held back and the man writhed under us. I dug the knife in again and with warm blood pumping all around my fingers, I grabbed the tip of the arrow and pulled it out, fast.

"Keep him still," I said. I went to the flame and heated the knife again. I returned and pressed it quickly and hard against the wound. He screamed. The blood flow eased and then stopped as the skin and his flesh melted together in the heat. The stink of blood and burnt flesh lay heavy in the air as he screamed for me not to stop.

"I see why Harold's men wanted you at Hastings," said Odo. "Come and pray with me."

"I'm not finished with this man, my lord," I said. "Let me prepare a poultice for the wound." I kept my head up, but heard an intake of breath, as if everyone nearby had been shocked by my words, by my not agreeing at once to what Bishop Odo wanted.

Odo pointed at me. "I'll not repeat myself. This man will live or die because of prayer, not because of some old magic. Come." He turned and departed, his long tunic swirling after him.

I looked down at the man still biting on the cloth, his breath heaving. I bent down to him. "You will live," I said. "Hold on to that."

The man nodded, his eyes wide.

I went after Odo. He was walking with a limp, holding men's shoulders and tent poles as he went. Everything outside was wet from another shower and there was a chill in the air. Dawn was not far off. A glow in the east could already be seen. Odo headed for a large nearby tent with wind spluttering torches outside it lighting our way. A small gold cross sparkled on the roof.

I followed Odo inside. A wooden altar of a thin-legged table with a yellow embroidered cloth covering had been placed at the far end. There was an open area in front of it where men could stand and pray. A gold box lay on the altar. Odo stood in front of it with his head down. He waved at me to join him.

As I approached him, he put a hand out to me. I thought he wanted me to hold him up so I held his hand. His palm was sweaty. He held my hand so tight my bones scrunched together painfully.

I should have been frightened. He could do anything to me, but I'd gone beyond fear that summer, living in the constant expectation of death or worse. I also felt a strange new confidence. He would not injure me. My mother's words about healers being spared what other suffer came back to me.

"Come, join me, let's kneel together. Saint Cuthbert's relics are here. Let's pray that his piety and obedience shall be an inspiration to all who mark his passage once again through these lands."

The Power of Synne

We knelt together. Was there really some part of Saint Cuthbert in that gold box? I didn't speak it, but he must have sensed my doubt.

He grunted angrily, then spoke. "Yes, it is true. We are taking the saint's relics all around the north of this troubled isle and thence to their home." He gripped my arm. I almost called out.

"I hoped you would be touched by the virtue of obedience here with me." He bowed his head.

I stared at the golden box. It had lines of multicoloured jewels embedded in its side, but was not big enough to hold many of the bones of any saint. But unwilling to express any doubt, I bowed my head and whispered prayers to the Queen of Heaven.

What Odo had told me with all his talk, though, was where we were headed: Dunholm, the resting place of Saint Cuthbert's relics. If Odo had managed to get the bishop there to agree for him to tour the north with some of Cuthbert's relics, he'd be expected to return them after his tour was over.

Everyone knew about the white church at Dunholm and how it attracted pilgrims from all over these islands and even further away. The life of the town probably depended on the relic's speedy return.

"You will now join my personal retinue of servants," said Odo. He released me. But only for a moment, as I felt his hand again, but this time on my back and moving down.

I winced.

So this was what he wanted.

14

The worst summer of Gytha's life was thankfully ending. The king was insatiable all through it, but now, at last, another slave had found his attention. This new woman was from a tribe in the east. Her eyes were different, and her skin yellow and her attitude defiant. Like Gytha's had been.

Gytha knew this woman could entertain the king. She also knew this would likely mean she'd be allowed out more, to the market and other places. And so, it happened. They sent only one guard with her those days, often an older man recovering from injuries. She'd been accompanied by two men on her first trips to the market early in the summer, but she'd never strayed, so it seemed they'd come to trust her.

That was their mistake.

Preparations were now underway for the All Hallows festival, which meant there were more traders than usual in the town. The market was bursting at the edges with everyone from Norse traders selling slaves or amber to dark, smiling men from Araby with sacks of aromatic spices she'd never even seen before.

Her guard was a pace behind her that day, his hand on the pommel of his old sword, when a tall man appeared in the distance, making his way through the crowds. Gytha's heart missed a beat. Was that Erik the boatbuilder?

It certainly looked like him from behind. She picked up her pace, afraid he might disappear. And for a moment he was gone as two king's guards came in from a side passage. She hurried to catch up as a flood of relief and expectation came over her and then she saw the man had stopped at a wine stall and knew it was Erik.

She glanced around. Her guard was behind her, his eyes on her, and she could not run from him.

She passed Erik and nudged hard into him. She stopped at the next stall and looked back as she looked at the leather bags hanging from the stall. Erik was staring at her, a big smile on his face. She gave him a short half-smile, shook her head, just a little, her gaze darting to the guard.

Erik turned away. The guard had his hand up, as if he was going to intervene if Erik tried to speak to her. He'd sensed something.

She walked on.

There would be little she could do to stop Erik and the guard fighting if she spoke with Erik. But men smiled and

The Power of Synne

gestured at her regularly in the market, and always she did the same, just walked on. Men stopped following her when they saw she had a guard ready to confront any man trying his luck.

She didn't look back, but she listened. There was no commotion behind her, which meant, thankfully, that Erik was being careful. An ale merchant stood in the path in front of her. He had a red beaker in his hand. He held it up to her.

"The best ale in the Holy Roman Empire," he said. He smiled. "Fit for a true lady."

She took the beaker and swallowed some of the ale, then coughed and threw the beaker on the ground.

"Are you trying to poison me? You'd kill the king's pigs with this in one night!" she shouted, then she bent over, coughed some more, and spun around. Her guard was just behind her with a worried look on his face. Behind him was Erik. She pointed at her guard.

"What use is having a king's guard, if anyone can poison me," she shouted. The guard came forward. His gaze shifted to the ale seller who started babbling, offering ale to the guard to show him he had not poisoned her.

"Rescue me," she mouthed at Erik. She checked that her guard was still distracted, then shouted, "Please."

She looked at the ale seller. "Perhaps I am mistaken. Whatever happened has passed." Erik had to have heard her.

But when she glanced around for him, he was gone. Had he figured out what she meant? She didn't dare look around again in case the guard mentioned she was looking for some man, but she was sorely tempted to do it all the way back to the hall. A sweet tingle of excitement had made her lose her appetite, too. She barely ate that evening.

And that night she slept alone and early. Her place in the king's bed had been taken, so she slept with his other wives and slaves, all of whom he took to his bed whenever it suited him.

They were friendly enough but they spied on each other like forest hawks, always looking for some morsel. And she had a problem. The king did not entertain travellers like Erik in his hall. He usually fed his own guards, important travellers, monks, and the families of his men and his local wives. Traders like Erik used the taverns near the marketplace to eat, drink, rut, and sleep. There would be no reason for her to go to a tavern at night. Finding him again would not be easy. He would have to find her.

She could walk around the royal hall. She had done it many nights after the king had dismissed her from his bed. She claimed her bowels needed walking to loosen, but she really needed time alone to stop the despair that overtook her occasionally. The king had threatened to share her with his men, which frightened Gytha deeply, as she'd heard about the damage a group of men can do to a woman.

If there was one good thing that had come from that summer, it was that no one said anything when she walked around the king's hall, past the guards at the front, half sleeping, to the stables at the side and then around to the stinking pigsty at the back and around the smithy on the far side and to the front again, where a guard, who appeared to be sleeping, called out her name, "Gytha, come, sing for us."

She kept walking around the hall. Had Erik worked out what she'd meant? Would he be here? The anticipation was almost unbearable. When she reached the pigsty a third time, a hooded shadow appeared in her path, making her jump. She knew who it was though and with her heart beating fast, she took his moon-pale hand when he held it out.

"Quick, I've a boat waiting. Are you ready to leave, sweet Gytha?" he whispered.

She hugged him so tight he had to push her away. "They will torture and kill us if they find us," she said.

"They won't find us. Come on." He pulled her after him. They went around the back of the pigsty and jumped across a stream that was more a midden. The smell was so strong there you could almost grasp it. They went past a fur traders' hall and were soon at the river.

"Give me your cloak," said Erik.

She gave it to him.

He threw it down near the edge of the water. Then he undid a skiff, the low-sided type for making short river crossings and urged her to get in.

"They will know where we've gone," she hissed at him.

"We'll leave this death trap as soon as we are out of sight," said Erik. Then he reached for her, put his hands around her, and pulled her to him.

"I had many dreams about you," he said.

They kissed. It was the first kiss she'd enjoyed in a long time. Would he be the one she'd been looking for? He was certainly strong enough and brave enough. Risking his life for her was a good sign. He'd probably found out she was a slave of the king's. And he'd know that any king did not like losing slaves, especially his wives who might be bearing a son. Kings needed sons the way they needed warriors.

But now was not the time to tell Erik her news.

It was the time to escape.

The Power of Synne

Around the first bend, the river widened, and another river joined it. The dark water became choppy as the flows mingled.

As they neared a sandbank, Erik threw away the oar he'd used to steer them and waited as they were taken swiftly onto it. He helped her off, asked her if she could swim. She nodded. Then he tipped their boat over and left her bag inside it.

He'd taken most things out of it and put them in a second bag, but she guessed why he would leave the bag behind. He wanted it to appear as if they'd lost everything and had been heading downstream.

"Come, we must move quick. We were seen leaving the town, and when they find this skiff, they will search for us downstream. That will give us a day or two to get away, no more."

"Where are we going?" she asked.

"Through the forest. We must avoid roads for at least a week."

"Do you know the way?" She'd heard it could take months to get through the forest, even to the next town if you didn't take a road or path.

He nodded, grinned.

"You are sure you know what you're doing?"

He pulled her to him. "Do you want to escape that bastard king or not?"

She pushed him away. He kept her in his arms. "You came here to trade?" she asked.

"I did. And my companion will meet us when we are through the forest. Just be thankful, Gytha. I know how to hunt and I know how to survive, and it is the right season for nuts and berries and rutting. We will not starve." He smiled. "But we won't have the luxuries of a king's hall. We may even have to fight bears. Are you good for that?"

She wasn't sure if he was being serious. Then he handed her a long knife.

"This is for you to cut your own throat if I'm overwhelmed by a pack of them. Better to die quick than watch yourself being eaten."

15

That night with Odo was one of the worst I'd ever been through. And that takes some doing. His tastes were odious. He enjoyed force, clamping his hands on my neck until I almost blacked out and then begging my forgiveness. I gave it, to get the whole thing over with. I had more than such indignities to think about.

He quizzed me about everything, too. He asked me about Dublin and its defences. I told him it had more defenders than London. It was a lie. I'm sure he knew that, as he scoffed at a lot of what I said. He also asked me about my home village and what had happened to my father. I told him he'd gone to war and hadn't been heard of since and that my mother was dead. He asked me the name of our village. I hesitated, but with no one from our family left there, I told him.

That was a big mistake.

Later that night, after his second pawing at me, which he seemed to think ended too quick, he became angry and spouted at length, while supping at his wine, about

England being full of vermin, people who defied their new king anointed by every leading English bishop and favoured by the pope, which forced him to make this armed procession, when he should have been on a simple pilgrimage to see the relics of Cuthbert.

I said nothing. It seemed the best plan. He sent me away soon after.

***

The following week was spent with Tate, Yann, and me walking behind the carts as the good Bishop Odo led from the front with a pack horse beside him with his golden relic box strapped to it under a leather shroud, which he would pull back to reveal the box to any passing peasant or in any lucky hamlet we went through. We headed north across moorland and then into a long sweep of dark forest, the type I was told filled most of the land beyond to the ice sea.

Odo only called me to his tent every second or third night. He told me he spent the others praying. His men pretended not to notice the frequency of my visits, but I caught one or two smirking when I left him each time.

Odo told me nothing about how long the journey would be. What I began to fear was that he was making it a slow journey and would dispose of me, Tate, and Yann when we came to Dunholm, in case we shared what he'd been up to on this procession.

Twice he had men we met in villages cut down and their bodies left at the side of the road for raising their voices against him. One man simply raised a fist as we passed and he was axed, his wailing wife and three young children left to mourn him. I suppose it is the way of kings to subjugate first and be kind later, but the distress it causes those left behind turned my mind to angry madness.

I chanted and prayed at night that others would not stand up against him. We whispered together about running into the dark at night, even if the chances of us escaping were poor and the likelihood of us at least one of us dying, high.

The night we heard the wolf pack was a night Odo called me early. He played his sick games and I'd moaned along with him to get it over with quick. This was the reason I was walking through the camp near midnight. I'd heard wolf packs many times, especially in winter when some of them are vicious hungry, but this one was louder and their singing howls seemed to come from all around the forest clearing we were camped in.

Tate and Yann were both awake when I got to the slaves' tent we slept in. I had not told them details of what the bishop did with me – I was afraid Yann would risk his life in some gesture for me – but from his eyes I knew he guessed the worst. Tate seemed not to care. From what I found out from her, she'd been subject to all the indignities you can think of as a woman, and her heart had long hardened.

"The wolves are loud this time of year," hissed Tate, after I sat down near her.

"They are readying for an attack," said Yann. "We'll need weapons if they get into the camp. They'll be looking for anyone weak. They want to eat tonight."

I reached under my tunic and pulled out the short kitchen knife I kept in a pouch. I'd been planning to cut my own throat if the bishop seemed about to share me with his men.

After plunging it into his heart.

"Take this, Yann." I held the knife out. "I know your left hand is as good as your right used to be." It was a small exaggeration, but I had seen him doing many things with his remaining hand and I knew he would appreciate my words. And the knife.

He smiled at me. "I will die to protect you both."

"Don't talk like that," said Tate. "The wolves won't get past the guards."

At that, a series of longer howls, one on top of the other, came. They were coming from multiple directions. The hairs on my back and on my arms stood up tall.

"They've surrounded us," said Yann.

"Be more quiet," said a low voice. One of the other slaves had woken. He was on all fours in the low-roofed tent and moving towards the entrance. He looked back. "Wolf packs in these hills can be fifty strong, or more. Start praying."

"Fifty strong," repeated Yann. "We don't have wolf packs that big."

The slave pulled open the flap at the entrance. Usually there'd be a guard who'd slap or pull outside for a beating any slave who dared open the flap at night. But all that happened this time was that a crisp breeze rolled in.

The slave turned. His hair was long and his beard too. "The guards are gone," he said, a surprised tremble in his tone.

"We cannot run into the darkness with a wolf pack around," said Tate, staring at me, reading my thoughts.

I pressed my lips tight together, sniffed. Was that wolf I could smell? It was certainly like it, that peaty-sweaty-iron-bloody-animal smell a pack of them give off. It was a memory of childhood journeys in fear through woods.

All the other slaves were awake now. Most were crouching, getting themselves to their feet, pushing their heads into the roof of the tent.

"The wolves won't get us all," whispered Yann.

Was he thinking we might find cover in a mass breakout and escape the bishop's men and the wolves at the same time?

We'd need good fortune on our side for that.

More howls sang through the air. Then an orange glow appeared in the distance beyond the entrance flap. I had to go outside and see what that was. Many others had the same idea.

We stood in a protective bunch outside. A row of guards was fanning out through the camp. Each of them was carrying a glowing torch. The light they gave off was like the dawn.

But this was an evil wolf dawn. A sliver of moon lit a dark moorland on the edge of the dense pine forest. I spotted Bishop Odo with five mail-clad knights heading for where the horses were kept. The horses were neighing wildly. The bishop had on his silver mail shirt and was holding a nail-embedded club.

You would not get up quick after a blow from that.

He spotted us and shouted something in our direction, but the wolf howls and the wind took away what he said.

Some of the slaves pointed at him. "Let's go after him," one shouted. "The bishop will protect us."

They did not know the bishop's views of slaves. Then I noticed one of the young slave boys staring at Tate with a mixture of longing and despair. My heart went out to

The Power of Synne

him. He was right to despair if he liked Tate. He would find no kindness there.

We went after the bishop. There was a mist beyond the camp. The grey evil we used to call such forest mists. I'd always hated dense mists and the fear that came with them, because of what they might hide: marauders springing out, wolves. I slowed my run, as the call of geese echoed above us. Geese fly together at night at this time of year, but there was something odd about these calls.

The wolf calls had stopped.

I looked around. Tate was ahead with the other slaves not far behind the bishop. She glanced back at me, her expression asking me what I was doing. I waved her to come back to us. Yann had stopped too and was near me, turning on his heel, looking around the camp.

"Have you seen a wolf yet?" I asked him. There was a tent nearby. I walked to it, bent down, tried to pull out one of the wooden stakes. Yann had come with me. He bent down to help. We pushed it from side to side to loosen it. The first wave of terror had subsided inside me. I was curious now. There was something strange going on. The mist may well be hiding the wolves, but why hadn't we seen any?

Shouts from the other end of the camp, where the cooking fire had been set up, made us turn.

A metallic clash of weapons and the roars of men came on the breeze, and sent the air out of me in a rush as a tingle of fear set my arms shaking.

"They are not wolves," shouted Yann. Tate was beside him, her face grim.

"Which way do we go?" she asked.

They were both looking at me. When had I become the leader? I spun around, looking for any clue as to what we should do. There was every chance that we were being raided by opponents of the new king, but it could also be some war band looking for treasure. Perhaps someone had talked about the gold box the bishop was carrying with him.

Either way, whoever was attacking us might not have any sympathy for slaves if they could not feed them. I'd heard about slaves being killed if they had any injury, as they'd be difficult to sell. That could mean Yann would be cut down. I had not shown him affection, I'd left Tate to do that, but I felt a bond to him. He had tried to me, to help us, and we'd been through so much together.

As well as all that, who knew what demands these raiders would make on Tate and me?

This all made the next few moments so anxious I was jumping from foot to foot ready to run, if I only knew which way to.

Then, out of the mist, came three warriors with their axes raised. They wore big wolf heads and had fur cloaks flying out behind them and were running towards us. I was hopeful for a moment they would head past us and attack the bishop and his men.

"Down, heads bowed," I shouted. It was the sign of submission that most fighting men understood no matter what tongue they spoke. With luck, they would not waste time killing us but leave that decision for later. Moments count in a fight. They would not want to waste them. I hoped.

My heart thumped as Tate, in the middle between us, reached out for my hand and for Yann's. Her head was bowed. Mine was still up. I peered forward. Was there something familiar about one of the men running towards us? More fighters were coming out of the mist behind the first three. Shouts echoed, then the beat of hooves sounded on the ground. The bishop and the personal guards that had been with him were riding into the mist with clods of earth flying in the air behind them.

"Stop," cried a voice. I blinked. My heart nearly burst. Standing in front of me was Magnus, the outlaw son of King Harold, who had abandoned me in Dublin.

I stood up, went to him, hammered my fists into the thick leather of his tunic.

"Where in Christ's name have you been, you bastard?" I shouted.

Magnus laughed and threw his axe down. He took me in his arms and swung me one way then the other.

"Huh, what about you? You should be safe and warm in Dublin," he said, whispering in my ear.

"Why didn't you tell me you were leaving," I shouted. I pushed against him, as hard as I could. He began talking to one of his men, over my shoulder.

"Tie up any of their men still alive."

I punched his chest, slapped his face. He released me. "And find the relic box," he said, ignoring me.

He looked at Tate and Yann. He had a puzzled expression. I was still deeply angry at him, but I was a little relieved too. We would not be slaves anymore.

"Meet my sister, Tate, who I told you about. She came to Dublin after you left me. We came here to look for my other sister. Yann came with us." That was all I was going to tell him for now.

Magnus squinted at Yann. "You've been disfigured." Many warriors do not want to be with an injured comrade, as if bad luck might engulf them, too.

Yann nodded. He looked ashamed.

"Men who cannot fight are useless," said Magnus. "Run back to Dublin, Yann."

The Power of Synne

"No," I shouted. He didn't get to order Yann away. "Winter's coming. He'll be dead by the time he reaches the coast."

Magnus shrugged.

I shook my fist at him. "I want him with us, Magnus son of Harold, you cannot be relied on."

Magnus laughed. "What does Yann say?"

Yann nodded. "I'll go," he said. "Magnus is right."

I raised both of my fists in frustration, shook them in the air, and groaned loudly. Men can be so stupid. "Stop this. If Yann leaves, Tate and I will go with him." I pointed at Magnus. "Is that what you want?" I ran my hands through my hair, making the curls flow wild around me.

Magnus's eyes widened.

"He can stay," he said. He glowered at Yann. "Can you do anything useful with one arm, Prince of Leinster?"

Yann held his hand out. "Give me your axe."

Magnus had a large axe with a large blood-stained handle hanging from his hand. He held it out for Yann, who took it and pointed at a body lying twenty paces away.

"I can finish off men who are injured by your warriors, so they don't have to slow down and fear being attacked from behind." He pointed at the man lying on the heath. "That one is still alive. Shall I finish him?"

"Go on," said Magnus.

Yann went to the man, who must have seen him coming as he raised a hand in a plea for his life. Yann planted the axe in the man's neck. Blood spurted and an end-of-life cough and gurgle came to us on the wind.

Magnus raised his fist as Yann came back to us. "Perhaps you can be useful," he said when Yann passed him back his axe. He bowed to me. "Wait for me at the Norman cooking fires. I will check on my men." And he was gone.

Tate, who had been listening to all this, grabbed my arm. "You cannot let him slide back between your legs after what he did," she said.

I looked at her, put my head to one side. "I won't."

16

They did not starve. Gytha was good at finding nuts and berries. They were lucky it wasn't winter. Wolves would have been a lot more hungry and desperate if it had. They met no one for ten days and emerged thin but alive in a tiny clearing in the dense woods. The smell and smoke of a cooking fire had attracted them from the other side of the wooded valley.

Erik offered his knife on the palm of his hand as a gift to the two men who confronted them, each of them with a slightly swinging hand axe. Three huts made up the farmstead. One of the men grabbed the knife, while eying Gytha as if he hadn't seen a woman in a long time. The other man ushered them inside the bigger of the round thatched huts. A woman inside near the back looked beaten down.

The men left their axes at the door. Both kissed the woman, one on each cheek, and Gytha knew at once what was going on. Both of these men were with this woman. It was not unusual, but such people often became outcasts.

That could be why they were living deep in the forest and not in a village.

The woman opened her arms to Gytha. She said something in a strange bark-like tongue, and Gytha noticed her eyes were different with a fold in each corner. She was from somewhere far to the east. The woman stopped talking and pointed at a black pot hanging over a smouldering fire at the centre of the hut. Gytha nodded and could not help herself smiling. The woman knew what they were here for. She pointed at the table nearby and went off to get bowls.

The food, a yellow vegetable pottage, was the best thing Gytha had ever eaten. It felt as if she hadn't eaten in a year. The smell of it alone set her mouth watering. After eating, a strange feeling came over her. Both of the men were staring at her. She knew what that meant.

She banged her fist on the table. "We will leave now, Erik. We cannot take more from these people."

Both of the men who'd welcomed them stood. One went to the door, picking up his axe as he went. Erik still had his face almost in his bowl, as if he wasn't aware of what was happening. The woman reached for his bowl, to clear the table, probably for what she expected was to come.

Erik grabbed her wrist, twisted it, and pulled the woman to his side. In his other hand, he had a thin, short knife. He held the tip near the woman's ear. She squealed and writhed. He kept her head tight to his chest while stepping back from the table so she had nothing to grab as a weapon.

"Open the door and let us leave, or her blood will dampen the floor here before you can kill either of us. We will not be your playthings." Erik pulled the woman with him as he moved towards the door.

Gytha stared at him, open-mouthed. All this had happened in moments. Erik was better at all this than she'd thought he would be. He was well able to stand up for himself. She went behind him after grabbing a kitchen knife from a bench at the side of the room. She was beside the woman as they neared the door. She pressed the woman's flailing arm down and held the knife up.

"Two neck holes will flood this floor so you will never want to live here again," she shouted. "Out of the way!"

The man near the door hesitated, but, after a nod from the other man, he swung the door open and stood behind it, as if waiting for his moment to pounce.

Erik rushed through the door with the woman pushed in front of him. Gytha stayed as close to him as if they were bound together by ropes. But it was fate binding them. When they got outside, the sun was setting.

"We'll take your friend into the woods and release her there," shouted Erik, turning back to the house. "Do not follow or she will die."

The two men were outside, standing by the door. They looked surprised, as if they'd expected an easy time forcing Erik and Gytha to their will.

Gytha's breathing was fast and heavy. She was proud of Erik standing up to those two men, but afraid too. Who knew what they would have been subjected to if he hadn't taken the woman?

When they reached the woods, Erik released the woman. She turned to him and put her hands together, begging him for something. Gytha was taken aback.

"Me, you," the woman said, pointing at her and then Erik, glancing back towards the clearing with fear in her eyes. Her meaning was clear.

Erik shook his head. Gytha did too, but when they strode off down a track she'd found, the woman followed them. And when Gytha looked back beyond her, she saw the two men not far behind. Each of them had a bow and a quiver of arrows.

"Let her come with us," said Gytha softly. "She can take a few of the arrows from those two following us."

Erik groaned. "Our troubles will double, Gytha. We'll have those two as well as your king on our tails."

"King tails," said the woman. She smiled, pointed at her ass.

Erik laughed. "She can come if she can keep up."

He started running at a loping, easy pace. It was the first time Gytha had seen him run. She knew by his stride that he would not be stopping soon. She motioned for the woman to follow and set off after him. They had no bags, just the few things in the pouch on their belts, and two knives now, enough to find food with.

They ran for most of that night.

The woman kept pace, but kept looking back. She wore a grim look, as if she'd learned suffering from a young age. Gytha was tired; her bones and muscles were aching by the time the moon moved a little across the sky. But when she looked around, she saw movement and knew they were being pursued and that their lives depended on their stamina now.

That was one of the worst nights of her life.

The forest didn't make her scared during the day, but she knew there were giant boars and wolves likely hunting, too. They liked hunting in packs, looking for the small, the weak, the injured, any animal in distress. Wolves in these forests had a taste for human flesh, she'd heard, from raiding farms and taking infants and small children.

The problem with loping through this trail was that it twisted and turned around giant fallen trees and rocks and tight clumps of bushes. You never knew what to expect when you turned a corner.

Which was why she was not really surprised when they came upon that bear running towards them. But when it saw them, it went up high on its hind legs, glanced behind it, then crashed into the trees. It was moving slower than bears usually moved because of a limp. Something or someone had disturbed it and was after it.

"Follow the bear," said Erik, his breathing laboured.

Gytha's skin prickled. A shiver ran through her. She hated big bears. One had swiped at her in a marketplace in England. That one was supposed to be tame. Its sharpened claws had left two scar lines on her shoulder.

Erik led the way.

The bear's passage left a trail of broken branches, but the moon, which had been high earlier, was flitting behind clouds now, making it impossible at times to see how close the bear was, and if they were catching up with it.

She guessed, with a deep shudder, that it was near, perhaps only a few strides away, when the earthy smell of that bear filled her nostrils. Erik had sensed it as well. He stopped running. He pointed at the thick undergrowth to the side and didn't speak, but she understood and pushed into the undergrowth. Gytha was breathing hard and fast now, her chest shaking from all the effort. She needed a rest. Badly.

The Power of Synne

They didn't have long to wait.

Gytha was still getting her breathing under control, trying to be as quiet as possible, when the two men pursuing them arrived on the path the bear had made. They were looking around as they came. Gytha was sure they could hear or sense the bear up ahead.

Perhaps the two men had. As they passed Gytha, both had their bows up and arrows with shiny, pointed heads nocked. Then they were gone past. Gytha leaned over and gripped Erik's arm. The woman on the other side had already done the same.

Erik shook his head very slowly. They were not to move. A few moments later, the roar of the bear echoed, chilling Gytha's blood almost to ice. The bear was charging, thumping at the ground hard so she could feel it through her boots. Every part of her said *run*.

Lots of other animals must have felt this too. A flock of birds rose into the air with a flapping noise while the screeches of other fleeing animals echoed through the trees. The bear's roars had changed. Gytha imagined arrows sticking out of it, enraging it. Then she didn't have to imagine it anymore.

The two men came running back towards them. One had discarded his bow. The bear was not far behind. A pale, wild-eyed fear had come onto their faces.

They didn't look around to see if anyone was watching. Bears run faster than humans. Everyone knows that. Not for long, but for long enough to catch all but the fleetest runner. The bear sniffed the air as it went by, as if it knew they were there, but preferred the thrill of the chase. Its pitiless black eyes were wide, taking in everything as it ran past them.

Gytha's mouth felt as if it had been filled by sand from an hourglass. She held herself still and on her toes. If the bear turned for them, they'd have to split up, and it would likely catch one of them in the trees. It would go after the smallest of them too – her. She wasn't that much smaller than the woman who had begged her way to join them, but the bear would know.

Prayers are good when you see death close up.

The hope that the Queen of Heaven would protect you was just that, a hope, she knew, after seeing men dying with prayers to her on their lips, but isn't hope better than none? So her mother told all her children. Where were Synne and Tate now, she wondered. Would she ever see them again? They were probably in some warm king's hall dealing with suitors. Lucky sisters.

17

It was night when Magnus found us again. We'd taken over the bishop's cooking pot and we'd boiled up a stew in the meantime. An older man told me Magnus never slept until he was sure guards had been placed all around the camps they made.

Magnus looked tired when he arrived and took a bowl of stew from the pot. He bowed and smiled at me the way I remembered, as if all the empty nights and the broken promises were nothing.

He looked into the bowl. "Your stew looks as good as ever," he said.

"It's better," I said proudly. "I put whatever I want in it now."

He looked at the bowl, then pushed more of the stew into his mouth with the wooden spoon. When he was finished, he walked away, sat with his men, and did not look at me. I was conscious of all the eyes on me and on him, everyone wondering what would happen between us. He'd told me before, and often, how important it was to keep your men on your side during a campaign. No special treatment for leaders was what his father had taught him and was what he practised.

"We found the bishop's tent," he said as he handed me back the bowl. "Come, let's go there. We need to talk."

I knew what he meant from the mischievous look in his eye. He probably expected me to share my body with him. But there was no way he was getting that from me.

"I won't pretend the last few months never happened," I said.

"Don't pretend. Just thank me for freeing all of you." His smile was back. It was distracting.

"Thank you," I said. I gave him a bow, held it briefly. I did appreciate being freed. But I knew this was not the thank you he wanted.

He pointed at Yann. "Does he lie with you now?" he asked, an angry edge to his tone.

I shook my head. I did not want him blaming Yann for my reluctance.

Magnus smiled thinly. "So, tell me, who keeps you warm at night? Who have you been with?"

"No one." I said it fast. I would not admit anything to him. He was looking for an excuse to get angry with me. "I can survive without that." I leaned towards him, poked my finger in his chest. "How many women have you left with a babe inside them since I last saw you?"

His face was red and getting redder. He did not like being thwarted. I knew that about him, but I needed to move the conversation on. And I'd seen him leering at the slave girls in Dublin.

"Let's see what your friend Yann has to say." Magnus spat on the ground.

Would Yann tell him something I didn't want known? It felt like I was standing on the edge of a cliff with a great fall looming.

"Have you been forcing yourself on these sisters while you've been tramping the moors?" Magnus raised his fist in front of Yann. My body relaxed. He was only asking what Yann had done. He was jealous.

Yann snorted. He looked angry now, too.

"I'm not the type who takes women against their will," said Yann. "Is that what you do?" There was a sneer in his tone.

I knew where this was going. "Magnus, no," I said forcefully. I raised my hand to stop him, but he wasn't listening. Maybe it was my refusal to go with him when he'd asked or maybe it was some need for him to show his men who was in charge, but whatever it was, he was in no mood for insolence.

He slapped Yann across the face hard with the back of his hand and with a snort that made clear Yann was lucky not to be properly beaten.

He pointed at Yann. "If you value your life, do not speak to me like that ever again." His words came out twisted with anger as if he might yet gut Yann.

Two of his men, standing nearby, were watching all this. They'd likely tell their comrades what Magnus had done. It would impress all that he was still strong-willed and willing to stand up for himself.

It did not impress me. I'd seen too many injuries and too many deaths caused by men unable to control their anger.

Yann held a hand to his cheek as his head came back from being twisted by the blow. I stepped to him, grabbed his arm, and hissed, "Be quiet now." I meant for him not to react to what Magnus had done.

Unfortunately, Magnus misunderstood my words.

"What, you have secrets now you don't want him to speak about?" he said with a laugh.

Yann laughed louder. It was the wrong thing for him to do. Magnus grunted and pulled a dagger from the sheath on his belt. With it out, he would have to use it or lose face in front of the small crowd of men who had gathered to watch the confrontation.

My senses came alive. The air was riddled with anger and fear. My skin pricked exactly as it had during my fight in London the year before. I stepped between Magnus and Yann. This was a stupid thing to do, as either side might attack you to get you out of the way, but instead of just standing there, I went up to Magnus and wrapped my arms around him and whispered in his ear.

18

They headed away from the track the bear had made. There was no point in trying to hide from a bear in the woods. It could smell you a league away. Humans leave a trail in the air Gytha had been told, which she believed too, after being beside men who had not washed in a year.

It was a difficult journey, ducking and weaving, avoiding branches, with thoughts of the bear and those two men keeping her moving, though her chest was burning inside and many of her muscles screeched for her to stop.

But it was the woman who'd joined them who stopped first. She went down on her knees and cried out, throwing her arms around, pulling at her tunic, tearing it so that it half came off her shoulder, exposing a large breast. Gytha knew what she was doing. Some slave women who thought they might have a chance with a man, someone who might buy them out, would risk a terrible beating from their owner to tempt a man they liked.

She'd thought about it herself a few times, so she couldn't blame her. And it was how she'd got Erik to help her, so she did not feel jealous at that moment. She'd seen Erik's good side, his concern for her, but he was a hard man too, pushing her always to keep walking, not to talk about hunger or thirst and never to complain about the noises in the woods. She thought he must have been born in woods like these.

Erik stopped and went back to the woman and shared water from the small waterskin that hung from his belt. It had kept them alive a few times while they were moving between streams, but all he'd allowed Gytha ever was a quick taste. This woman glugged at the skin and he did not stop her. When he took it back, he did not offer it to Gytha, he just pulled the woman to her feet.

He pointed at himself. "Erik," he said. He pointed at her.

"Ambr," she said in her weird accent. She did not look at Gytha. That was the moment Gytha became angry.

Erik's gaze was fixed on her breast. Gytha supposed he'd grown tired of their rutting. Men like him were like that. They found it so hard to resist when something is laid out in front of them, they forget everything else.

They kept going only for a little longer that afternoon until they came to a stream. They walked alongside it, Erik rushing forward, until they saw a small clearing beside the water in a narrow gap in the woods. Ambr quickly made eating expressions with her hands and went off. She was going to forage. Gytha followed her. She was good at it. She pulled her tunic up to form a wool basket held with one hand, which she started throwing berries and seeds into. Gytha copied her. They had piles of hawberries, redberries, and redseeds when they arrived back at the stream.

Erik was standing in it, washing himself. Naked. When he saw them, he smiled, stuck his tongue out. It was clear what he wanted.

The two of them.

It was a chilling moment, one filled with risk. He might lose any affection for Gytha if he liked the woman more, but she'd always felt a deep attraction to him and standing there brazenly, he looked good, especially after that fight they'd been in and their rush there to survive.

Ambr poured her pile of berries and nuts onto the ground near the water and stripped off. Her body was lithe, her skin the colour of ripe butter. Seeing them touching each other pushed a twist of jealousy deep into Gytha's mind. There was no escaping it. She had to join them.

19

I did not look back at Yann as I went, but I could feel his gaze burning into me. We'd never rutted, but I knew he wanted me. That was why I didn't care what Tate and he did at night that left them panting. I knew who he really wanted.

When we reached his tent, I told Magnus something that made his ardour cool.

"You cannot have me whenever you want any more, Magnus. Things have changed between us." I stopped. He snaked his arm around me in reply. I slapped it away. "You get one night, this night, with me, that is all, and no more until I know you are true."

"Have you gone mad, woman? You will do what I say." He laughed.

I pointed at him. "You'll not laugh if I curse you; all your plans will turn to dust. I can do that now. I learned how to from the seers at Tara. They taught me many things. Be careful, Magnus son of Harold. If I curse you, I will scream it, so all your men know it too."

He stopped laughing, stared at me with an expression like poured steel. His men would believe in curses, even if he didn't. He'd not want them to know I'd cursed him and their mission. I watched his eyes, could almost read his mind as he considered beating me or just taking what he wanted and not caring what I screamed. I stared back at him. I'd taken a gamble, but perhaps not that much. I could change his fate. My power was real. I could make things happen. How else could it be that he'd found us and rescued us? There was no other possibility. I'd pulled the threads of our fates together again with my prayers for a rescue.

He smiled and reached for me. I raised my eyebrows and shifted fast away from him.

"What is your answer?" I asked, pointing at him, my finger shaking.

"You're not the woman I left in Dublin," he said. "But I like this new Synne."

"Do you agree to what I said?" I needed him to agree. "You get one night with me."

He sighed. "I agree." He said it as if the words burned him. Then he narrowed his eyes and held his hand out to me. I went to him. Another of my wishes had come true.

He left me panting that night, as if he got his revenge on me by taking me hard. He enjoyed me three times. We barely slept. When we were both sated, he talked, his tone different to what it had been earlier that night.

"Our fate is twinned, Synne. Finding you here proves that. Believe me when I say I left you to protect you."

"What happened down south?"

"We lost a battle, many good men. I cannot go back to Dublin empty-handed. That is why I stayed away," he said. Then he stopped himself. I was supposed to be grateful. From him, these words were nearly an apology. And all the explanation of what he'd been through I'd likely ever get.

But I knew why his luck had been bad.

"You made a mistake leaving without me," I said.

He grunted as if he knew it.

He was gone by the time I woke. I ached all over from the rough way he'd taken me. He'd been like that before, always after some bloody fighting he'd been involved in, but this was worse, as if he thought that night with me would be his last. I ached deeply too, from remembering the time when I'd loved him every night, when I'd put up with anything to be with him, and how my heart had hardened since he'd abandoned me.

He was right about it. I was a different person now. He'd given me crumbs. I would do the same to him.

Fearing for Tate and Yann, I went to find them. They were sleeping under a cart nearby, tight together like puppies. I woke them and we found a young man making pottage in a large cauldron on the other side of the camp. Many men were hanging around him. Dead bodies had been collected and wood had been put around them to make a bonfire.

After we'd eaten, Magnus appeared. He eyed me warily at first. When I bowed my respect to him, he smiled. He had a dishevelled monk with him who was wearing the muddiest, blood-streaked habit I'd ever seen. Magnus called me to him.

"This is my monk Edward, named after the old king," said Magnus, pointing at the monk.

I gave him a low bow. Monks like respect.

"You're lucky to have escaped Bishop Odo," said Edward.

I nodded.

He had a sly look on his face. "What do you know about this box of relics he's been showing?" asked the monk.

"He said it's Saint Cuthbert's relics."

"He should not have taken them from Dunholm," said the monk. There was bitterness in his tone. I knew this type of talk. It came from people who'd lost family in a battle or some skirmish.

He took a step towards me, put his head to one side. "Did he force himself on you?" he asked, a curious look on his face.

I shook my head.

The monk snorted. "We must take the relics to a holy well to wash them clean of all the Norman stink on them," he said.

"Where do we have to go for that?" asked Magnus. He sounded surprised.

"Not far, my lord, and on the road to Dunholm. You'll be welcomed well with open arms by all villagers there and it'll be a lot easier to get the church folk at Dunholm to take their relics back if we've cleansed them at the holy well."

Magnus sighed. "We don't need a lot of men for the blessing?"

The monk nodded. I noticed the sour smell of sweat was even more pronounced around him. Who knew how long it had been since he'd washed?

"We'll take them to your holy well, but my men must go straight for Dunholm. We must catch their garrison off guard before they get warned we're nearby."

He was looking at the monk warily. Was he concerned about being spotted at the well and informed on, or was there something else troubling him? He was right to be concerned, though. Bands of warriors using hit-and-run tactics only worked if the enemy weren't waiting for you.

***

It was a two-day ride to Saint Cuthbert's Well. I slept in Magnus's tent, but we did not rut. He did not even ask. Most of his men stayed with us until we left them at a crossroads. Yann, the monk, and two of Magnus's best men came with us down a narrow side path heading into a deep vale in the heathland, which you would miss if you didn't know it was there.

The monk nodded at a man we saw on the way down that twisting path through an ancient oak forest. We came to the well, a bubbling outpouring of water from marshy ground, at the lowest point of the vale as dusk drew in. The monk had told us already we would stay the night at a farm nearby.

We tied up the horses and the monk led us by half-hidden stepping stones to the source of the waterlogged ground. One of the guards stayed with the horses. The other one, a giant, carried the relic box covered in a dirty woollen blanket. I asked Yann and Tate did they also not want to stay with the horses. They didn't. Yann did not trust Magnus. Neither did Tate. Yann had overheard talk in their camp that those unable to fight should be put out of

The Power of Synne

their misery, fast. Tate had her own reasons for not trusting him. I figured what they were from her expression.

As we walked to the water source, Tate motioned me to her.

"You know it was at Dunholm that Father died?" she asked.

I was taken aback and stopped. I put my hand out to grab her. I'd completely forgotten about father dying at Dunholm. It was so long ago I'd been told and we all knew so little about what had happened. "Dunholm, yes." I let out a low groan. "What do you think it means we find ourselves in his footsteps?"

Tate gripped my arm. "I don't know, but it must mean something. You're the one who should know these things, having your gifts and all. Much use they have been to us so far."

She had a point. Still alive, being alive was good, but everyone expected more when you supposedly had powers and gifts. I did too, though finding my sister Gytha would be enough for me.

"There is a good reason for all this happening to us," I said. "There has to be." I'd been searching for my sisters for so long, it felt strange that questions about my father had returned.

I blinked. A dim flaming torch was coming towards us across the marsh. Or was it a ghost light, a will-o'-the-wisp, those lights people see sometimes in marshes? I squinted. The light grew. Someone was approaching the well from the right side. I wasn't sure if it was a human form, then I knew. It was a thin rake of a man. Like something from an old tale.

"Who goes?" shouted Magnus.

No reply came but the man did not stop.

"'Tis the well keeper," said the monk. He moved beyond Magnus and put his hand up in a greeting. The well keeper acknowledged him with a slight bow and then stopped on the far side of the bubbling water. He bowed low for Magnus, and for the rest of us, too.

"What brings all tha to the well?" he asked.

Magnus pointed at the guard. "We bring Saint Cuthbert's relics. They need to be cleansed of Norman trickery before we take them back to Dunholm."

The man peered at me. A look of recognition passed across his face and for an odd moment, I thought I recognised him too, as if we'd met in a dream.

He spat into the marsh, peered at me, and said, "You've lost more than one, 'aven't you?"

I nodded. A wave of memories came pouring up as if his words had opened a door. We used to have a village fool who would say mad things to people. Mad things you later realised were true. This well keeper reminded me of him.

The Power of Synne

"You'll find what you need by listening to a howl," he said, his voice turning at the end into a perfect wolf howl.

Magnus grunted loudly in obvious bemusement that the man was talking about me rather than what he was here for. Why is it men always think they should come first?

"Can you wash the relics of Norman guile or not?" he asked in a testy tone.

The well keeper put both his hands out. He wanted to take the box and had no problem with its weight when Magnus's man, after a nod from Magnus, passed it to him.

The well keeper placed the box into the water, held it under. His hands came up empty.

Magnus shouted, "What have you done?" Groans echoed around us from the loud to a shocked whimper.

The well keeper laughed, then pulled his dirty tunic down from his neck, as if presenting himself for slaughter.

20

Erik had the best of it for many nights after that. Gytha also enjoyed the freedom to explore Ambr's body at the same time as enjoying Erik's, though she knew it was giving in to every thought the monks said was impure.

It took them seven days to reach a river heading west. Their progress speeded up on the final days, as Erik became sated with the pleasure of the night and they set off earlier on those mornings. It took another three days, the first spent building a raft from tree fall branches, to reach a village.

The raft leaked so much Gytha was sure they would all drown. Every moment on the water she was dogged by horrible thoughts about drowning. It was hardly a raft at all after a few days, more like they went downstream holding onto branches held together by tendrils all moving under their hands as if it was all alive. Her fear turned into a constant stomach ache, as she became resigned to her fate.

Then, for two days it rained non-stop. Ambr did not like the rain and begged them by signs to wait it out under the trees, but Erik shook his head. The day the rain stopped, they made a big ceremony of lighting a fire. Erik had a tinderbox that Gytha had used before. Erik said she was quicker at it than him. She reckoned it was just because she gathered properly dry moss and leaves for the first sparks. She was also good at blowing just right.

Ambr made cooing noises as the tiny flames appeared. She'd collected small sticks and she built and grew the fire while Erik and Gytha went to hunt for something to cook and eat. Their best bet was finding a wild pig. They spent half the day circling the woods, looking for animal trails, but ended up with just one silver eel they caught in a stream as a flash of sunlight caught it twisting through shallows.

It tasted as good as anything she'd ever eaten when it was properly cooked. The head was the only part they didn't eat. Ambr buried it and whispered something over it as if she was thanking the eel. The next few days were easier after that. The forest thinned, which made Gytha fearful they'd be seen, that she'd be taken back to that king, but when they did meet people again, no one showed any interest in the new arrivals.

Erik spoke enough of the villagers' tongue to work out where they were. They would have to make their way across another forest to find the great river and his trading partner, but he was a lot happier now.

Six days later, they found the village his partner should have gone to. The man was not there. Neither was the boat Erik hoped would take them downstream. He talked to the owner of some small barges tied up at a nearby sandbank on the river. One was being loaded with furs. The owner had no interest in giving passage to any of them, even if Erik worked all the way. The owner had two bear-like companions who both carried axes on their belts to discourage anyone thinking of trying to steal anything.

Ambr was the one who got them passage. First, she sang on the bank as the older man was packing away the last of the furs. Then she sang again, a more plaintiff song. The man put down a bundle of furs and came to stand near her.

After Ambr finished her song, he told them they could travel down to the sea on his barge, if Ambr sang like that every evening.

Erik agreed. Ambr smiled, then poked Gytha and opened her mouth. Gytha was not a big singer, but she hummed along when Ambr sang, giving depth to the song, Erik refused to even try singing with a snort and a violent shake of his head.

Two weeks after that, with Christ Mass approaching, and snow flurries in the air, the moment when the barge owner expected to sell his cargo neared. Gytha had been thinking about what they might do next. It was her dream to find her sisters, but could she persuade Ambr and Erik to go with her on the journey or head off alone? It would be better if they were with her. She'd enjoyed the last few weeks. They'd become a friendly, embracing trio, reminding her of all she missed with her family. She'd wondered at times if she'd be better off if it was just her and Erik, but the singing had proved that idea wrong. She had to accept that Ambr was useful.

To persuade them to join her mission she could make promises, she knew that, or plead with them to go with her, but the thing that might work to keep them together, was the power of the happiness she knew they felt while travelling and sleeping together.

She told Ambr about this plan, hoping she'd go along. Ambr had been catching their tongue quickly and got the idea of sisters, saying she too had a sister.

"We can go to England," said Gytha, on the morning of the day they were due to arrive at the coast, and the small port where traders came from all directions to buy furs this time of year, when demand was high with winter approaching.

Erik was listening. "We'll go north," he said. "I'll take you both home."

Gytha laughed. "You have a wife there already, yes?" she asked.

He looked at her with anger twisting his face. "Of course," he said. "Do not fret. She will do as I say."

"I'm not coming with you to be your second or third wife and wait curled by the door while you fuck all the others," she said. "I'd rather kill myself." She spat those final words out.

He laughed. "Where did you get this spirit of yours?"

Ambr was listening. She sat beside Gytha and pointed at her.

"Me and Gytha, sisters," she said. She put her hands in front of her and entwined her fingers.

Gytha did the same thing with her fingers. They touched their hands together with their fingers entwined and smiled at each other, ignoring him.

"You'll not survive long without me," said Erik. He was wide-eyed and on the verge of violence.

Gytha made a breaking apart motion with her fingers, then pointed at herself and Ambr. "We don't care," she said.

Erik scoffed.

Ambr shook her head, scowled, put her hand out.

Gytha held it. "Perhaps you are right. You can come with us, and we can all go to your home after we find my sisters," she said, as if defeated.

The Power of Synne

Erik looked puzzled, then smiled. He would get what he wanted. His women available to him any time he wanted them.

"Good," he said.

"You will help find my sisters first?" asked Gytha.

Ambr nodded. "Sisters first," she said nodding.

Erik shouted. "You are good at this," he said. "You should lead a tribe." He laughed. Gytha shrugged.

"Where are your sisters?" Erik asked with a resigned sigh.

"We'll look for them near York, where we were born. Someone may have heard of what happened to them here. That is our best hope."

Ambr was looking from Gytha to Erik. She put her fist to her heart, closed her eyes, and pressed it into her chest. Then she held it towards Gytha. She was pledging herself to Gytha.

A warm feeling came over Gytha and a smile grew on her face.

Erik frowned, stood. They were at the front of the long wooden barge, so there were not many places he could go.

Gytha went down the barge after him.

"I must find my sisters. They are everything to me," she said when he turned to her, putting his hand out to stop her coming too close. She pushed up against his hand, grabbed it, and put it to her breast.

"You like what have got with us, don't you?" she said, a grin on her face.

"I can get this anywhere," he replied, his tone dismissive.

"Then we must part ways," she said.

He grabbed her wrist, pulled his dagger from his belt with an easy motion. He'd been pretending to allow her to decide her own fate. He held the blade towards her. "Stop this stupid talk about sisters. You will both do what I say. We will go north. I saved your slave skin. You owe me. You will repay me."

She stared into his eyes. She could not let him win. Not like this. She would be a slave for ever if she did. She went up to him until his blade was pressing into her chest.

"If you force me, the first chance I get I will cut my own throat," she said softly.

He laughed, moved the blade, pulled it back as if to slash at her.

"Do it. See if I care," he said. "You've taken leave of your senses, Gytha, because there are two of you. Do not think for a moment your wishes come before mine. That is a mockery of me and any warrior worth his salt." He pulled the blade away.

"I will not cut you today but know this: if you continue with your insolent demands, I will make those words the last you hear and feed you after it to the fishes." He spat into the water.

Gytha didn't reply. She was frightened but angry too. She knew Erik was well capable of extreme violence, but she'd imagined he cared a little for her and their happy days together. That it meant something.

Ambr stared at her with sorrowful eyes. She may not have understood everything Erik said, but she knew what had happened.

It was late that evening when they reached the small port. The barge owner let them sleep one last night on the barge, tucked up beneath some loose furs, but he ordered them off in the morning. Ambr sang a final song for the man as they went.

Gytha stayed quiet all this time, kept her head down as any good woman was supposed to do. Erik boasted as they went through the small port town that he knew all the boat builders here and that his countrymen from the far north passed through this port regularly and they would do his bidding.

He turned to Gytha and Ambr as they reached a rundown-looking hall, its thatched roof dark, rotting and sliding off in places. "You are both my slaves. Remember that and you will be fed and treated well." He sniffed.

Gytha wanted to spit in his eye, but she looked down instead. She'd noticed he kept his dagger further back on his belt now, making it more difficult for someone in front to grab it. Was that because of her threats, she wondered.

When he pushed open the door of the tavern, a stink of sweat and ale wafted towards them. Erik smiled as if he recognised and loved the smell. Ambr's nose wrinkled.

"You're lucky I don't rope you both together and put a neckband on you both, like some here do," said Erik. "But if you run or raise a hand to strike at me, I will do that and tighten your collar too, so you struggle to breathe. Do you understand?" He made a motion with his hands about tightening something around his neck.

Ambr looked at him as if she had no idea what he meant, but Gytha had seen her expression when he was talking. She knew.

Inside the ale hall, there were only a few free people as well as slaves carrying pitchers of ale and bowls of pottage.

Erik pointed at a bench at the side of the hall. "Wait there," he said. He shook his fist at them, then turned to the room to see if anyone was watching. Two of the men at other tables raised their fists acknowledging him.

Gytha and Ambr sat. They didn't talk. Gytha was trying to work out what had happened to Erik. Was this his plan all along? Had he rescued her to claim her as his property? Was she a fool to think he'd liked her? Had he just been caring towards her to get her to do what he wanted and not cut his throat in his sleep? She felt a total fool. Her mother would laugh if she'd heard about this.

She watched as Erik went around the room, stopping at tables, sitting at some, talking to the men at them, each time pointing over to where she and Ambr were. Gytha caught the eye of two men staring at her. One, a giant of a man, gave her a wink, then went deep into conversation with the other man, while glancing occasionally at her.

She knew what was happening.

21

The well keeper stuck his tongue out at Magnus. He put his hand on the hilt of his dagger. The monk reached out and grabbed Magnus's arm, holding it so tight his knuckles whitened. They all stood like that for a moment, waiting for violence to erupt.

I peered down into the water, then went closer and put my hand out. I slid it into the ice-cold water, felt down and down until half my arm was in water and someone behind laughed at my stupidity. But then I could feel the top of the box, gnarled and slippery. The well wasn't deep. It was a shallow hole with water coming in from the back and going out from the front. I laughed.

"It's here," I said, splashing at the water and smiling with relief. There would be no need for anyone to die.

The well keeper applauded, reached into the water, and together we pulled out the box. I stood. Tate and Yann clapped me on the back, hard, too hard. I coughed. The monk was praying loudly. Magnus had his mouth wide open as if he'd just seen a miracle.

The Power of Synne

I laughed. Tate spoke for me. "Synne always had powers I did not understand. Her mother told us about her gifts but we did not know what to believe." She pointed at me. "Synne is blessed by the Holy Mother, and our Father."

The monk stood straight. "Only the church decides such things," he said. "Do you believe you are blessed in the eyes of Christ, Synne?" He put his head to one side.

I knew this was a trap. The church loved to get people to admit heresy.

"I do not," I said. "I saw a flash under the water, that is all. It's no miracle." Was she trying to get me into trouble?

Tate stuck her tongue out at me. I could tell she was jealous, as she'd been so often when we were young. Any slight thing could set her off.

As if a signal had sounded, a hound began baying. We all looked around for the source of the plaintive howls. It sounded as if the animal was injured. The undergrowth and trees around the hollow hid where the dog might be.

"I'll see to it," said Yann.

Magnus put his hand up. "Have you befriended the hounds here?" he asked, a quizzical look on his face.

"No," said Yann.

"Go then. But stop the howls. It will attract everyone in this valley and beyond to us."

Yann went back the way we'd come.

"Your relics have been cleansed, my lord," said the well keeper with a low bow. One of his hands shot out in front of him after he gently deposited the box at Magnus's feet.

Magnus groaned loudly, reached in the purse tucked behind his belt, and gave the man a small coin. I did not see what it was.

We all went back to our horses. Yann was there with a large grey warhound beside him. The dog eyed us as if we were all the enemy.

"You have set that hound's mind to you," said Magnus. "Did you sleep with it?"

Yann didn't reply to the barely veiled insult. We mounted and rode. Clouds had gathered. It looked as if it would rain again. It was cold enough for hail too.

The hound followed as we went back out of the valley, heading fast towards Dunholm. A rain shower caught us, but we kept going, our cloaks soaking and icy. We sought out a fire as soon as we found a village. Magnus and the monk prayed in the long house of the village. He was known there. After we ate, all crowded together at rough wooden tables, I was able to spend time talking with Tate. Magnus was with the village chief, deep in conversation, both of them looking around as if they were being spied on. Yann was with the dogs.

"I thought you were keeping Yann busy," I said. "Not the dogs."

"He lost interest in me after Magnus claimed you," said Tate. She laughed. "I think he was only wooing me because you were near. Trying to make you jealous, as if he could." She rocked from side to side. "You know that is the best gift Mother gave you, your power over men? You look like you don't care what they think of you, but you do, don't you?" She sounded jealous and angry. I'd have to be careful. Whenever I'd heard her like this before, she was always getting ready for a fight.

We did not need that now.

"So, it's a gift that Magnus abandoned me, and is only rutting me now because he came across me on the moor?" I laughed, leaned close to her, so only she could hear me.

"What do you think he'll do if a child starts in me?" I said, matching her angry tone. "He'll abandon me to the wolves. That's what he'll do." I went close to her ear. "Or perhaps give me a knife to cut it out of myself."

"You think he's that bad?" Her face didn't show much concern. I wondered was she pleased I had so little sway over Magnus.

A tap on my shoulder made me turn. It was one of Magnus's men.

"You will sleep with Lord Magnus in the head man's bed," said the man. "Go now and prepare for him."

Tight-lipped, I nodded. There was no way I could dispute Magnus's wishes. Not now. That time would come. All I had to do was wait.

The night passed with Magnus's usual energetic rutting passing mercifully quickly. A few groans for me, and he assumed I was satisfied. But everything had changed between us. When he was finished, I tried to remember what he was like when we first met. He wasn't like this, all curt, brooding, his mind somewhere else. I know the prospect of imminent death distracts some men, while others it gives energy to.

***

We spoke a little in the morning before he went out to check on his horse.

"Do you expect more easy victories?" I asked. "And to gather men as you go on?"

He shook his head. "I've seen enough to know victory is never easy."

"More men will die."

He nodded.

"Will it be today?"

"Perhaps. We will be outside Dunholm by evening. Most of our men are already there, in the woods outside the city."

"The defenders will know. There'll be no surprise."

"Yes, and they'll have sent for reinforcements. But if we hit and run before they arrive, we have a chance."

"You will not hold what you capture?"

"No." He raised his hand. "Stop. You sound like one of my liege men. Leave such matters to me, Synne. You are not expected to help with military planning."

I nodded. I knew he would not take kindly to even a hint of an argument. And that was another of his failings. I'd heard a lot of talk in the taverns in Dublin about raiding. Many men thought they were masters at it. They almost all spoke about the importance of surprise and ruthlessness, the only ways to win at it, apparently, though some had other ideas, like cutting off the head of the beast, assassinating the leaders of wherever you wanted to raid.

I helped Magnus put on his mail shirt. He wore it every day recently, even though it was wearingly heavy. I knew what that meant. Any moment we could be attacked. Arrows might fly and axes come too. I was glad I didn't have to wear one though.

Always expecting the worst is not a good way to live. Though some who grow up that way get used to it.

I'd grown up wishing my father would return from raiding and fill our house with the laughter and affection we'd known before he left. Mother changed when he didn't return after that dark summer, and I knew why. She missed him. We all did. And though she didn't talk of it, and she pretended not to miss him, it was obvious she did.

I thought about what I'd feel if Magnus was lost in a raid. I'd hung so many of my hopes on him once, it would be hard to see them all finally dashed, no matter what he'd done to me. I whispered a prayer under my breath as he kissed me goodbye. He must have heard it, as he touched my cheek before he went.

The next time I saw him, he was in a rage.

22

Gytha and Ambr sat and waited. Men hovered around like flies around a dead dog, but none sat down with them. They knew what was going on. The giant who had winked at Gytha finally came over with his ale cup tight in his fist.

He reached out to Gytha. Gytha stared up at him. She thought he wanted her to bow for him, but instead he grabbed her chin and, with his other hand, he held her forehead and forced her mouth open. He wanted to see her teeth. They were a good sign of how well she'd been reared and taken care of. Rotting and missing teeth meant other illnesses could be lurking too.

Gytha didn't close her eyes. She kept her gaze fixed on his forehead, as if she had the power her mother's mother had, to curse people, bring the goddess of ruin on them. Many times, too many times, she'd wished she had that power.

A thick stench of stale sweat wafted from the giant. He stank worse even than Erik after a month in the forest.

Being pounded regularly by him would be endless torture. Her stomach tightened at the thought. When the giant reached for her breast under her tunic, Erik intervened with a hand on his arm.

"You pay up before that," he said with a leer. Behind him, Ambr was coughing and retching.

The two men went back to the other table and talked, head to head, until Gytha spied the giant's purse coming out and coins being handed over and him grinning over at her. Ambr had disappeared, clutching her stomach.

The thought of being stuck with that monster made Gytha want to vomit, too. Ambr had been clever to get away. Gytha hoped she'd run at her first chance.

The giant was coming for her. He grabbed Gytha by the arm and pulled her with him. No formalities. No talking. Just taking what was his. He wanted what he wanted and he wanted it fast.

Outside, it was dark. Spluttering torches near the doors of a few alehouses lit the path. The wind was beyond icy. Ice underfoot crunched. Winter was here. They'd missed the All Hallows festival while they were wandering in the forest. Erik had talked about wanting to be home for Christ Mass, that he hated All Hallows. She'd disliked him and his opinions, but they were connected by hard experiences, their fates seemed intertwined. Now she was with a walking nightmare and had no idea where he was taking her. Was he even a Christian?

The giant dragged her along the main street until they reached a house with a dark thatched roof half sliding off, almost reaching the ground. Two guards with spears, not axes, sat on stools outside the door. The guards had surly looks and wore pieces of wolf skins on their heads.

As Gytha heard the giant talking with one of the guards, her heart sank. They sounded like Germans. They might take her back to where she'd spent all summer escaping from. How stupid she'd been to trust Erik. She'd had many chances to cut his throat and had taken none of them. German slave traders often came downriver to buy slaves. Was that why he'd brought her here? Was this to be her fate? Had their whole summer escaping through the forest been a sham?

She'd had nightmares on many nights in the forest, always with men laughing and chasing her, dragging her back to the king.

As she was pulled towards the hall, Gytha saw a flicker of movement to the side. It was Ambr. She'd followed. That gave her hope.

Inside the hall, it was dark with only one source of light. A man was sitting at a table at the far end near a glowing brazier with red sparks coming from it. The man looked similar to the giant, although he was not as big, and his beard was longer. The giant pushed her in front of the man and they spoke in a fast, dismissive way to each other.

It was not the same German she'd learned during her captivity, but she heard enough similar words to work out what they were talking about. The giant was explaining why he'd spent so much coin on Gytha.

They planned to sell her upriver. They'd get a good price for her there. And a king he knew was looking for someone exactly like her description.

She wailed inside, then made her mind up. She could not go back. She would likely be tortured as an example to other slaves and would end up praying to die. But how could she escape? She peered into the darkness around her.

There was no one else visible in the house and the giant was paying no attention to her. Perhaps he was right not to worry about her escaping. There was no other way out of the house and with the guards at the front door, she would not get away easily.

After a lot of argument, the man who'd brought her here stood and went away without looking back. The giant pointed to a table at the other end of the hall and motioned her to go to it. It had round wicker baskets under it, similar to the type she'd seen used in many places to store food. She knew what he wanted, for her to find something for him to eat and drink and serve him.

She went where she was told. The only food was loaves of hard bread and mounds of cheese. She cut some bread and cheese for him and served it on a giant wooden platter with ale she found in a wooden cask. After she served it, she stepped back and bowed. He grunted in approval. She kept her head down. In one hand she held the knife she'd cut the bread with pressed close to her thigh. She wanted so much to use it.

Perhaps she could get close to him, smile, lean forward to kiss him and then cut his throat, fast. But as the moment to do it came quick, her courage deserted her and her hand trembled.

She had practised the slicing motion when she was preparing the food. It had seemed so easy to do but now the moment was here she could not. Would he die quickly? Would the guards hear him dying? Would they impale her with their spears?

As she stepped back, she realised she had to do something fast. If she didn't do something now, she might never get another chance.

The giant looked at her, his eyes narrowing. He held his ale horn up and grinned. She walked forward to take the horn from him. The knife lay hot, almost burning, in her left hand. She held out her right to take the horn. He looked at her suspiciously. Could he hear her heart beating, guess her thoughts?

A squealing noise shattered every expectation pressing on her.

Someone had come. She turned quickly. One of the guards was pushing Ambr in front of him. She was squealing as if she'd been stuck with a spear, but when she saw the giant, her expression changed. She smiled and winked at him and as she came up the room, she swayed flirtatiously.

Gytha's mouth opened in amazement. Was this the real Ambr they were seeing or was this a show?

The giant grinned, waved at Gytha to come to him. Gytha knew at once what this meant. He wanted to enjoy both of them together.

23

I was at the back of our marching line, riding slowly, when we encountered the Normans. Magnus was in the middle. He'd allocated a horse to Yann and Tate after two days of my badgering. We were on a narrow path through a dense black pine forest and had recently crossed a rocky stream bed. The Normans were hiding in the trees as we came to the bottom of a low hill. The first I knew of the attack was the shrieks and the bellows from some of our horses as arrows plunged into them. This was followed by shouts and groans from some of our men.

I've seen many men survive arrows, but that day some of ours at the front received four or five and looked like practice dummies before they fell over. Magnus shouted orders as his men fell.

The following moments were frantic. My heart jumped into my throat. I feared that any moment would be my last. The Normans hadn't even broken cover and our men were whirling on stricken horses and crashing into the woods on each side of the muddy path.

Yann and Tate were beside me.

"Into the woods," shouted Yann. "We can escape south."

I followed them into the woods, urging my mount after them. I had no intention of leaving Magnus until I knew his fate. He'd treated me badly, time and again, but we were connected, our fates wrapped tight together. His appearance again in my life that autumn showed that clearly. How can it be that a man who should be at the other end of England appears at the right time to save you, unless your fates are entwined?

I grabbed Tate's arm as we passed close, our horses touching. "Flee. I am staying with Magnus."

"And if he's killed?" said Tate, leaning to my side, her gaze on the now-empty path except for three horses stuck with arrows, two half-down and writhing. Two men were also on the ground, groaning.

"If he's dead, I'll come after you."

"We'll stay with you if you don't come," said Yann, his breathing fast as his horse turned, and he scanned the path behind us.

"The Normans are coming," he hissed, pointing at the woods on the other side of the path. Steel helmets glistened through dark branches as Normans came towards us. We had moments before they were on us.

"We have to go," hissed Tate.

"Go," I hissed at Yann, who was staring at me. "Save my sister and yourself."

Tate pulled at his arm. He blinked, looked distraught, and then they were gone and I was alone, and it began raining. A heavy downpour too, as if the gods were weeping.

Fighting in pouring rain changes everything. Men who thought they should win a skirmish could lose their confidence.

Anything could happen.

I leaned down and whispered to my horse. The Normans broke out of the tree line opposite.

There were twenty of them, at least. Our men, Magnus among them, were in the woods to each side. I could see one or two of them, near me, that was all. The Norman leader, a bear of a man, came charging towards us on his horse, his heavy sword up, ready to cut off the head of the first man who stood up to him. I held my breath, the suddenness of it all overwhelming.

Spears whistled from our side as the Normans closed on us. Two of their number fell.

My breath spluttered in my throat. Two Normans on horses had seen me. One, wearing a dented iron helmet, pointed at me, let out a shout, and came towards me.

I knew what was coming. With no one to protect me, I might be dead before night.

If they caught me.

I kicked my horse, broke back onto the path, and headed down the hill, kicking my horse into a canter first on the rough swerving path. I glanced back, just about able to keep control of my horse as I did. One Norman was coming after me. I kicked my horse again, wondered if I'd see Tate and Yann ahead, but I didn't. The path was empty. They must have found a way into the woods. I remembered there was a deep stream coming up. I kicked my horse to go faster and bent down along its neck as we rode towards it. With luck, the Norman didn't know what was coming. Hopefully, I would get across it quicker.

I urged my horse to cross the stream fast, which it did, but it lost its footing and slowed on the rough ground beyond. I turned. My pursuer was coming. He was closer than I'd realised. What had happened to the other Normans I had no idea, but I was grateful.

I watched him coming. I'd been chanting in my mind the spell the seer at Tara had given me.

My horse was snorting, breathing fast, shaking, as I was. It was almost blown from the race to the stream. He was a better horseman than me. I would not outride him. I slipped down from my horse.

I could run into the woods, hide.

The pursuing rider was in the middle of the stream. He was nodding his head, his iron helmet glistening. He'd sheathed his sword so he could ride fast, controlling his horse with two hands. I looked beyond him. He was definitely alone. He urged his horse to move on, but then it stumbled and he was almost thrown, slipping down to one side. I had my chance. I pulled the dagger Magnus had given me from its sheath and ran for him, my daring surprising me.

But you cannot hesitate when you have an opening. You may never get one again.

The man put his hand up to ward me off. He'd been almost sitting upright, but he slipped to the side again because of that. I had to be quick. If he got to his feet, I'd have no chance. I avoided his hand and came at him from behind, yanking hard at his cloak to unseat him as I'd seen others do on the battlefield.

And without hesitation, I jabbed fast and hard with my dagger point into the exposed pale flesh at the side of his neck as he slipped slowly down. He needed only moments to right himself. My blade went in so easy, breaking the skin like cutting into an apple. My dagger was almost pulled out of my hand by him falling, making my cut into his neck wider, like a red mouth opening.

His scream turned into a wild death cry and his hand found my thigh to push me away, and then he slumped down, slowly, heading for the water. Blood was pouring from his neck.

A shout echoed from the path we'd just come down. Magnus was coming towards us, his steed moving fast. He was leaning down, getting ready to dismount in case I needed him.

I didn't.

I hadn't killed a man since London, but this felt good and right. Some recompense for the difficulties the Normans had put me through. I knew too, deep inside, that it was either me or the Norman, and that if it was him, my death might not have been as quick as his.

Magnus jumped down from his horse as the Norman finally fell face forward into the stream, the thud of his skull hitting a rock echoing into the trees.

"You haven't lost your skill with a dagger," said Magnus.

He stared at my hands. I lifted them. They were bloody and shaking violently as if I had no control over them.

I put them in the water, then raised them high, made tight fists of them, but still they shook. Tears welled inside me, but I would not release them. I snorted instead, over and over, as if something bad was releasing inside me.

Magnus pulled my arms down.

"You didn't need me to save you, did you?" he asked.

I didn't reply. Some of his men had appeared on the path.

The Power of Synne

"We won, my lord," one man shouted. "I'll add this one to your tally."

A cheer went up as his men gathered around. I could not tell them who had killed this man. They would not believe me anyway. They needed to see me as a weak woman, needing protection. Even the blood on me would not convince them.

After all I'd been through since returning to England, I knew now I had real power. Power a woman was not supposed to have. I was protected by the slip of fate that made the strong vulnerable. The chant had worked. Women are not expected to be powerful, to take their chances, but I had, and I felt something strong and powerful coursing through me.

It reminded me of something my mother had said. How a healer could take lives as well as save them. But it was a power I'd never expected to feel.

I could kill without hesitation.

24

Gytha waited as the giant mounted Ambr. The other man had been waved away.

The giant turned and waved Gytha closer. He had no fear. His lust controlled him. Gytha glanced around. The guard was gone. She smiled, made her face look as if she wanted to join in. Her hand with the knife was pressed flat into her thigh. She moved her other hand. Surely he'd notice something was wrong, and cry out? Blood pounded in her ears. Desperate to distract him, she leaned her face far forward as if she wanted to kiss him, then pushed her tongue out seductively. His face rose to her, his neck extended.

The blade slid fast across his neck like a hot knife across hard butter. Blood spurted towards her in a red fountain. Gytha felt for a moment that she had seen all this before, but she hadn't. Ambr was splattered with the blood too. Gytha got her share. The giant rose and shook like a dying bear, tried to shout, but only a gurgle came out. The light died in his eyes a moment later and his arms flailed for a few moments until he flopped to the floor with a thud like a sack of wheat falling over.

Ambr slid like an eel from beneath him as he went down. She groaned disgust at it all and scrambled to a waterskin nearby and poured the contents over herself. She was naked. The blood mixed with water glistened on her as if she was a wild animal in its birth throes.

She stood up straight, grinned, and raised her fists. She was happy at what Gytha had done.

Gytha was worried someone had heard him hit the ground. She kept looking at the door.

It was time to leave. They had to find a boat.

They covered the giant in a wolf skin to make it look as if he was sleeping, if a guard looked in. Then they found their tunics and wrapped themselves in a wolf skin cloak each. They found them at the back of the hall in a pile. But they found no coins after a quick search and did not want to stay longer to look. The back corner of the house had a hole near the ground, but it was too small and would take too long for them to make it any bigger.

Ambr pointed at the hole in the roof where the smoke from the fire drifted out. Gytha went to some leather belts on a bench nearby. They tied a few of the thick ones together. Gytha's hands were fumbling. She was jumping inside her skin at every rustle or noise. Images of what his men would do if they found the giant's body filled her with dread. They had to move fast.

She raised Ambr up as if she was a feather. Ambr reached high and pulled herself through the roof hole, holding the central beam. She had attached some belts together. She hooked them around the thick, blackened beam. Gytha pulled herself up. At one sick moment she heard a creak, as if the beam might break, but Ambr reached down and helped pull Gytha up the last part of the way until she could latch her arm around the beam.

Then she was up.

The icy cold outside tickled like cold fingers at her face. She forced herself not to groan, to lie flat on the cold thatch roof and shimmy towards the back of the hall. Voices echoed from the front. One man was laughing. Another joined him. Their voices were clear in the cold air, as if they were close enough to touch.

The ripe smell of the thatch filled her nostrils and the wind seemed like a beast at her back. This moment would shape their lives. She had shed blood wilfully. She remembered then what her mother had said and wondered if either of her sisters had shed blood too, if the prediction their mother had made about what would happen if the three sisters were blood-soaked. No, there was no way Synne would kill anyone.

In her mind, Gytha said a prayer to the Queen of Heaven and to the fates that twist all our lives, hoping the men would not discover the blood-soaked body until the morning.

Wishful thinking.

As they lowered themselves down at the back of the building, straight into a stream, muffled shouts came from inside it.

Gytha's mind raced. What would they do? She hissed at Ambr, who dropped into the dirty water beside Gytha and moved away like a frightened cat. A moment later, Gytha went after her. It was dark and cold and the water stank, but the stream led to the harbour and that was where they had to go. They might catch Erik before he got away with the coin he'd sold them for. They needed coin to escape. If he was alone, they had a chance if they struck first and hard. He would not be expecting violence from them. It was a risky plan, but Gytha really wanted to see his face when he realised they'd escaped. And she wanted the coin he'd sold them for.

She was to cut his throat too for betraying her. Such betrayals had to be avenged. She could have killed him before, but he didn't deserve it. Now there was no question about it. It had to be done and not just for revenge. He could come searching for them. Better to finish things with him. She slapped Ambr's shoulder.

"We'll find Erik," she hissed. She went towards an alley on the right leading away from the stream. The wind here was colder if anything, but she was warm inside from all the madness they'd just been through. And from the thought of finding Erik.

"He'll be at an alehouse spending coin," said Ambr.

Gytha remembered where the alehouses were, on the path leading up from the harbour.

Only two were still open when they walked up the path. Gytha was nervous. She'd heard shouts in the distance. A hunt might have started for them already. They had to find Erik quickly. By the morning, every alehouse might have been warned about them.

At the door of the first alehouse, a thin man with an axe in his belt looked them up and down.

"No need for more girls here," he said with a surly tone, as they went to push past him.

"We're looking for a friend named Erik," Gytha said. The man shrugged. "He has red hair." He lifted his hand to bar their way.

"Try somewhere else. Your friend's not here." He seemed very sure of himself.

They walked on. The next alehouse didn't have a doorman. Inside, it was quiet. A woman appeared from the darkness as they stepped in. She had a dagger in her belt.

"Name Erik?" she said, when Gytha told her who they were looking for. "He's not here." Her tone made her think she knew someone called Erik.

"You saw him?"

"An Erik got into a fight with one of my girls last night. I kicked him out. Try up the street." She pointed with her thumb.

"Does that sound like the Erik you're looking for?" she asked.

Gytha smiled. They went to the next alehouse. It was almost in darkness. Only the red glow of a fading fire could be seen through a crack beneath the locked main door.

"We go in?" asked Ambr.

"Yes." Gytha pushed at the door. It was barred. She put her hand on it. It felt a little warmer than the air. The candles had not been out for long.

She knocked lightly. There was often someone awake on an alehouse floor who would come to a door just to see who it was knocking so late.

No one came. She shivered, knocked again, louder. A scuffling sounded and a woman's voice called out from the other side of the door.

"Go away. We're not open."

"I need to find someone, tonight," said Gytha. No one replied. It seemed as if they weren't going to get in.

She knocked again, louder.

And again.

And again. Until finally the voice spoke again. "If you keep disturbing us, you'll get the taste of a blade."

"Is Erik the boat builder there?" Ambr said angrily. "Tell him Ambr is here."

That would wake him up.

The cold had taken the edge of Gytha's anger by this time, but it wasn't gone and must have been etched on her face as Ambr looked at her and raised her fist in support.

Gytha knocked again. A shout came from inside the tavern. She recognised Erik's voice. Someone had found him and roused him.

She stood to the side and flattened herself against the wet sod wall of the alehouse. Ambr stepped back and waited in front of the door. She looked pensive.

A few moments later, the door creaked open and Erik guffawed.

"What in the god's names are you doing here?" he said in a dismissive tone, drunk tone.

"I need your help, Erik," said Ambr. She had her most alluring smile on.

Erik fell for it.

"Come in."

But Ambr beckoned him to come out. She pulled her wolf skin off her shoulder and shoved her tunic aside so her bare skin became visible.

He stepped forward as if she'd snagged him with a hook. In his hand was a dagger pointed towards Ambr's heart.

"You're supposed to be looking after your master," he said. His words were slurred.

Gytha raised her blade. She smashed the round end of the handle into the back of his head. No hesitation. The way it should be done. No thinking about it. She'd learnt that. She had to make sure he wouldn't get a chance to swing his knife at either of them.

He went down hard, smashing his face into a thick slick of mud.

Gytha smiled. He deserved that.

Ambr was on him in a moment, looking for the purse on his belt.

Gytha bent down, felt along his belt too. Men often attach a pouch, like a second purse inside their belt. Ambr looked at her. Her face said enough. She'd found nothing. Gytha kept looking, a feeling of panic coming over her.

Had she risked attacking him for nothing? Then she felt it. A lump lodged between his belt and his stomach. She pulled it out.

The purse had a finger of silver coins in it. Her heart leapt. This would be enough to buy them passage almost anywhere, but now they had to move Erik's body. He wasn't dead yet, but he would not be coming around soon. Should they finish him off?

She looked at Ambr, raised her knife. Ambr shook her head. Gytha nodded. It would take a hard heart to cut a man's throat when he was out. She wondered if she'd regret this moment. She opened her mouth, closed it, the desire for revenge pulling her one way and memories of him pulling her another. Then she remembered her mother's admonitions to not be cruel to her sisters, just because she was the oldest.

Ambr held her hand out to her as if she understood the dilemma. When Gytha took the hand, Ambr pulled her up and away from Erik. She hesitated for only a moment, then rose. She had to trust Ambr. Now was not the time to break their bond.

Ambr cooed as she looked inside Erik's purse. Then, with a wide and warm smile, she passed it back to Gytha.

It was a real struggle to drag Erik's body around the side of the alehouse, but they had to move him, and eventually, with stops and starts, they'd moved it out of sight. He would be found in the morning, but not by anyone passing. He was still alive and breathing, but as softly as a sleeping cat. Gytha stood over him as they curled him under the overhang of the thatched roof, a place where drunks slept things off.

Thoughts returned about cutting his neck wide open and watching him die. Her urge to kill him was undeniable, after all he'd done, his terrible betrayal, but she resisted. She would leave it to the Fates to decide what would happen to him. The decision felt right.

Gytha stood. "We have to find a boat. We can pay for our passage now."

They arrived at the harbour as the rain started. Dawn had not arrived. A thin crescent moon barely lit their path. A glimmer of candles from fishing vessels at the end of the wooden quay showed where some were getting ready to set sail.

The first fishing vessel had one old man coiling ropes in the dim light from a candle. He laughed when Gytha asked did he take passengers. They went to the next boat. A man who was working on a net on the long deck also laughed when she asked for passage. He raised his hand and pointed at them.

"You runaways?" He put his head to one side and grinned. Gytha could almost see silver coins in his eyes as he spoke.

She shook her head. "We are free women, searching for our husbands."

He looked them up and down. "We take no passengers," he said after a few moments.

The third fishing boat was the same story. The last had no one on board.

They walked back along the quay, their heads down, the rain picking up as if to tell them they had no hope. The pouch of silver would be of no use to them if they could not spend it.

As they reached the end of the quay, two women appeared walking towards them. One had a coil of rope on her arm. She held it high to part cover her head. The other, a smaller woman, had her head down as if she was examining the wooden boards in front of her.

They are here to deliver rope, thought Gytha.

"Morning," she said as the two women passed. They didn't reply. As Gytha and Ambr headed up the slope towards the alehouses, they would almost have to pass where Erik was lying, she turned her head. What she saw made her stop.

The two women who had just passed her were going on board the last fishing vessel.

"Wait," she called out to Ambr. "We didn't ask them."

"They are servants," said Ambr. "No woman owns a fishing vessel."

Gytha was not so sure about that. She'd seen two vessels with all-women crews in England. Someone had explained that was usually because their husbands had been called off to war and had died. So many men had died at Hastings and in previous battles, women were forced to do things that menfolk usually did, especially if they needed food and it was usually provided by a husband's work.

"We have to go back," she said.

Ambr followed her, grumbling all the way about the rain, wasting time, dawn coming, and telling Gytha that she would kill herself first before being taken to face charges of killing the giant and almost killing Erik the boatbuilder.

They arrived at the final fishing vessel as one of the women was untying the rope attaching the ship to the quay.

"Can we pay for passage out of here?" asked Ambr.

The woman kept going without reply, didn't even look at them, but the other woman moved closer. She had a green streak in her hair. The rain made her look like a sea creature.

"How much you runaways got?" she asked.

"Whatever you need," said Gytha.

"Show," said the woman.

Gytha pulled out the purse and showed her the silver coin. As soon as she did, she realised her mistake. This was all happening too fast.

"Throw the purse here," said the woman.

"Where will you take us?"

"England, that sounds like where you're from, yes?" Her face was as hard as the stone path that led up to the town.

"Will you take us to York?"

The woman bent over and laughed.

"We take you to London. You can find your ways from there, I'm sure."

Gytha hesitated. The purse was all the coin they had. She should have hidden some. She felt stupid and desperate. Did she have a choice?

"Give," said Ambr with her hand out. She was looking back towards the town. Gytha knew what that meant. Trouble.

"We'll help with the fishing and get some fish when we leave you, yes?" she asked, trying to extract something extra from the bargain.

The woman pointed back towards the town.

"Maybe we leave you here so you see what happens to runaways. It's not funny. The men here love to make women pay for stepping out of line." She held her hand out.

"You won't turn us in?" said Gytha.

The woman shook her head. Gytha nodded, then jumped across into the ship. She passed the purse to the woman with the green in her hair. Ambr was beside her a moment later.

"Go to the back. Hide under the boards, quick," said green hair.

The boards at the back, laid from side to side, allowed someone to stand on them and repel boarders, climb a dock at low tide, and also act as somewhere for cargo to be stored or for people to shelter.

They pushed in among tightly wrapped bales. The stink from the bales was like a pile of dead animals.

"Beaver," said Ambr, sniffing hard. She pushed her back up against the bales.

This was why they were going to London, Gytha realised. They weren't fishing. They were fur traders. Perhaps the fishing was a cover, so they didn't have to pay duties.

As they slipped away from the dock along with the other fishing boats as the tide turned, they heard shouts echo from the town. Ambr smiled as the shouts faded and they headed into a grey haze off to the west.

The two women kept well away from them, busying themselves rowing at first, then raising a square sail on the single mast. The sail flapped, but did not fill.

Gytha looked around when Ambr pulled urgently at her sleeve. A long ship was being rowed from the harbour straight towards them. Behind it, the sun was rising.

25

The road to Dunholm passed through a series of wooded vales. In every one of them, we met villagers who cheered us and gave us hard bread and aleskins when they saw we weren't Norman. Magnus treated me differently now, warily. We both rode together in the middle of our line. I knew he'd seen me kill before, but what I'd done this time was different. I could have run, avoided it, but I didn't. In London, I'd had no choice. I'd killed this time because I wanted to.

Tate and Yann appeared soon after we set out. They'd been watching what had happened from afar. I was relieved when I saw them, but felt guilty too about what I'd dragged them into. And also about the deaths I'd caused. I told Magnus how I felt.

"To take a life when you don't have to requires guts," Magnus said, staring at me. I knew what he meant. But guilt still twisted at my stomach like bad ale. I could have just injured that man. I saw dead faces in my dreams now, too. And every morning before I opened my eyes, I thought about what I'd done and I prayed for that man, whose name I did not know.

Magus spoke about other things as we rode. "You will do what I say at the next skirmish," was something he repeated, more forcefully each time. I nodded but said nothing. The third time he said it, he reached across and held my upper arm tight.

I tried to shrug him away, but he would not release me.

"I am not your slave, brave Magnus," I said.

"You were lucky with that man. First cut lucky. It's unlikely to happen again. I do not want to bury you, Synne."

"Have no fear for me," I said, a sharpness to my tone that surprised even me.

He laughed. "You're getting your bloodlust," he said. He grinned.

I knew what he meant. Sometimes I wondered if there could be a different way, where we didn't have to fight or watch others fight for us, but everything seemed to be shaped by violence and death. And if it was my turn to inflict it, so be it.

An ache filled my heart that day, a deep and relentless desire to see Gytha, to have her see how much I'd changed, and to talk to her about what had happened. I do not know where this urge came from, but it felt as if I had a limb missing, her not being with us. Finding Tate and being with her had made it clear to me that I must find Gytha. She was the one I'd shared my real problems with. She was the one who listened. That ache for her inside me was like the one you get after carrying water every day. But this was in my mind, not in my arms.

"You can leave us, you and your sister," said Magnus, that night as we lay in the tent listening to rain beating off the leather, soaking through so that it was wet if you touched it, close together to stay warm after he'd satisfied himself inside me.

"I might," I said. I was still angry at him.

"You may be pregnant," said Magnus.

"I am not pregnant. I take herbs. A baby will happen only if I want it to come. Only then," I said forcefully. I needed to believe it too. The herbs could work but not always.

What would I do if I left him? I could not go back to Dublin now. My road led forward. I needed to find Gytha. I had to find her. I was as sure of that as anything I'd ever been sure of.

I didn't tell him about the dream that kept coming back. I didn't tell anyone about that. I knew that seeing a lord or a king in a dream can be a good thing, but the dream was bloody and ugly. I could not speak of it.

The Power of Synne

The next day we came to a wooded ridge. Streams of smoke rose high in the grey sky beyond it.

"Dunholm," said Magnus, pointing at the smoke.

I shivered, didn't reply. It felt as if I was watching myself all that day. As if I knew something was coming for me, for us, something the smoke signified, like a rune mark on a door.

"Are there Normans there?" I asked.

"They are everywhere here," he replied. "We'll shelter at a village outside the town before we test them."

He was more cautious than I'd remembered him. I'd asked him again about what had happened down south, but he still told me almost nothing, except that he'd been sent up here by his mother to see if the north could be woken.

I knew from his sullen face when I asked him about the south that the campaign down there had not gone well.

He needed a change in his fortunes. If all his family could spare to raise the north was him and this small band of raiders, things were going badly for them.

They would need a true run of good fortune to turn things around.

It was early evening when we arrived at a defendable village, a place of stout wicker walls and closed and spiked gates, defended by a few men with axes and little else.

The guards at the wicker gate, like all the other village guards we'd met, cheered and clapped our horses' necks and the woollen breaches that clad our legs.

Our horses were taken from us to be fed and watered. Almost all of our men, except for the two who watched our horses, we were seventeen companions at that point, were escorted to the long hall of the village, where we were shown to seats in a half-empty hall. Thankfully, there was a fire going. For that, I was grateful.

We'd had a mild winter the year before, but this one was colder than I remembered only a few weeks after Christ Mass. What a Christ Mass we'd been through with barely enough to eat, never mind celebrate anything.

We sat and waited for the villagers to join us. A crackling brazier piled high with pine wood was set beside us and ale provided, though it was weak.

Voices came to us from outside the hall. It seemed there was an argument going on. Magnus, who sat close beside me, didn't comment on it. I expect he was used to causing dissension whenever his war band stopped at a village.

Who can blame people who just want an easy life, not to have to stick their necks out for a lord?

I put down the mug of ale and whispered to Magnus.

"What do you tell everyone you're fighting for?" I asked.

The Power of Synne

He spoke slowly when he replied. "It is a good thing to fight and root out these invaders."

"But your family were invaders in the past, no?"

He became angry then, as if he thought I should know what was obvious to him. "I seek revenge for the death of my father too, and for my uncles and many others."

"Most people in this land do not care about your wish for revenge."

"Perhaps, but the Normans have inflicted wrongs on many. They want to take everything, to own everything, even our women," said Magnus. "That is what most people here understand. The Normans want every daughter, every house, every farm, every meadow and byre, to say they own it all. Then they will give it to their supporters, and any man who tries to stop them will be put to the sword. Wait and see."

He banged the table. "And worse than that is to come, from what we know of how they rule. They will tie all men to the land for generations, sons after sons and on for ever, and require them to ask permission to leave their home for any reason." He shook his head. "We must fight them. That is what I tell our followers."

Yann had slid along the bench to come close to Magnus.

"What plots are you coming up with?" he asked Magnus.

Magnus gave a thin smile. "No plots," he said.

"I must go and see to the hounds," said Yann, looking at me. "Keep some broth for me."

He stood and was gone a moment later. Tate slid along to where he'd been sitting. She waved in his direction, but after looking up, I saw she was calling a serving girl to us, who was carrying a steaming blackened pot.

She put it on our table. It was filled with broth. She filled one for Magnus.

I took two bowls. One for Yann. Tate, as usual, looked after herself well.

Villagers arrived then to fill the hall and share in the pots of broth. Every seat was taken soon after and while we ate, we listened to a piper playing a plaintiff tune.

It was after more ale arrived that I realised that Yann had been gone a long time and I stood. "I'm going to see where Yann is," I said.

"Sit," said Magnus. "I'll send someone."

He waved one of his personal guards to us and whispered in his ear. The man nodded, touched the hand axe hanging from his belt, and disappeared among the tables.

Storytelling followed, but I was still uneasy. It was all good humour around us. But what had happened to the loud dissension we'd heard earlier? And why did the top

The Power of Synne

table have eager youths at it, not elders as you'd expect at a large village gathering?

The crowd had thinned too.

It wasn't until a horn blew that I guessed what was happening.

The sound cut through the hall like an axe through a neck. Our party was about fifteen strong at that point. Two of these had gone to look after our horses, two others were scouting ahead watching for Normans.

A small man, half my height, near the entrance, blew the horn. The noise made everyone in the hall stop what they were doing. Some men raised their fists. Magnus and his men came to their feet slowly, stumbling. They still had their weapons. Swords came out and axes came into hands and we stared, dumbstruck, as a double row of Normans in dull mail shirts and helmets came filing into the hall.

They had their axes resting in their hands and did not seem intent on an immediate attack. From the back, a man in a shiny mail shirt and wearing a striking black helmet approached us as his men lined up on each side of the hall. Beside him walked a boy, perhaps ten years old. The boy's eyes were wide, his hands clasping and unclasping.

Magnus had his right hand up high, his palm open, in a signal to his men not to start fighting. The man in the black mail shirt came towards us. He had a sullen expression on his face.

"Are all you men loyal followers of King William?" he shouted in a rough Norman accent, as he came near, looking along our line of men.

Magnus waved the man to come closer, bending forward as if he didn't hear him. As he bent, he held his sword out, the blade flat on his hands.

"We are in your debt, brave Norman," he said. "What can we do for you?"

The Norman came to Magnus and poked him in his leather-clad shoulder with his stubby finger.

"Are you the band of thieves who waylaid my brother out on patrol?"

"I've not heard about such an incident, my lord," said Magnus, his head up now. "Tell me more. What have these thieves done?"

"You are a liar," said the knight. He reached for Magnus's sword.

Magnus swirled the sword out of his reach, as if he was practiced in this feigned handover trick. He stepped forward and a moment later he had the sword point at the Norman's neck.

"Tell your men to put down their weapons or you'll be breathing through your neck in a moment."

The man growled, then dropped his sword and cried out, "Wait for me outside, men."

The Power of Synne

It wasn't what Magnus had asked for, but the effect was immediate and perhaps better than them putting their weapons down.

I stood beside Magnus.

"How did you find us?" I asked the Norman.

"We have spies everywhere," he said with a Norman sniff that meant the man had a high esteem for himself and none for us.

"Take your sword from my neck, sir." He pointed at the table we'd been sitting at. "May I sit and try some of the ale?" He was calm for someone who might soon die.

Magnus slid his own sword back into its mottled leather scabbard. He pointed at the bench.

"Join us, Norman. There is no need for any of us to die tonight."

"Your men look ready to run," said the Norman, as he sat.

"Yours look tired and worn out, which makes me glad," said Magnus. "They can all submit before I string their worn-out guts around this hall."

"You'll be lucky," the Norman scoffed.

"I am lucky."

Magnus was clearly used to this banter, but my heart was racing. We had this in our power, but there were a lot of Normans outside. Our chances of escape were thin. Was there a way we could escape our fate?

"Did you come from Dunholm?" I asked him.

The Norman looked at me as if I was a slug that had just been pointed out to him.

"Who is this?" he asked, squinting.

"A healer who travels with us," said Magnus.

"Your woman?"

"Not mine, not anyone's. She heals for pay."

I was taken aback by Magnus's willingness to disown me. Was he saying this to save me if he and his men were killed tonight? His face was stony. It felt like a betrayal, but was it?

The Norman laughed. "I heard they have women healers in the north," he said. "Perhaps she can help me before we get to other matters."

I could not stop my distaste. My face twisted with repulsion at the idea of helping him. A fight to the death might be imminent, but this man wanted me to assess him for a cure?

"Don't look so shocked, healer. Come here. Look at my leg."

Before I could object, he raised his knee onto the bench and rolled up his muddy brown breeches above one leather boot.

A scab, about the size of a pigeon's head, oozed pus below his knee. Parts of it were yellow. How he walked with it I did not know. Strangely, the sight of it made me want to laugh. The man was in pain and because of that, I was valuable to him.

"I can save your life," I said. "Because you will die within a few weeks if this is not treated. I see the blood sickness has started in you already."

"Make no predictions. Just stop the pain," he said. He straightened, turned to Magnus. "You see, I have nothing to fear from your sword. I am dying anyway. You can cut my throat any time you like. You will likely do me a service."

A noise made me look around. I wasn't sure when it had happened, but all the villagers in the hall were gone. There was only us and the Norman and our men left at our table.

I sniffed. Was that a burning smell?

Magnus had his dagger out. "You may be willing to die but are you willing to have your eyeballs pushed down your throat until you gag?"

The man laughed. "Hold your blade still, sir. If you do not release me, all your men, and all those who we captured on the way here, your scouts, the men looking after your horses, the man who looks after your dogs, they will all be burnt to death as well as everyone here." He laughed. "You will put down your weapons and I will lead you outside before this hall burns to the ground." He put his arms out wide. "That is what you will all do. And accept your fate. You have no choice."

Anger and dismay filled me. I looked at Magnus. His mouth was open. He looked baffled by what had happened.

I raised my fist. "Let's watch him die first," I said.

Magnus nodded.

26

The sun was well up by the time the pursuing ship caught up with us. There would be no arguing with the men on board, either. Gytha stared at them as the ship came closer. One blessing, at least, was that Erik was not among them. His cruelty at this moment would be hard to bear. A trip back to Germania, probably in chains this time, would mean a fate worse than death for Gytha.

She should have cut his throat when she had the chance.

Shouts echoed between the two ships in a language she did not understand as they came close together.

"They only want the two of you," said the woman who captained their vessel. Then she smiled. "I've asked them what they will pay for you. I told them you have cost us money already, and that we must be compensated." She looked over Gytha's shoulder. A row of other fishing vessels, they must have been from other ports, were sitting in the water not far away, their sails down, riding the swells.

Gytha hadn't noticed them before, being focused on the ships pursuing.

Shouts came from that other ship. They must have noticed we were heading towards the group of fishing vessels. And that one of these vessels had shields all along its side facing them. It was protecting the fishing fleet. And its large sail was going up. And then it was swinging in their direction as oars had appeared and then it was moving fast through the water towards them.

They were a half league apart but the pursuing vessel turned away. All eyes were now on the ship that had forced their pursuers to abandon their hunt. Gytha felt a wave of relief, but not for long, as the new vessel with the shields along its sides bore down on them.

"Say nothing," was Ambr's advice as the other ship came alongside.

Gytha was scanning the faces to see who they were. They looked mostly English faces, perhaps a mix of English and Danes, but the most striking thing was that there appeared to be more women than men on the ship. And the women bore axes on their shoulders as if they weren't afraid to use them.

Their captain pointed at Gytha and Ambr as the two ships came close together in the swells. Gytha stood up straight, ready for whatever was to come. Whatever happened, it was better to be back in the hands of English people than to be going once more to the slave huts of Germania.

They were waved forward by two burly looking women who motioned them to jump into the other ship despite the swells pulling them apart every few moments. When Ambr shook her head, a rope was thrown to them and one of the burly women jumped into their ship as if it was no big deal. She tied the rope around Ambr and walked her to the side where the two ships met. She almost threw Ambr over to the other ship as they rose together with a swell.

Gytha did not need help.

She was wondering what these people would do with them. Would they demand payment, seek to sell them as slaves, make them work? That would be the best outcome, to work for them and get to some port in England.

What happened next was unexpected.

As soon as they were both across, they were seized and bound, their ankles tied tight and their arms tied behind their back. They were left like this, back to back.

"We are free women. You cannot just rope us up," shouted Gytha as they were pushed into the bottom of the boat and a young man was set to watching them. No one replied to her. She stopped asking as she saw they were heading back east to England.

She'd almost forgotten about their hurried departure from London. Had their descriptions been circulated along the coast and a reward offered for their recapture? That was how many slaves were returned to their masters for punishment.

***

With a sinking, dread feeling, she watched, wet and tired two days later, as the wooden palisade wall of London and its long bridge, still scarred with burn marks, came slowly into view. They were pushed ashore near the same dock they had left from, though the queen's ship was no longer tied up there.

It was a rainy grey mid-December day when they were taken to Westminster Hall, which was now surrounded by leather tents on the landward side and by a row of long ships at a wharf in the mud on the riverside, as if the Normans were expecting London to be attacked at any moment.

"Why are we here?" she asked the guards who pushed them towards the main door.

No answer came.

They were taken inside the hall and a messenger ran off after they arrived. She did not hear the exchange that sent him away, but soon after, a tall man with a strict Norman haircut, shaved high at the back, came to see them. He had a similarly tall guard with him, who had two axes hanging from his belt and multiple scars on his face.

The first man pointed at Gytha. "Take this one below," he said. Then he walked off.

Gytha's dread tightened inside her. They were surrounded by Normans.

Gytha was taken tightly by the arm and pushed down some stairs, along a corridor, and into a room with only a high narrow slit for sunlight and disturbingly, a selection of evil-looking weapons on a long table.

She was manhandled roughly and tied to a wooden pillar with her hands behind her back. A yellow candle provided a little light, enough for her to see the many bloodstains on the earth floor. They looked as if they were laid on top of each other with different shades from different times.

The man who'd brought her here sat down on a stool after tying her up and set about sharpening the weapons. First a dagger, then a sword, then a thinner dagger, then an axe. All of this was probably meant to frighten her. It succeeded. He acted as if he didn't even hear her when she asked to be released, for water, or to pee. Eventually she let it flow hot down her leg, and her shame mixed with her fear to make her tremble, softly at first, then more, until the man turned to watch her with a hint of a smile.

She bit her lip and braced herself to stop her weakness entertaining him.

As the room darkened and the day ended, the man finished with his sharpening and began moving his weapons around on the table, lining them up as if getting ready for someone to come.

She was cold, hungry, and scared when the door finally opened and a young monk in a clean black habit walked in. His skin was sallow and pockmarked.

The monk approached her and smiled thinly.

"Tell us everything about your sisters and we may release you, Gytha, my child. But hold anything back and I will return here tomorrow to see if you are still alive after my friend uses his tools on you." He licked his lips, as if he might enjoy it if she suffered.

His accent was Norman, but there was a hint of something else, too.

Gytha tried to put a brave face on it. "Who are you, Father?" she said softly.

"I was sent by the pope to root out the heresy that pushed deep into these lands before our brave King William took them under his cloak of protection. I am Bishop Rutilus, defender of the faith."

Gytha stared at him. He was very young to be a bishop.

"Come on, Gytha, talk. I don't have all night. I must be at vespers soon. Tell me everything."

Gytha started with the easy stuff. How she'd grown up with her sisters and how their father had left them and how she'd been captured by slavers. At that point, he stopped her.

"I want to know about the heresy your mother and your sister Synne practised. Tell me more about the powers they claim," he said. As he came closer, he pointed at her with a thin finger. "The devil is well known to sneak into women's hearts and force them to do wicked things in his name. We know this. We only need your confirmation of this."

Again, he smiled.

She hated him and she hated herself too in that moment. Fear came clutching at her throat and moving inside her like an animal, restless, telling her to do what she was asked to do, and quickly too. Fear was in control. This man was one of those who would do anything to get their way. She could smell it from him. She could not stand against him.

The torturer, as that was what he surely was, stood behind the bishop with a dagger in his hand, running a whetstone along its edge so the blade sang. It was a noise she would not easily forget.

Gytha shook her head. It was a small shake, as if she didn't want to say no, but had to; something compelled her.

"No, no, my mother was not a witch. She was not a heretic. None of us are," she said, soft at first, then loudly, her legs shaking as she spoke, something inside telling her to be quiet, just give them what they want.

"That is not what your sister, the one called Synne, says." The bishop laughed. "Think. We already have her sworn evidence accepting she is a seer, and descended from seers, spawns of the devil, who use his dark powers to see the future." He said each word angrily, putting his face close to hers, grabbing her jaw at the end and making her look at him.

"We need you to tell the truth too, to shame the devil and his works. To show whose side you are on." He was shouting now.

She stared at him, her mouth half-open. The man behind the bishop was looking at her fixedly, his head bent to the side, his eyes wide, as if he was enjoying her distress.

"Please, let me go. I've told you everything," she said. She knew it sounded like begging, but she didn't care. She would do almost anything to escape this place.

"You will be going north tomorrow, Gytha," said the bishop angrily. "Someone wants to meet you up there." He grunted in frustration. "He will decide your punishment.

We had plans for Christ Mass, which have been set aside because of you," he said, breathing fast, angrily. "We must go north with you. The faith of this nation has been called into question by resistance to the rightful King of England, powered by the devil himself. This cannot be allowed."

She was left tied to the stake all that night, though her tormentors disappeared. She was given no water or food.

***

The following morning, when she was reunited with Ambr and after being fed some watery pottage, they were put on pack horses and a rope was placed around their bodies and they were set in a chain linking them to the torturer's horse. He rode behind them on a much larger mare.

She wondered why they'd been put on horses, as prisoners and slaves usually walked. All she could guess was that they needed to get quickly to the north. Why, she had no idea. They travelled with only a few guards.

27

The Norman in the black mail shirt laughed. He pointed a black glove at Magnus. "You and your men have a chance to live, sir. Do not throw it away. Submit at once and your lives will be spared."

It was one of those moments when the threads of the future swayed and lurched and anything could happen as they twisted. Magnus looked at me. I smiled. That a son of the last rightful King of England would look to me for what to do was astounding. I mouthed the chant silently, praying to escape this trap. Magnus watched my lips, a frown on his face as he tried to work out what I was saying. And then, all at once, many shouts echoed.

It was the Norman who first realised that the smell of fire was completely gone. He stamped his foot. "Let me free. I will tell my men not to attack you. Do you agree?" he shouted.

Magnus nodded. It was better to let the Norman go.

We all went to the door and the Norman opened it. Behind it were our men, each with an axe or a sword, all ready for a fight. When the door swung open, a few of us, including me, gasped. The Normans were lined up outside, but without their weapons. Behind them, a mass of villagers with torches, pitchforks, and long-handled axes stretched away in all directions. There must have been a hundred people, villagers and others, people from the surrounding countryside most likely, mostly men, but some women, and they all had ash-smeared faces, as a symbol of their willingness to die. The threads of fate had spun for us.

The Normans had downed their weapons. Had their leader been captured by us contributed to their desire not to die?

The Norman went straight to his men. "You gave away your weapons?" he shouted.

One of his men stepped forward.

"We were told we had to down our weapons to save your life."

"Who said this?"

The man pointed to one side. Yann stepped out of the crowd. I smiled.

"Do not blame your men," he shouted. "It was obvious to all that you had been captured and that you would prefer to live." He raised his good hand in the air. "And it turns out to be true. You and all your men will live to fight another day. No one has to die tonight."

The Norman shook his head, as if death, at least for his men, would have been preferable. Then he muttered an order and led his men out of the village.

When they were gone, with hoots and shouts accompanying their departure, we headed back into the hall. I was shaking and cold after all that had happened. One of the village women came to me.

"You lie down," she said. "There is the sweating sickness about that makes people shake. You need rest now. You have it proper. Come with me."

I licked my lips. There was a strange taste in my mouth. My mind was clouded too, as if it had fallen into a well of deep tiredness.

The woman led me to a sod-roofed house along the path. She brought me inside. It wasn't until I was lying on a straw mattress with a sheepskin over me that I knew she was right about being properly ill. I was shivering badly when Magnus came to see me. He left soon after. He'd whispered something in my ear, but in the fog that consumed my mind, I cannot tell you what it was.

The woman fed me thin hot broth. It probably saved me, and soon after, a great heat consumed me and I fell into a series of sweating dreams like I'd never seen before. This was clearly because the chant had taken all the power inside me to weave and warp our fate as I had wished, leaving me vulnerable to any contagion.

***

Days later, I told her about the ingredients for a healing potion, but the woman kept giving me broth. Soon after, the broth tasted like the ingredients I'd told her about, so I didn't push any more for mine to be made.

I dreamt of my mother many times during those days. She had given me so much, my knowledge of healing and my heritage as a seer, and the powers I was still learning to use, but which undeniably worked.

I dreamt I was with her in a strange house. She was getting a broth ready, cutting onions endlessly and placing them in an almost overflowing pot. A baby was crying somewhere. I wanted to go to it, but my mother shook her head and put a hand out to stop me. I tried to reason with her, but no words came out of my mouth.

She kept putting onions in the broth.

It started overflowing. I wanted to go to help the crying baby. She wouldn't let me. She was trying to warn me about something, but I couldn't understand what she was saying. I woke. It was night. I was sweating. It felt as if the house was rising up into the air. I could not sleep for a long time after that. The night seemed endless.

After that, the pain came. Sharp, deep inside me. I know we must accept pain, that it is part of life, and we must not complain about it or blame anyone for it. This is the healer's code. We accept it all and live with it and placate it with broths and potions and prayer and wait for it to pass, a storm or a season, depending on what pain we receive.

***

The torments lasted three weeks. Everyone said I was lucky to make it through, that many had died. When it was over, I was thin, like a twig. Tate visited me often. She kept pushing hard bread into me and though I missed Christ Mass, she said it was the worst feast she'd ever seen here, no extra food, just thin broth on Christ Mass day with mutton bones in it as the village was forced to share everything they had with us all. She was sure some of the villagers cursed us.

She kept some of the bones for a special broth she prepared for me. She said she'd prayed over it, though she knew her powers were not like mine.

The broth tasted good. It helped me, I am sure.

Magnus came to see me eventually, when I was mostly better. I was sitting up with a pile of blankets all around me when he arrived. He had a wineskin with a little harsh wine in it. He filled two small wooden beakers and passed one to me.

"We have warned the whole of England with our victory here," he said, a big smile lighting his face.

I wasn't sure that what had happened with the Normans was such a big victory, but if he wanted to call it that, so be it.

"Weapons and men are coming out of so many hiding places," he said, his smile radiant.

"What is your plan? It is mid-winter," I said.

"We march on Dunholm. A small force of Normans hides there. They've well overstayed their welcome. They ravaged everywhere around them. Edgar, the Aetheling, is calling for a proper uprising. We will lead it up here in the north. The Normans can be defeated, Synne. We've shown it. Our victories will prove it. Perhaps we will lure William here. Perhaps..." He stopped, looked around, as if he was scared of the words that might come out next. A hope that dared not speak its name.

"What about his brother Odo?"

"He might be still at Dunholm. That is why we must act soon." He leaned closer to me, excitement visible in his eyes. "The Normans have sent out raiding parties in every direction. They steal all they can, including daughters and wives."

"Can we defeat them?" I sat up further.

"Yes, I've called the Scots to come and help. A great alliance is building, Synne. We have a real chance. The throne of England can be restored."

There was a light glistening in his eye. A dream of the restoration of his family. I felt good for him. Everything could change with a few more victories. We had to believe it.

"Someone has come for you," said Magnus.

I sat up straighter, hope rising inside me. Had Gytha found us? It would change everything if she was here. The hole in my heart would be filled, at last.

"It is Bjorn," said Magnus. "He came all the way from Dublin to see you in the middle of winter." Magnus shook his head. He did not hold me in much regard. I knew that, but this annoyed me.

"Send him to me," I said. Next to Gytha coming this was not as good, but certainly I wanted to see Bjorn.

As Magnus walked away, I called out. "Did he arrive with many warriors?"

"Ten, I'm told," he replied.

Not a lot.

Bjorn did not come to see me until that evening. I assumed Magnus would see meeting me as an unimportant part of Bjorn's visit here and would detain him talking about Norman battle tactics or the chances of getting more help from Dublin.

When Bjorn arrived, he bent down and greeted me with a hug, despite me having been sick for weeks. He had no fear of catching anything from me. He had a great belief in his own invincibility.

After greeting me, he told me what had been happening since we'd left Ireland. An invitation had arrived for me to travel to London. This was the reason Bjorn had come to find me. The invitation had been sent by word of mouth, one man passing it to another, so I knew it might have been a lie, but what he told me was enough to see me wanting to rise up that moment and confront the Normans.

The message claimed I could be reunited with my father if I sailed for London at once. How they had found out who my father was and how they'd brought him to London shocked me. That the Normans were concerned about me at all was both exhilarating and terrifying.

Bjorn did not want to stay here if Magnus was planning to build a revolt against King William.

"I was warned I must do no more to set the Norman king against us." He looked troubled.

"What else have you done?"

"We helped Magnus and his family in the south. It did not go well. He and his brothers argue all the time."

So that was why Magnus had changed. We sat in silence as a squall of rain battered into the thatch above us.

"He has men and belief. It's not over," I said.

Bjorn touched the thin gold torque around his neck. It had a knot at each end and was usually covered by a cloak when travelling, but presumably he'd uncovered it for his meeting with Magnus and his men.

"I swear to you, Synne, your name has been cleared back in Dublin. The seers at Tara sent word that no action should be taken against you." He reached his hand towards me. "I am here to pass on this news."

I was glad of his message but concerned that the Normans knew about my father. Had they been looking for Gytha, too?

"Where is Tate?" I realised with a sinking feeling that I hadn't seen her in days.

"I heard she went out looking to find food." He looked uncomfortable.

"We're running out?" I had a sudden urge to rise from the bed and look for her immediately.

Bjorn knelt beside me, put his hand out flat to stop me rising. "I did not mean to distress you."

"I need to know where Tate is. Go, find out." I waved my hand. As he headed for the door, I shouted after him. "Ask Yann. He'll probably know."

I waited until he was definitely gone, then rose from the bed and put on the dark blue tunic I found hanging on a peg. It had to be for me. The house was small and the old woman who lived in it was out a lot of the time, visiting other houses healing and helping with childbirth and winter ailments. I walked up and down the barely dry mud floor. The house had sod walls and a thick thatch roof, so it was like living in a cave.

The walls were damp too and the fire in the centre of the room was almost dead. I found a pile of dried turf in a corner and put some on the fire. I wanted to warm myself before they returned. I did not have long to wait. Bjorn and Magnus came back together.

"You should be in bed," said Magnus. His haughty demeanour had returned.

"I have to find out where Tate is," I said, matching his tone. "Do you not know?"

Something flashed across Magnus's face. Perhaps it was surprise at me throwing this question at him. Either that or rage. One benefit of being sick was that it allowed me to stay well away from him at night.

"If you're feeling better, follow me to the village hall." He turned and was gone before I could say anything else.

Bjorn helped me put on my cloak. It had been hanging on the back of the door. What happened to my old tunic I did not know. My boots, cleaned, were near the door too.

"What's happening in the hall?" I asked Bjorn.

"All I know is that a messenger arrived and after that, Magnus wanted to come and see you."

I wondered if my outburst had stopped Magnus from telling me something. I make so many mistakes. Was this another?

It was icy cold outside and dark. Only the glow from candles behind a few doors showed where the village houses lay and a larger glow from the hall where we'd had our confrontation with the Normans.

Two guards with axes on their belts waited at the door to the hall. They were stamping their feet and looking around nervously. I wondered was there a reason. Surely the Normans would not attack us on a night like this?

When we went inside, the crowd hushed. Magnus was standing near the top table. He'd been telling the packed room something.

He waved me forward as soon as he saw me. "Come up here, Synne. It is good you hear this with everyone else."

I went up the middle of the room.

"Hear what," I shouted. I'd lost all caring about what people thought about me and about a woman speaking up.

"Just listen, woman," someone replied for Magnus. I knew that many people did not like women speaking up, preferring us to have the demeanour of slaves, heads down, speaking only when spoken to, and then to only answer questions simply.

I stood among the tables, crossed my arms, and waited for Magnus to speak.

He waved at us all to calm ourselves.

"I received a message from the Normans this night," he said loudly. He paused.

Someone shouted, "Get on with it."

"They've taken hostages and are holding them at the bishop's house in Dunholm. They demand we surrender, or the hostages will all be killed, one new one a day until the end of January."

That was five days away.

"Who are these hostages?" I asked. A sense of foreboding had sneaked up on me as he spoke, as if I knew something bad was coming.

"Your sister is one. Yann from Dublin is another. And some of the villagers they captured sniffing around."

I put my hand out to touch the table nearby. I needed to touch wood, to pray to all the gods for Tate and Yann. Things had moved far beyond what I'd expected. That they'd captured Tate and Yann from under our noses was sickening.

"We must take Dunholm and release the hostages," said Magnus loudly. Cheers greeted his words. No matter how improbable the outcome, some people are always ready to cheer something stupid, if it's said with enough confidence.

Magnus turned to me. "You stay here. We'll return when we have freed your sister and the others."

It was my turn to be stupid. "I'm going with you. I have to." Each word was filled with spiky conviction.

His mouth opened, but before he could say anything, I turned to the room and shouted, "I know a way they can be released without any of them dying. Do you want me to go along with Magnus and make sure this happens?"

A ragged cheer went up. Magnus could not leave me behind now. He sat down, acknowledging I had succeeded. But what would that success bring? Could I deliver on my promise?

That night I didn't sleep much. Magnus stayed away from me. I wondered if he'd found some woman to satisfy him. I didn't care. I spent most of the night chanting and praying that we would succeed.

***

We set out the following morning, early. It was raining, of course, but our cloaks all had thick hoods and rain would just mean fewer people out on the roads to spot us and gallop to the Normans and tell them we were coming.

The road to Dunholm went through a thick, seemingly endless forest. The land was mostly flat now with occasional rivers and streams we had to ford. The rain lasted all that day. We arrived at Dunholm at dusk. Magnus would not wait until the morning to attack.

"By morning they'll be ready for us," he said to the group of men at arms gathered around him. Many looked at me with wariness as I stood nearby. "After we get inside, we'll go straight to the bishop's house where they're holed up," said Magnus, his tone firm. We did not cheer him, but each man raised a fist in front of him, signalling his agreement. I did too, but the man beside me laughed.

I nudged him. "I can fight," I said. "And if I save your life, you can thank me."

He turned away with a disgusted grunt. Acknowledging he might need help from a woman was a step too far for him.

The town of Dunholm, the usual location of Saint Cuthbert's relics, was not a military fort, like many towns, but a river port with a large wooden church, where pilgrims gathered from all corners of the land hoping for cures for all manner of ailments. There were likely few pilgrims there in winter, especially at a time of war, but there would be monks and nuns there.

We dismounted to approach the town on foot. I was hungry and ready to do whatever was necessary to find shelter and food. Perhaps this was what Magnus planned on. Desperation is a good whip.

As we drew close to the town, the crescent moon, which had been out and pale against the dying light, became obscured. A foggy crown appeared around it. I knew what that meant. Fog was coming in from the sea. In winter, fogs held sway all along this coast, and sent tendrils far inland, through marshes and bogs.

No one pulled an axe or a sword as we moved forward and many of the men could be heard muttering, praying, their heads down. The need to fight as a man is thumped into boys from an early age and they knew what that meant – an early and painful death for many.

Magnus came beside me. "No arguments, you stay here with the horses. If we need your skills. I'll call you." He stepped back. He did not want to hear my answer.

"All the hostages will die if I don't come with you," I said. "You want that on your head too, as well as your defeat down south?"

His expression changed, twisting towards rage. "What happened down south was not because of me." He glanced around, as if concerned at who had heard my accusation.

There was only one sure way to get him to agree. "Let me come with you and you will have someone to blame if this goes wrong." I said it slowly.

He groaned. "I don't need anyone to blame." He paused, breathed in hard. "I want to protect you."

"To protect me, you must win here, Magnus. You will win if I am with you." I said it quickly, then beckoned him to me. He looked strong, glowering, brooding, troubled by what lay ahead, his hair wet, curling around his forehead. I knew it was a risk claiming I could help, but I also knew that if you believe fate will help you, it will.

It was time to encourage him. My illness had also dissipated my anger with him. It was time to show him that.

I kissed him like I'd not kissed him in a long time. There is something about the prospect of imminent death that makes you see life differently, put petty squabbles aside, and realise that each moment is precious and will never, ever come again.

He responded with his body pressed into mine. A cough from one of his men pulled us apart. We would not be rutting in front of them.

"We've been spotted, my lord," said the man. He pointed through the trees.

The wooden palisade wall of Dunholm was visible as a dark patch rising in the distance. Little of the town could be seen, though the crescent moon above showed the road clearly. What the man was talking about was a string of yellow torches in a line above the closed wooden gate to the town. They had not been lit when we first saw the wall.

There was activity above the gate, too. People were moving around. Then the sound of a horn echoed distantly, carried to us clear in the cold air. The whole town would be waiting for us.

"Fast march," shouted Magnus. We moved forward as one along the muddy track to Dunholm. No one paid me any attention. If Magnus wanted me with them, that was his decision.

The disturbing skin-crawling feeling I'd experienced listening to the sound of arms clashing had not gone away since the battle at Hastings. But I'd learned one thing since I'd arrived back in England, I could shape outcomes. This day would prove how much.

Some of our men split away, heading through the trees. That left a small band of us, about twenty, to storm the front gate. It suddenly seemed a ridiculous plan. How could we even get close to the gate with so many men above it ready to deal death on top of us?

Only the thought of Tate and Yann being held captive behind those walls pushed me on. And this was not London we were storming. It was a town unlikely to have many troops stationed on its walls. If we were nimble and got over the wall quickly, we would succeed.

We were walking fast towards the main gate when a flaming arrow soared above and fell not far in front of us.

They were getting the measure of us.

The Power of Synne

"Spread out," called Magnus. We spread our line out between the marshy river bank and the fern-covered ground in front of the forest. My mouth felt dust-dry as anticipation of death curled around inside me. I should not be here.

Stop. I would do everything I could to save my sister. I must not lose her.

I had to do this.

A shout went up from one of our men, a roar of disgust. I squinted at the town, wondering what the man had seen. There was something going on above the gate. Someone was holding something up.

A slimy dread gripped at me inside as I made out what was being held up. It was a head.

Please, no! Don't let it be Tate or Yann's. No! I wanted to race forward, find out if it was one of them.

Magnus did not react. He was busy giving hand signals to the men on either side of him.

More fire arrows rose, arcing into the sky from the town. Then came a roar from the town, its defenders signalling their defiance. The head that had been held up flew high in the air, fell on the path in front of the closed gate, and then rolled towards us.

Another wave of arrows went high. These whistled. Groans followed from our line. They had our range. I looked around. Some of our men had been struck.

Then I was pitched forward, flailing, and a flash of pain came.

28

The rain started in the early afternoon. They'd been riding for a month, their progress slowed by stops at every major town. Travelling in winter was always slow. This was worse. Gytha had it in her mind that they were being taken to York, but she didn't know where they were going. They could be on their way anywhere up north.

Bishop Rutilus was unpleasant company. He spent a lot of time talking about his plans to bring real Christianity to the north of England. Parts of the country had lapsed into idolatry and devil worship, he claimed. Only men like him could save the people.

"How will you do that?" Gytha asked him.

"By spilling the blood of Satan's deceivers." He looked happy at the prospect. He reminded Gytha of the look she'd seen in some men's eyes before battle. Bloodlust is not a pleasant thing, especially in people who preach about God loving us all.

The Norman guards with them seemed to shun him, which meant he was left alone for most of the day, as well as during the evenings when they ate, and in the mornings when he prayed before they departed too. He also prayed each night, out loud, when they arrived at whatever village hall would take them, before they slept in the straw among the vermin. Not once did they pay for their accommodation or food. Everything was extracted under threat of violence.

They arrived in York just before Christmas. Ambr and Gytha were allowed to walk around the town on their own after that. It didn't take long for Gytha to work out why. The town was mostly empty and had Norman guards on every wall. They would not get far if they ran. Winter meant tracking them would be easy too. It was not the time of year to run. It was the time to put up with things. Gytha remembered, with a numbing sadness, the visits she'd made to York with her mother and sisters many years before. The town had been peaceful and bustling, with singers outside some taverns and pie sellers shouting their wares. The pies had been delicious too, hot and juicy.

They were lucky now to get a small bowl of pottage once a day and horsebread and thin ale later in the day. It was the worst Christmas she'd ever experienced.

On Christmas day there was no extra food for the likes of them, though they did see, and smell, a pig being roasted in the hall they stayed in that day, and they got cabbage broth as night fell. There were too many hungry mouths in the town for prisoners to be well-fed.

One good thing, at least, was that neither of them was raped. The bishop had a fiery tongue about such things and promised to have the cock cut off any man who raped anyone, woman, girl, or boy.

They did not see Bishop Odo, though he was expected to arrive at any time.

***

January arrived with an icy grip, but snow held off and they huddled together in the back of the hall most days, helping carry wood and feed the animals during the day.

Bishop Rutilus kept a close eye on them, encouraging them to pray for a good outcome when Bishop Odo arrived.

Three weeks into the new year, they were roused early one morning.

"Put on your boots and cloaks. You are travelling," said the Norman who kicked at them in the straw they were sleeping on in the hall.

Again, to their surprise, they were given horses, though this time the horses were packhorses more suited to carrying supplies. At least they were sturdy, sure on their feet, though they had to help feed them and help saddle and unsaddle them because their party was even smaller and without stable boys as they headed north again.

Few people were on the road in January, not just because of the fog and icy rain, but also because of the blood shed by a new Norman governor of Northumbria, Robert de Commines, who'd installed himself in Dunholm with a force of mounted knights and was taking anything that pleased him from the surrounding countryside.

Gytha had discovered all this while helping in the kitchens during their time in York. She'd heard rumours that Bishop Odo had travelled to Dunholm to be with this new rapacious governor and realised that was probably where they were going.

The journey was one of the worst she'd ever been on. What would have been a five-day ride in summer, ended up taking a full seven days. Winter, she was even more sure than ever, was best spent in your house or in the local hall, living off whatever stocks of food you had or were available close by.

It was not a time for travelling.

Many days they ended up wet through from icy rain, their hands rigid from the cold, even when kept under their cloaks. On the final night, they found refuge in a village, which had a tavern already crowded with men and women almost covering every inch of the straw matted floor. From the people there, they heard whispers about raiders from the south, who were looking for villagers to rise up against the new Norman overlords.

Bishop Rutilus shouted at the woman who said that at their table as they downed a thin stew. He did not want to hear about such things. They were the words of the devil.

They arrived at Dunholm the next day. It was almost the end of January. The following day they were paraded in front of Bishop Odo, a tall man with a heavy black tunic and a gold cross hanging around his neck, enough gold to probably buy the entire town they were in.

The bishop's house they were taken to was low-roofed and had blackened roof timbers from decades of smoke. They were pushed forward to stand in front of a long table at which Bishop Odo was eating stew and bread. She could smell the stew. It made her stomach rumble.

Gytha and Ambr hadn't eaten that day yet. But they'd got used to waiting for food and they knew not to beg.

"Are you the sister of Synne, the healer?" asked Odo.

"I am," said Gytha.

Odo wagged a finger at her. "Prove it, tell me what she is really like."

"Raven-haired, clever as a hawk, what else do you need to know?"

"Will she listen to you?"

Gytha shrugged. Odo's gaze fell on Ambr, who stood beside her.

"Who is this?" he asked.

"We've been travelling together."

"She knows your sister?"

Gytha was not sure how to respond. Was it better to lie to protect Ambr, make her seem valuable, or tell the truth?

She shook her head. Odo turned to the guard standing behind him and said something Gytha did not hear.

Then he pointed at Gytha. "You will stay with us," he said. "We need your companion for something else."

His guard, with another, came around the table, grabbed Ambr and took her off, kicking and screaming.

29

I woke under a tree. Magnus was bending down to me. "I knew this was a bad idea," he said.

I tried to get up, but there were several cloaks over me. At least it wasn't raining.

"My horse?" I asked. I did not want to lose my horse.

"He threw you. He's good. Are you in pain?"

Slowly, I felt my body, my arms, and legs. There was some pain, from bruising most likely, but nothing sharp, nothing preventing movement.

"No more than usual," I said with a wince and a smile.

"Good, we need you on your feet. They will send men out to take us soon."

"Did you see what they threw over the wall?"

He looked at me with a sad expression deep in his eyes.

"Was it… Tate's… head?" I asked, barely able to say my sister's name, not really wanting to know if it was.

He shook his head. His movement was filled with sorrow.

"Who?"

He reached for me. I pulled my hand out from under the cloaks.

"Yann," he said softly.

I groaned loudly. A twisting, sinking feeling rose inside me in a wave of sadness that threatened to engulf me.

"No, not Yann. It cannot be. Why would they do that?" Was this a bad dream? *Please, let me wake and see his smiling face.*

"They did it to send us a message."

"What message?" I snorted. How stupid that Yann's death was a message.

"A message that we'll all die if we try to take the town." He straightened his back, his expression hardened. "But what it really means is that they are weak." He gripped my hand. "We must wait, be ready for the signal that will come. Our men will be in position soon."

One of his men came running towards us. As he came near, he pointed back towards the town. The pale glow of the sun going down had spread all around the town. Magnus, illuminated by the sun, looked haggard, as if he'd barely slept recently. We both gazed towards the walls of the town. Beyond, towards the forest, a spiral of black smoke rose into the sky. It did not look like the smoke from cooking fires we saw every day rising from villages. This was a wider, darker column of smoke.

"It is time," said Magnus. "Our chance is come."

I gathered my strength, stood straighter. "I may not be able to kill many Normans," I said. "But I can still save men injured in battle."

Magnus didn't reply. I could see that his mind was elsewhere, somewhere in the midst of the coming battle.

He put his hand out to me. "Swear you will stay out of the melee, or I will tie you up and leave you here." His tight-lipped expression made it clear he meant what he said.

I felt an urge to argue with him, but his words gave me enough leeway to get involved in some other way.

"I swear it."

He straightened, nodded, hurried away to round up his men.

This time, when we went forward, our men carried their circular shields in the air above their heads. They were locked together. Not one of our men had a bronze plate or boss on their shields. Most had worn, slashed, and discoloured leather shields providing limited protection. But it was far better than nothing.

Arrows thwacked down on us, but not as many as before. I stayed back with the horses at the treeline, with the stable boys. Our men had two ladders with them. They got as far as the wall, then threw the ladders up fast.

The first men to run up fell back with arrows and stones raining down on them. I said a prayer that Magnus had not gone up first. Some of our men moved away from the gate then, some going to one side and others the other way. It was a desperate tactic. Our attack was being split.

But it would also split the defenders.

I watched the road leading to the town. I kept thinking about Yann, wondering if his body could be reunited. I felt sick and gloomy at these thoughts and fearful too for Tate and for Magnus's fate. How much more suffering was on its way to us this day? How could any good come from this?

My mother had always looked for good, the sunshine that would come after rain, but I could sense no sun on its way to warm this cold day of death and despair.

Then I saw it happen.

The gate of the town creaked open. I could hear it faintly.

Above the town, the smoke from fires inside was growing thicker by the moment, and was now streaming from more locations.

Riders appeared in the gate. Four guards wearing mail shirts and helmets followed by three other riders a little behind. One of the four was a dark-haired woman. A red-haired woman rode beside her.

My heart skipped.

Could that be Tate, but if so, who was with her, who was beside her? My heart was beating like a trapped bird.

Who could it be? The riders were moving fast. I blinked. Could it be?

I ran towards the road. I did not care that I had no weapon and could be ridden down. If who I thought was here, I had to see her clearer.

One of the riders was Tate, I could see her now. That thought cheered me – she was alive – and Bishop Odo was with her, but the other woman, the red-haired woman, she looked strangely like Gytha, from her hair colour and the way she held herself.

But I had to be wrong. It was some trick. I was seeing ghosts.

Was I?

I reached the road and stopped, holding my cloak tight around myself from the bitter wind and leaning forward from my exertions, but my head still up.

I'd seen women who looked like Gytha many times from across a tavern or down a street, and each time it had been like this, my hopes raised, then dashed.

They were only an arrow flight away now, cantering towards me, probably on their way to a clean escape from the fires engulfing Dunholm.

The riders pulled up.

The road between us was no more than a muddy track. The riders were staring towards me. Surely, I couldn't have put any fear in them? That was when I felt the hoof beats.

I turned. In the distance, a group of riders was heading towards us. A raven banner flapped among them, and clouds of steam rose from their horses' breath. I ran the other way, towards the riders coming from the town. They wheeled in the road. They were perhaps thinking about heading to the woods, but then some of our men, with Magnus in his shiny mail shirt among them, broke out of the woods in a line. My heart soared. Magnus had found his horse and was riding towards us through the winter-thinned ferns.

On the far side of the road the river flowed, the water black as night. The river was too wide and running too fast for fording on horseback. Beyond it, dark clouds gathered, filling half the sky with the promise of an evil storm.

Tate put her fist up as she came forward. The other woman raised her hand in triumph. Both were rosy-cheeked from the cold. My breath caught in my chest, burning, painful, but I kept running, my boots crunching on the frozen mud. I had to get to them fast before any

The Power of Synne

violent confrontation, when I would be swept aside in a moment.

Bishop Odo was walking his horse towards me. He raised both his hands, reins still in them, showing he had no weapon. His guards, behind him, all held just their reins too, as if they were in no danger from anyone.

"Synne the healer, greetings. You have a rare skill for turning up at a ripe moment," shouted Odo, as I slowed, then walked to him as we came close, my breath puffing steam.

"Bishop, let my sisters go, you are surrounded," I shouted between breaths. There was only a small chance he'd agree, but I had to try. I did not know who the other approaching riders were, but hopefully he did not either, and might assume they were not his supporters.

But instead of agreeing, he laughed, and shook his head like a hungry dog.

"So now it is you, taking any chance, who gives orders to the rightful rulers of this land," he said, mockery dripping from his tone.

He looked happy. Why? His guards still had neither sword nor axe out, though they looked ready to trample me, their horses grunting and breathing loudly as they all walked closer.

I stood still. I'd come to him too fast and Magnus was too far away to stop them doing whatever they wanted to me. And who knew what the other riders would do when they arrived.

But I could see my sisters now. Tate looked pensive, eyeing the road behind me and Gytha was beaming at me as if she'd glimpsed heaven. My chest filled to bursting at the sight of her, warmth spreading through me despite the cold and the danger we were in.

I'd found her. I'd found them both. We were reunited. At last.

"Tell those men" – Odo waved towards Magnus – "I am doing Christ's work here and will release your sisters when we get to the next town." He pointed dismissively at Magnus, now riding slower, as some of his men, also on horseback, fanned out on both sides of him.

I stared at Gytha. She looked different, older, thinner, but still she had defiance in her eyes.

Magnus's voice came clear to us in the icy air.

"Harm your prisoners and your heads will all be on spikes at the town gates by morning," he shouted.

Odo looked at me. "Tell him what I said."

I turned to Magnus. He'd pulled his horse to a stop just beyond Odo's riders who were almost encircling me. He looked at me as if to say, *I told you to stay out of this*.

"Magnus," I shouted. "Bishop Odo has my sisters. He says he's doing Christ's work." I was glad he was here.

Whatever had happened between us, this moment would prove if he'd stand by me.

Magnus slid from his horse, walked to me through a gap in the horses around me, his hand gripping the pommel of his sword hanging from his belt. "Greetings, Bishop Odo, I see you left your men to die in the town."

"I did not bring those men here." Odo held his head high as he spoke. "I do my best to prevent bloodshed, Magnus Godwinson. I'm a bishop of Christ, appointed by the pope, as you well know. I'm on a sacred mission. You will not detain me."

He'd remembered who Magnus was.

"Synne," called a voice from my past.

Gytha had slid from her horse. She came running towards me. Seeing her smiling face was like watching the sun come up after a dark, cold night. We embraced like bears hugging. "Stefan?" she asked, looking around.

"Dead." I hated to say it.

She shuddered, groaned.

"I saw our father," she whispered in my ear, as if trying to cheer me up.

I pulled back, stared into her eyes. No, she must be mistaken.

She pulled me close again. "Mother told you he died but she told me the truth." Her whispered words came fast and held conviction.

The idea was ridiculous, but a seed of doubt had entered my mind. The men around us were watching us, leaning forward on their horses, trying to catch our words.

"A week ago, a party of warriors passed us riding north. Father was with them. I could not go after him or say anything." She looked at the men around her.

My knees felt odd. Could any of this be true?

"Synne?" Magnus shouted for me.

He was in conversation with Odo, who was still on his horse. They both had wolf fur on the collars of their cloaks, though Odo's was thick, new, deep black and Magnus's was ragged and stained.

"Come," I said. I held my hand out for Gytha. As she took it, a shiver rose right up my arm. Her warm touch brought back memories, our hands fitting together like gloves. We walked towards Magnus and Odo.

Tate had also slipped from her horse. She came to the other side of me.

"My sisters must be freed, Odo," I said, hoping that he'd fear Magnus and his men. I put my fist to my breast, then held it in front of me. I was demanding they be released.

Odo spoke. "Have you seen who's behind you?" He looked amused.

I spun around.

The other riders were close now. I'd imagined the raven banner must be something to do with Magnus, but he also turned and did not look pleased.

The man riding at the front was a giant with a war axe hanging from his hand. He wore a mottled black sealskin cloak with the thick hood up, his long blond hair streaming out from the edges around his face.

He looked different to any of the men I'd seen recently, but there was something strangely familiar about him, as if I'd met him in a dream.

Bishop Odo was the first to greet the man, whose horse came to a halt within spitting distance. His men, there were at least ten, all dangerous-looking, splayed out behind him as if he was the tip of a spear.

"Jarl Erlend, may Christ be with you. You arrived in time." Odo walked his horse forward. "Thank God and I thank you for your quick response to our call."

This changed everything.

Magnus no longer had the upper hand. If this jarl intervened for Odo and the Normans, Magnus and his men would have a real fight on their hands. Magnus might die. My reunion with my sisters would be a fleeting moment of joy.

"Greetings, Bishop. I'm looking for someone," said the jarl. "A young woman." He was staring at me.

I felt uneasy. It couldn't be me he was looking for, could it? Could it be something to do with what had happened in Dublin or on the way here? My mind raced through possibilities.

"Meet Synne, the healer," said Odo. "The others are her sisters."

The jarl laughed as if Loki the trickster had just played a joke on him.

"All your angels and saints have answered my prayers," he shouted, raising his axe.

I stood still. I did not like the sound of this.

"Synne," Tate hissed at me, but I could not take my eyes off the jarl. He walked his horse forward and as he did, Bishop Odo waved at his men to move aside.

The jarl's horse breathed thick steam into the air. I could smell its stinking sweat now too. They'd ridden hard to get here. "I've been looking for all of you." He pointed at me, then Tate and Gytha.

"I'll take them off your hands, Bishop," he said, his voice commanding, expecting no resistance.

Magnus grunted, walked in front of me.

"I am Magnus, son of Harold. Synne is my woman. You will not be taking her anywhere." His sword was in his hand, up and swinging a little, ready to thrust.

That satisfying moment, Magnus standing forward for me, lasted a weirdly long time as the threads of all our

The Power of Synne

fates knotted around us. My skin prickled then as if something was crawling beneath it.

Erlend leaned from his horse, his axe at the ready. "These women are spawns of the devil. You want to lose your precious life for one of them, Magnus, son of Harold, the stupidest man who ever wanted to be king?"

My breathing spluttered. I had to say something, fast. My voice was thin when I started but my fear disappeared as I spoke.

"We are not spawn of the devil. That's a stupid lie."

Erlend laughed.

"Devil spawn, do not deny it. You're the daughter of a seer, and she the daughter of a Queen of Denmark who refused to be baptised and her bloodline cursed because of it." He leaned down. "I know where you came from and your cursed bloodline."

Doubt blossomed inside me. Our mother had said we were from a royal bloodline. Did this explain why she'd said so little about it and about the rumour of being cursed?

Erlend grinned, showed his broken teeth as he watched me. "I see the look on her face. She knows I say the truth."

Magnus grunted loudly, angrily. "Get down from your sickly horse and fight me or I'll cut you down and cut your head right off, you ugly, stupid son of a rabid dog." He stepped towards the jarl's horse and raised his sword, holding it as if he was going to run the horse through.

At that, the jarl's men let out a series of whoops like sea birds fighting. The jarl raised his axe and slid from his horse in a moment.

He stepped back from Magnus. I thought this meant he didn't want to fight. Then he lowered his axe and ran the tip of the blade across the muddy track in front of him, creating a line.

"If you're ready to die, come for me, Magnus, loser, son of a loser, brother of more losers, all ugly stains on this land. Your woman is mine now. Run away, be a coward and accept you are a weakling loser or die choking on your blood."

Magnus blinked at this tirade. He'd know it was meant to get him to rush into an attack with his reason impaired. He looked around at the jarl's men.

"You, all of you, prepare to watch me kill this dumb ox," he shouted as he pointed at the jarl with his sword. "We shall see which of us God picks, and which of us the healer will ride with."

It was a fight over me.

I did not want it. I did not want blood flowing because of me. Some women enjoy such things, but I'd seen too many terrible wounds and too much death from stupid bravery and axes and swords to want more.

The Power of Synne

"Jarl Erlend, kill the traitor and my brother will reward you," said Odo. He looked at the sky as if something had distracted him.

I felt the hard icy spit of rain. I knew what was coming.

Magnus and Erlend faced each other on the muddy track as the circle of men grew around them, different groups in different parts of the circle.

Magnus moved first as the fighting chant rose from almost every throat. "Kill, kill, kill, kill." The blood rousing chorus.

His blade sliced air.

I could hardly breathe. I'd noticed a bloodstain on Magnus's leggings. It was wide and looked recent. He was injured. I sucked in icy air, the cold wind pushing all around me. He had to win.

The jarl's axe swung next. Anything in its way would be split apart. The blade went through the air like a ribbon of silver.

My breathing stalled.

Magnus leaned back. The jarl's blade missed him by a cat's whisker. He was already swinging at the jarl's throat. His cut was parried by the axe shaft the jarl held up with both hands. I did not want to watch this, but I could not look away.

The jarl held his axe in one hand. He lunged, swiped it by Magnus. The blade caught Magnus's arm with a glancing slice. Both men stepped apart. Blood dripped from Magnus's hand. It twitched as he held his sword. He'd be lucky to be able to keep going like this. My throat tightened as if I might stop breathing.

The jarl rushed forward. His axe swung for Magnus's blade. Their weapons clashed. The sword fell from Magnus's hand.

He stepped back, his foot slipped, he fell sideways into the mud. Near quiet descended. Only the rising chatter of birds could be heard. This had ended quicker than I expected. The jarl smiled, raised his axe to split Magnus in two.

I reached for the bead hanging warm under my tunic, gripped it tight and screamed, my other hand high in the air.

"Stop." My voice went on and on, higher and higher, extending the word, demanding I be listened to. The jarl glanced at me, his axe poised, and then a great whoosh sounded and from the nearby trees a flood of starlings rose fast into the air and swooped down towards us, as if I'd summoned them with my shout, and everyone looked towards them, watching as a dense black cloud of birds swooped to us and then away and then back again like a crazed animal had been loosened.

And then the hailstones started. Giant icy stones. They hit my face and head like audacious slaps.

The jarl still had his death blow up and ready. Magnus was still under him. None of this had distracted him, but it had scattered many of the men around us, changing the moment. I walked through the hailstones, ignoring their bite. I knew it well. I put my hand up to the jarl's chest. He could kill me on a whim, but I didn't care. Better to die than watch this stupid moment play out and see Magnus's blood and gristle and his death in my eyes.

The jarl's eyes were wide as he stared at me.

I knew what he was thinking, even if he was a follower of Christ. Flocks of swooping starlings mean change is coming, fate is intervening. They are roused by the dragons under the earth shifting in their long sleep. Everyone knows that.

"They trained you well at Tara," said Erlend. "But move aside, seer." He had bloodlust in his eyes. He wanted to kill.

I had to be quick. "Stop or the birds will come and eat your eyes out."

The starlings swooped.

The jarl's axe came down a little as he watched the birds. I'd stopped him, but he was still ready to kill.

Magnus was grunting, perhaps from pain or perhaps from the thought of how close his death was and who had saved him.

"Do not shed any more blood, Jarl." I pointed at the trees. "You have seen my powers." I waved my arm, feeling he needed another push.

My first scream had worked, and when it did, I felt strong, like iron, and more sure of myself than ever. I had real power. I could not doubt it. I had more power than my mother ever had, too. I could even smell moss and old leaves, the smell of the starlings' winter nests. I was connected to them.

I made my mind go gentle, then screamed again, one hand up and waving for the birds.

The starlings swirled near, and the hail came thicker too.

The jarl stepped back, almost stumbled. There was shock and real fear in his eyes.

He raised his axe as if to ward off the birds, took another step back. The mud was icy and slick under us all. He had to be careful.

I had my bead in my hand. It felt hot, as if a fire within it was giving me strength. I pulled the leather string up and out from my tunic fast and yanked it hard so the string broke. Erlend stared at my hands, a puzzled look on his face. I slipped the leather string out of the bead, thought for a moment it might catch, but it didn't.

The jarl laughed at my stupidity. His arm went back, as if he might throw his axe, but he hesitated as the birds swooped again. My hand went back. I flung the amber bead at his eyes with all the force I could muster.

It was a small chance, but a real one. I could not kill him. But I could distract him.

The bead did not strike him in the eye. He moved to avoid it, but it did hit his face and he winced, loudly, and in that moment a dagger landed in his thigh. I spun. Magnus had thrown it. He was on his feet and rushing forward with his sword in his hand like a spear.

"Do not interfere," I shouted. My hand swept around towards his bodyguards as my voice rose. "Or you'll hear me scream every time you sleep, and will know that the birds will come soon for your eyes."

The faces of his men still around us, all wet and white, went even paler.

Magnus was on the jarl. His blade pushed in, then swiped one way, then changed direction and its tip slid up and across the jarl's neck so that blood spurted wildly into the mud. The birds cawed at that, as if a feast had been made for them. I could smell blood too.

The jarl's eyes dimmed as his axe fell from his hand. I sighed deep inside. We'd done it. Magnus hugged me and his men whooped. I'd helped, but the death blow had been his.

The jarl's men put his body over his horse and walked away, sullen, into the night. They had no appetite for more fighting.

Odo stared at me.

"You're the first true seer I have met," he said.

"And you will go back south now if you value your sleep and your life," I said. I did not want to see his face ever again.

He rode away without another word. I bound Magnus's wound with a strip from his tunic as I watched Odo go.

I looked for the bead I'd thrown then and asked my sisters to help me. We didn't find it in the dark and stopped looking quickly. We would come back the next morning.

We had to get Magnus indoors and resting. He went up on his horse with the help of two of his men. I went up behind him to steady him. We rode through the last of the hailstorm towards the town. Some buildings were still smoking. But the hail had stopped the fires.

I looked back. Tate and Gytha were walking behind us, holding each other, smiling.

"You did help a little," said Magnus as we rode. "My men will thank you. My family too."

"A little? Ha. You are alive thanks to me."

He smiled. "I would have been happy to die for you," he said softly. "I nearly did."

A warm glow filled me. This was what I wanted to hear. "So, you will make me your queen?"

"I will."

"Of where?"

"You will see. With your powers, Synne, men will flock to us. We will be unstoppable." He smiled. "We'll rid these lands of Normans together."

My heart thumped lightly in my throat. The prophecy would be fulfilled. What had seemed impossible was possible.

Before You Go!

Please do **write a reader review on Amazon for this book.**

Reader reviews are more important than ever.

Thank you very much if you can.

https://www.amazon.com/Power-Synne-Destinys-Embrace-Book-ebook/dp/B0CXMMFRFK

And look out for the three novels in this series!

Thank you!

Printed in Great Britain
by Amazon